LITTLE BROTHER

Also by John McNeil:

THE CONSULTANT
SPY GAME

LITTLE BROTHER

J O H N   M C N E I L

Coward-McCann, Inc.
New York

Library of Congress Cataloging in Publication Data

McNeil, John.
 Little Brother.

 I. Title.
PR6063.A2586L5   1983   823'.914   83-1914
ISBN 0-698-11227-X

PRINTED IN THE UNITED STATES OF AMERICA

FOR MARY

1. Route 128

1

There is no escaping Route 128 in the electronics settlements that encircle Boston. It was there through the window, past the sprawling factories of Norwood, climbing on spindly concrete legs behind a Pizza Hut sign that barely glowed under the brilliant sun. The automobiles moved slowly up the incline, as if even 55 mph were an effort, and trembled lazily in the afternoon heat.

There had been a long silence while Leitner studied a file. Now he coughed and Toby Sorenson forced his wandering gaze from the freeway to find cold eyes on him. He had no idea what the file contained, but Leitner's low voice and threatening stare meant trouble. It was a well established fact at Eastern Semiconductor that the quieter he spoke the more serious a mess you were in. A man had to be a lip reader, so it was said, to realize he was fired. Sorenson leaned forward in the chair.

"I'm reminded we had a company car stolen last year," Leitner said softly. "From the lot outside this very building. A fancy executive Buick, all the options. Almost new, if I recall." He peered closely at the file. "Was it recovered? I can't find any mention that it was."

"We got a full reclaim on the insurance," Sorenson said.

Leitner turned several pages, his mouth tightly pinched. "Did we also get a reclaim on the electric typewriter that somehow walked out of Sales"—he looked closer still and his voice became all but inaudible—"eighth of January last?"

"I believe so."

"Nice to have a chief of security who *believes*," Leitner murmured. "So reassuring in this age of uncertainty we live in."

His office was in the seat of power, on the top floor of the Executive Building. It was of the extravagant size regarded as essential by vice presidents at Eastern Semi. It could have swallowed Sorenson's cramped quarters, in one of the less favored administration annexes, several times over. The window framed a long avenue of factories with little pretense to being more than sheds, where companies discovered new areas of electronics as fast and furiously as the pharmaceutical business turns out new drugs. Around them, wastelands of parked cars. At the end of the avenue, a trail of neons and rooftop billboards offered an escape from the assembly lines in the familiar comforts of hamburgers, donuts, submarines, and thirty-one flavors of ice cream. The single word BEER clung to a precarious construction of timber. Just beyond, Route 128 arched its back over the haze.

"Still, why should you care? What's it to you if unauthorized persons stroll into the plant to help themselves? The insurance company always coughs up, so why should you give a damn?"

"That's not my attitude, Mr. Leitner."

"We spend millions a year on product research." Where another man might have thrown his arms wide, Leitner was content to cup his fingers. "Let's hold open house, invite the world and his dog to see what we're doing."

"We've tightened our procedures since the typewriter went.

Closer controls at the gate, more frequent spot checks. I copied you in on the memo."

"So it couldn't happen again, is that what you're saying?" He struck an attitude that urged caution, his head at an inquiring angle, eyes searching.

"No security is ever perfect, but . . ."

He seized on the hesitation. "But now we have this business with Wiley."

"Who's Wiley? There are over five thousand people at this plant, Mr. Leitner. For all I know, we've got a dozen Wileys."

"This one is a department head in Research and Development." He revolved his chair to the window, to give the monotonous roofs, the distant freeway, the benefit of his attention. "This morning he had two computers in his laboratory. How many do you suppose he has now?"

Sorenson closed his eyes.

"Humor me. Try a number."

"One, I guess." It was what the bastard wanted to hear.

"Come now, with your smart new precautions, how would that be possible? All those spot checks, et cetera." He turned back from the window, counting on upstretched fingers to be sure he was understood. "This morning, Wiley had two computers. After a lunch I suspect was on the leisurely side, but we'll let that pass, he found he had two."

"I don't follow."

"One of them seems to have grown, Sorenson, that's the problem. Your problem. It's grown enormously, in the space of the hour Wiley tells me he was out. Let's say a couple of hours. It's still swelled up like a prize pumpkin." His mouth drawn in a thin white line, he examined Sorenson's face for some moments before asking, "In your considered opinion, do computers do that?"

"I'm not a technical man, Mr. Leitner."

"Take it from me, they do not." He proffered a barely perceptible sigh and held his head as he had previously, soliciting more. He was a man who rationed his gestures. Anyone at the plant with the misfortune to sit across the desk from him would have recognized the stare, the pitying, removed look of a doctor about to pronounce a fatal condition. When his patience ran out, he sighed the same sigh and touched a button on a telephone. His office had no less than four telephones; he chose the one in hot-line red.

"Tell Mr. Wiley," he informed his secretary, "the cavalry's on its way."

The other well-established fact about Leitner was that he waited until you reached the door, escape in sight, to issue the *coup de grace.* "One last thing . . ."

"Yes, Mr. Leitner?"

"Don't bring me back bad news." Head down, he was writing in the file as he spoke.

Outside, Sorenson could taste the diesel fumes from 128. The cars spilled from the front parking lot the whole company complained was inadequate, onto the balding grass around the flagpole. All around were buildings that had happened along as they were needed, in no particular style except that none looked remotely like any other. This was, he supposed with too much detachment to be bitter, what they had once called greener pastures back in the Boston Police Department. It paid better than the police, the hours were more civilized, the people you mixed with were, for the most part, a cut above the addicts and dropouts in Roxbury. All it entailed was guarding the shop and dealing with executives like Leitner. It was an absolute *mother* of a job, but what else could an ex-cop find for himself at the watershed age of forty?

The laboratory was on the most distant boundary of the site, a good ten minutes' walk at the easy pace the sun encouraged. Sorenson left his car where it was. Wiley had no business involving the front office. Wiley could damned well wait.

2

Five years after turning in his badge, he retained the eyes and instincts of a detective, even if some of the instincts, as he understood only too well, were more of a hindrance than a help. On opening the laboratory door he hesitated there, peering in with the meekness of a stranger. Every cop has his personal darkness at the top of the stairs, the places that make him uneasy, self-conscious, distort his judgment. Most patrolmen had an aversion to ritzy apartments; they could think of nothing but whether their shoes had muddied the carpet. On the company territory he covered now, Sorenson was like that with laboratories. It must be the untidiness, he thought, the shambles surrounding too much learning, that set his teeth on edge. If he lived to be a hundred he would never understand how Harvard graduates and the like could be such slobs.

A man bustled over, plump and thirtyish, sweating profusely.

"It's about time," he hissed from the corner of his mouth.

"Mr. Wiley . . . ?"

"I lost count of the number of times I called your office." He illustrated with vague shakes of the shoulders. "What do we have to do around here to get service?"

"I guess I was at lunch. Same as you, Mr. Wiley."

"I had them page the staff restaurant for you." He mopped his brow with a damp handkerchief, then added pointedly, "Twice."

"You should've tried Burger King down the avenue. That's where I go."

Wiley spun on his heel as if to say he found the company uncongenial. "It's over here," he snapped, and led the full length of the room, muttering to no one but himself how his research program was in tatters because of this.

"You fight tooth and nail, and for what?"

Over the laboratory hung the faint but distinctive smell of electricity—at least that's what Sorenson took it to be—sharp and burnt, like the smell of an amusement arcade. There was cable everywhere, all sizes of cable, from thin ribbons to bundles of wire as thick as a man's arm. It lay in tangled heaps on the shelves, in dead coils on workbenches; it spread like a gray undergrowth of jungle vine over the floor. Wiley and his crowd must *hoard* cable. Surely, too, they had more expensive equipment than they could possibly use? Instruments covered with controls and dials and often dust were scattered heedlessly on every available surface, with the discarded air of toys after Christmas. Why were so many empty containers piled up to the walls; did they never throw them away? Did the wastebaskets that overflowed with computer printout ever get emptied? A loop of cable snagged his foot; he stumbled. God, he thought, what a pigsty.

"Isn't it incredible," Wiley said when they came to a desk in a remote corner. "I still can't believe it. What did I do to deserve this?"

The computer on the desk looked ordinary enough: scarcely larger than a portable television and rather like one. A label over the keyboard gave the model name, Zylec 10. The delivery carton was still beside the desk, and the white plastic bubbles used for packing foamed onto the floor.

"Is this the machine the fuss is about?" Sorenson ran a finger over the keys.

"What does it look like!"

"To be honest, I was expecting something rather bigger. The way Leitner told it, one of those giant computers that fills a whole room."

Wiley regarded him quizzically.

"Swelling up, Mr. Wiley. Like a pumpkin, isn't that the story?"

Wiley glowered and held a finger and thumb fractionally apart. "I work with devices this size," he uttered contemptuously. "I don't need to fill a room."

"So what's your problem?"

He was aghast, needing to swab his brow again. *"What's my problem?"* Only fumbling in his trouser pockets after the handkerchief prevented a dance of rage. "One of my IP-3s is stolen, and when the security chief deigns to show up all he can say is, what's my problem!"

"Hold it a minute. You've had a computer stolen?"

"The message finally gets through."

"Then what's this?"

"That?" He sneered at it. "That's a cheapo desktop machine. I don't need it, I don't want it. The guy who has mine used it to bluff his way in. It was his passport to the plant, Mr. Sorenson, do I make myself clear?"

"Perfectly."

There followed a time, Sorenson had no feel for how long, when he was incapable of coherent thought. His knees seemed ready to buckle under him, his mouth went bone dry. As the nausea passed he had one of those unnerving moments of *déjà vu.*

Wiley was watching him intently, curiously. Somehow, he'd gathered his wits sufficiently to examine the computer, look in the packing case, at the empty but grimy floor under the desk. It was the oldest ploy in the detective's box of tricks: when all else fails, search. Had he been careless and laid a hand on the damned thing? Hell, he had a feeling he had. Wiley was still subjecting him to the same close stare. He resorted to the second-oldest ploy in the police armory: when the public gives you trouble, turn on the heat.

"Did you touch?"

Wiley retreated into a look of mild shock. As if he would. "What do you think! I know better than to touch."

Sorenson directed an appeal to the others in the room. He had paid them scant attention until now, except to notice how they'd stopped work to follow his every move when he came in.

"Anyone happen to touch this?"

None of the young men seated at their desks and workbenches bothered to reply.

"Give me a break, fellas. It's a simple enough question."

Still no response. They brought to mind the bystanders at a road accident. The same atmosphere of vicarious interest, the same mass retreat into dumb obstruction when the appeal came for witnesses. He counted six; there might be more out of sight behind a partition wall; not one was a day over twenty-five. Dressed in jeans of course, and open shirts stuck with badges espousing the usual causes. He didn't need to get close to know the slogans would all be about Survival or some such thing. Save trees, save the whale, save humans as long as they were someplace else. Perhaps he saw them with a jaundiced eye, but he couldn't rid himself of Leitner's words. *Don't bring me back bad news.*

"You heard the man," Wiley said.

"Never went near it," someone called.

"Don't understand computers," another added, which drew snickers.

Wiley was furious. *"You!"* he yelled, like a taunted teacher. "Dickerman. The chief of security is after your balls."

Across the laboratory, a youth rose unwillingly to his feet, started their way, then froze in a fit of indecision as if about to take to his heels.

"Dickerman is the idiot who accepted delivery," Wiley spat.

"Is he, indeed."

"Dickerman sat over there like a jerk," Wiley went on, his voice swelling to a roar. "Dickerman contrived to see damn all while my lab was being plundered. If you don't roast him alive, I sure as heck will."

Dickerman had at last summoned the nerve to come over. "How was I to know?" he moaned, blinking through thick pebble lenses.

"What's your job; what do you do?" Sorenson demanded.

"Me?" He was unable to stop blinking and was now standing on one foot. "I'm a research analyst."

His beard had every sign of being recent, presumably to hide the acne it didn't yet cover. But, give him his due, it took courage to wear a NO NUKE POWER badge in a corporation with a whole division devoted to nuclear control systems. Courage or innocence.

He fought a moment of stammering before explaining, "My specialty is bubbles. You know, bubble memories."

"No, Dickerman, I don't know," Sorenson said wearily. "Do you have an office, Mr. Wiley?"

"Along the corridor."

"Then I suggest we three continue there." Quite suddenly, he could take no more of the laboratory.

The sign on the door said Wiley was HEAD OF IMAGE PROC-ESSING, and he wondered without much interest what it meant. The photo displayed on the filing cabinet showed a wife as plump as Wiley, with four daughters who were unashamedly fat. But the real love of his life was obviously the house: he had cut off the family legs to get the roof into the frame. It was a fair-sized property, in what looked to be one of the leafy executive heartlands, like Lexington, and he must be mortgaged up to the eyeballs to pay for it. As any cop knew, those were the very worst people to deal with after a theft.

"Let's run this through from the beginning," Sorenson said. "In plain English, if you don't mind, no jargon, no bubbles." He prepared to take notes, as was his habit, on the back of a visiting card cupped in a hand. Dickerman sat beside him. Wiley was hunched at his desk, as sweaty and pink as in a Turkish bath.

"I got back from lunch at two," Wiley began. "Maybe it was closer to two thirty, who cares? I spotted the Zylec out there but didn't bother at first, why the hell should I? This is a big plant; I assumed it was a delivery to the wrong department, nothing sinister. Eventually, and I mean a very long eventually"—he looked daggers—"it occurred to Dickerman to say something. That's when I got the nagging feeling deep in my gut. About the guy who made the delivery, I mean. You know the feeling? The butterflies that tell you something is not right? Like you arrive home and there's a window open that shouldn't be. I've had it happen and there's no feeling like it in the world—you feel like you're about to throw up."

"Who did he say the computer was for?"

"Me. My name was on the delivery docket. Believe me, that was a man who knew what he was after. He turned up very conveniently, didn't he just, at a time most of us were out. When I checked the inventory I found an IP-3 missing." Now he came close to tears. "Jesus Christ, you fight tooth and nail for a development budget and they give you just enough funds for two lousy prototypes. Now one of them's gone."

"Two, you said?"

He made an anguished nod.

"I'd like to see the other." Sorenson rose to his feet.

Wiley waved him back to the chair. He unlocked a drawer in his desk with the ritual of opening a vault. The key went instantly back to his pocket; he patted his jacket to be sure it was safe. He placed a white tissue on the desk and unfolded it as delicately as if unwrapping a gemstone. Resting in the center was a square of plastic the size of a postage stamp and little thicker. "Don't touch," he gasped as Sorenson reached out. "Don't so much as breathe on it."

"That's a computer?"

"A microchip. I take it you've heard of such things?"

"Yes, but I've never seen one." Sorenson could just discern the faint circuits beneath the surface, like a skeleton of numberless small bones. He shook his head ponderously over it and gave voice to his thoughts. "How am I supposed to stop people stealing objects that small? This isn't a goddamned bank."

"We all bear our crosses," Wiley sniffed. The microchip went back into the desk. He locked the drawer and rattled it a few times to make sure it was secure.

"Is the IP-3 for image processing?" Sorenson asked.

Wiley arched eyebrows so pallid they were almost invisible. "Does it matter? It's somewhat involved."

"If I'm to locate that missing chip, I'd like an idea what it does."

Wiley issued the protracted sigh of a sorely tried man. "Our main interest is handling the visual information from space missions. The ground station gets back a data stream contaminated with noise; the problem is to reconstruct the picture." He regarded his wet handkerchief with dismay before dabbing it to his forehead. He believed he was wasting his time. "The big advance

here is shrinking most of the essential processing onto that miniature computer, the IP-3." He looked askance. "Is this helping
any?"

"Not really."

"It's all about reading order out of chaos," Dickerman added
enthusiastically. "Have you seen those color blindness tests
where . . ."

"I'll make you a deal, Mr. Sorenson," Wiley broke in. "You
recover my computer, I'll organize a free seminar for you on
image processing."

"You might just have to do that." Sorenson held his gaze until
Wiley glanced away. He didn't like pale eyes at the best of times,
and Wiley, he thought, had a stare like a limp handshake.

He kept them both in suspense while he went over the notes
he had jotted on the card. "It was a straight trade," he said then.
"His computer for yours."

"In a manner of speaking."

"So why did he do it?"

"Why? He left behind an ordinary home computer costing at
best three thousand. Our prototype chip was the culmination of
several years' work. Call it half a million."

"*Dollars?*"

"That's about what the competition would pay to get hold
of it."

Sorenson gaped at him, seized by a deathly chill from somewhere deep in his stomach. The figure shocked him; he was as
disturbed by his own lassitude. The first question you ask, he reminded himself furiously, is *what was it worth?* That's what gives
the inquiry its shape, its perspective. How else do you know if
you're investigating petty theft or grand larceny? Long moments
must have passed before he turned on Dickerman so fiercely he
made him wince. "You saw him right?" He could hear the desperation in his own voice. Wiley caught it too, and leaned back in
his chair, arms folded, with a vindictively smug smile.

"He just walked in, Mr. Sorenson, dumped the packing case
on the nearest bench, and shouted was there anyone called Wiley
in the house. The docket looked okay, he asked if I would sign it.

I was all alone in the place so I signed. Heck, I wouldn't have unpacked it if I'd known."

"You unpacked it?"

"Somebody had to."

Wiley made a noise like a sob. This wasn't news to him, but it hurt hearing it again.

"What did he look like?"

Dickerman sought for inspiration. "He had this service kit . . ." His fingers snapped with a bony crack as he remembered. "Know the sort I mean? A Samsonite case with screwdrivers and pliers and so forth."

"The guy, Dickerman, not the fucking case."

"He was just a fucking guy. Who the fuck notices a guy who delivers computers?"

"In other words, you can't describe him."

He subsided into a defiant shrug.

Wiley's window had sight of Route 128 sandwiched between the blank walls of a neighboring factory. Sorenson went there to be away from them, pressing his face to the glass and staring out at the great Mack trucks hauling their heavy trailers up the elevated section. Interstate transportation of stolen computers . . . if it wasn't a federal crime, it should be. The damned thing could be anywhere by now, concealed in a pocket on a plane to any one of a hundred destinations. And what if it was still in the plant, unlikely though that was? You couldn't strip search five thousand people; the labor unions wouldn't have it.

He lounged against the wall, arms locked, acting as calm as he was able. "What's the market for hot computers, Mr. Wiley? I presume it's the same as for stolen works of art? A very small group of buyers rich enough, crooked enough, to write the requisite fat check."

While he gazed out, Wiley had found a box of Scotties at the bottom of a drawer and was wiping a fresh tissue on his forehead, down his cheeks, under his pudgy chin. "I figure maybe ten major corporations might be interested. By the back door, naturally, and that's not counting foreign interests. Between these four walls, I'd prefer to keep quiet about the foreign angle. But they're respectable businesses, just like us. I presented a paper at an image-processing conference in San Francisco . . . last October or whenever. I can let you have the list of delegates. I gave none of the details, you understand," he hastened to add, "nothing of commercial value."

"Are you implying you whetted an appetite in San Francisco? Aroused interest of the wrong kind?"

Wiley only pouted as he screwed the tissue into a ball and dropped it in the wastebasket. He felt he had volunteered more than was good for him, that much was plain.

"What do you suggest I ask the delegates, Mr. Wiley? Have they just funded a half-million heist at Eastern Semi?"

He rose to the jibe. "You might start in your own backyard," he said. "You might enquire how a phony delivery man got past the gate, passport or no passport. Did any money change hands, that's the question you want to ask—any *graft.*" He stroked his thumb slowly, greedily, over his fingers.

"You mentioned a docket. May I have it, please?"

The yellow form that emerged from Wiley's pocket was crumpled and damp. Sorenson smoothed it on the desk, throwing him a darting glance of disapproval. The scrawl in a bottom corner was indecipherable, presumably Dickerman's doing.

"Business Computers Supplies Corporation," he read. "Ever heard of them?"

"They're not in the book," Wiley said. "I'm way ahead of you. I tried that number and all I got was a 'no such listing.' Draw your own conclusions."

"Still, it looks official enough. It fooled Dickerman, I guess it fooled my man on the gate."

"Your man is too busy harassing the likes of us to *need* fooling! Have you any idea what goes on down there? He checked my car trunk last month, even the tool kit."

"A routine search, that's all . . ."

"What's he think, I'm stealing pencils or something? I'm a department head, for Christsake, and I get frisked like I was a two-bit clerk from Accounts."

"He's only doing his job, Mr. Wiley."

"Meantime, a stranger gets the red carpet treatment by waving a scrap of paper could've come from an instant printshop."

"I'll be investigating what happened at the gate."

"You will, huh?"

Sorenson had no more to say on the subject.

"You want my opinion?" Wiley shouted as his anger erupted. He took it out on the desk, thumping with a fist. "The considered opinion of a person this company pays to *think* for a living? You ought to take a long, hard look at your contingencies. Frankly, mister, they stink."

Once more, Sorenson found his eyes drawn to the photo looking down from the filing cabinet, the Wiley women on their Lexington lawn. The camera never lied, he decided. It was true about fat little prigs being the worst, the ones with mortgages bigger than they could handle. Did they have to take it out on the rest of the world? A show of dignity seemed in order. "We're not all paid for our opinions," he said as he left. "But we manage, Mr. Wiley. We manage."

Back in the laboratory, he sent one of the research assistants off in a grudging hunt for polyethylene sheet and Scotch tape. He smothered the computer in the polyethylene and stuck a strident DON'T TOUCH label across the front. A final look at the state of the room and he knew how hopeless it would be to search for clues. But he puttered around anyway for a while, examining the floor, making inconsequential notes on the back of another card. All conversation had died as he entered. He was watched from every desk. So he wrote slowly, with ceremony, the way a patrolman writes a traffic ticket. It lends authority.

"You were asking about image processing . . ."

He discovered Dickerman behind him, standing on one foot like a nervous schoolboy.

"Only out of interest, Dickerman. I don't intend to major in it."

"Did you ever come across those color blindness tests? Know the ones, those cards with the mess of bright spots?"

Sorenson nodded.

"You're supposed to be able to read a number." His face gave a hint of a flush, throwing his freckles into relief. "Me, I can't. I see the world like you see a black and white movie, Mr. Sorenson. But I've learned to live with it, what else can you do?"

"And that's what this missing chip is for? Reading colored cards?"

"Well, not exactly. The principle's the same, though."

"Just what I needed to know." Sorenson squeezed his arm in a charitable gesture.

Dickerman was reluctant to go. "About the Zylec . . ."

"I'll get one of my police buddies in to dust for prints. Chances are it won't lead us anywhere, but it has to be done."

"And then . . . ?"

"How do you mean?"

"It doesn't belong to anyone, right?"

"That's the way it looks."

"I don't suppose . . . ?" He changed feet, his eyelids fluttering under the magnifying-glass lenses.

"Dickerman . . . be my guest."

*   *   *

In his office, he found a note asking him to call Leitner. He called and was told a meeting was in progress. No, it wasn't possible to disturb Mr. Leitner, not for the rest of the day.

"But he requested me to find out," his secretary cooed in her lowest of voices, "if you're likely to be at home tonight. We do have your number."

He nearly gave her a straight yes. Instead he said, "I can arrange to be."

3

Leaving Norwood for the Cape, Route 128 takes a wide, easterly sweep, keeping its distance from Boston. At Quincy, it comes up against the Atlantic. Since there are no electronics factories out to sea, 128 has no reason to go further. Which is why, some say, it ends there.

Sorenson lived at Quincy, a few blocks inshore from the Squantum Yacht Club. He called it an apartment for want of a better term; it was actually an upper floor, take it as it was, with shared use of the bath below. Until recently this had been a family house, though not, he soon came to realize, a happy one. Fitzgerald, who owned it, was the only other occupant, a widower with a slender government pension. From snatches of conversation when they met on the stairs, it seemed there were three married sons, but there had been no evidence of them since Sorenson arrived, no visits, not even cards at Christmas. Fitzgerald had wanted a tenant, he said, to keep the upper rooms aired and in case, heaven forbid, he fell down one day and couldn't get up. His peace of mind was more important than the rent, or so he claimed. His ideal was someone sensible and regularly paid, not too young, not too wild. A woman was out of the question. So Sorenson suited him and he suited Sorenson, because he kept to his cramped back room and asked no personal details beyond those he was entitled to know.

"No loud rock music," had been his opening words when Sorenson came with his baggage. He stood there, a gaunt shadow in an unlit hall. "You did say you weren't married?"

Sorenson nodded.

"I won't have married folks, all they do is fight. And the same goes for kids, who needs them, messing up the paint and the yard. How old are you, anyways?"

"Forty." Not quite, but on the phone Fitzerald had stipulated that as the minimum age.

He had felt the old man's stare on him from the gloom, deciding if he spoke the truth.

"And not married? You go for men or any of that nonsense? I won't have fags in my place."

"Divorced."

Fitzgerald stepped forward onto the stoop and eyed him head to foot. "You coming in, or are we standing here all night?"

Off the upstairs living room a somewhat nautical balcony overlooked only other houses like Fitzgerald's, with wood sidings bleached pale by the corrosive Atlantic air. They blocked the view to the ocean but it was impossible to be unaware of its closeness. It was because of the ocean that he stayed in Quincy. While there he learned to read its moods. Sometimes he would lie on the bed for hours and do nothing but listen to it. He was tired by the years of wandering since leaving Elaine; the Atlantic seemed as good a reason as any for calling a halt. Quincy, he told himself firmly, was the final resting place.

He walked out on marriage about five years before, in Peabody, near the northernmost limit of 128. Within days of running off with Cindy Fernandez he'd quit the police to try his luck in industry. If you are tearing up an old life, he'd thought, it might as well be done properly . . . it was called burning your bridges. Sorenson soon learned not to play with fire.

Elaine had prophesied that it wouldn't last; she had a phrase for his madness. When she saw such frenzied affairs among her friends she called them "Mayfly Romances," they fluttered briefly and died. But even she, in her blackest moments of damning him to hell, could never have imagined it being over, stone cold dead, in so short a time. When he came back from the plant six weeks later, Cindy Fernandez had left. Her clothes were gone, her books, every smallest possession she had brought to the apartment they shared. She left no note of explanation. It was as if she realized she had no right to be in his life and had tried to erase all traces of ever having been there.

For Sorenson, there seemed little else to do but move on and keep moving on, from one anonymous apartment to the next. A casual observer of his progress over those years might have seen him in the role of itinerant worker . . . following Route 128 ever southward as the jobs at the electronics plants took him until, like the freeway, he reached the sea and had to stop. At Quincy, he had chanced on Fitzgerald's advertisement in the *Globe* classifieds. It was so rude—so impossibly restrictive on who was acceptable—he felt compelled to rise to the bait. When he was handed the doorkey—and he knew it was crazy—it seemed as if he'd been granted admission to the most exclusive establishment in the state.

"Did I remember to say no women?" Fitzgerald had asked. "I want no fooling around, not right over my head as I sleep."

They sat on either side of the gateleg table in his back room, splitting a single can of beer.

"Never?" Sorenson made it sound more like agreement than a question.

Briefly, it seemed Fitzerald might relent. He gazed deep into his beer, weighing whether he was being unreasonable. Then he nodded as slowly as a man falling asleep and sucked at his gums. "Take it or leave it. I don't have no visitors to disturb you any. Seems only fair you should act likewise." Extending his glass, he sucked loudly and thoughtfully. "Mailmen and the like excepted, and even he comes pretty rare." Then the vestige of a smile, one of the few Sorenson ever saw from him, and he jiggled the glass in invitation.

Sorenson clinked it with his after a pause for decision that was too brief for the old man to notice. He was weary of breaking faith, having people break faith with him. The contract was struck—provided Fitzgerald kept his side of the bargain, he would do the same. And since in his two years at Quincy not a single visitor apart from the mailman had called at the house, he remained true to his word.

4

The evening of the Wiley fiasco, a single thought dominated his mind. In the car driving back to Quincy, it became an obsession, and on reaching the apartment he knew what he must do. He unplugged the phone from the jack by the bed, moved it to the living room, plugged it in there, and placed it next to the television. With the set switched on, he reclined in his usual position on a voluminous scatter cushion placed on the floor, his back propped against the wall. The phone had to be where he could see it. This was his private show of daring, his way of facing up to Leitner. For several minutes he stared, challenging it to ring. Only then did he turn his attention to the screen.

His evening routine was constant and had been for longer than he cared to remember. First thumb through the channels with the remote control, pausing on each station to see if it caught his eye. The sound had to be off—he preferred it so—he browsed like a man gazing in through shop windows for what would draw him inside. If he found nothing worth watching he would choose a movie from the video library instead. It had grown over the years to fill the alcove behind the set and now overflowed into the otherwise empty spare room. He could view the classics, *Casablanca, North by Northwest* and *Psycho,* as often as others might read and reread cherished novels, with the same pleasure in the discovery of the nuances, tricks, only a scholar of the art could detect.

The movies lost out that night, the black and white trapped him the instant he dialed channel 5. A news report obviously, the picture was too poorly lit, too immediate, to be yet another police series. The black and white was for real; Hollywood versions al-

ways looked fresh from the car wash. Real black and whites had
the filth of the city on them, eating deep under the paint like
rust; they were shabby even when clean. Perhaps it took a cop to
see it.

The lights on this one made their slow flashing twirls. Blip . . .
blip . . . blip. It was in a scruffy street, the sidewalk lined with the
drifters who gathered from nowhere when a patrol car screeched
to a halt. A shooting or a stabbing, he guessed from the position
of the car: way out from the curb at an urgent angle. Quickly, he
wound up the volume.

". . . who neighbors here describe as a quiet boy. Ten-year-old Kurt
took a handgun from a bedroom drawer in the early hours of today
and shot both his parents dead at point-blank range. His sister,
Karen, eleven, was the target for three further shots. She escaped
with a flesh wound, said not to be serious. She told police Kurt was
quote very upset last night. She says her father took away a TV
game Kurt was playing with when he refused to go to bed and it
quote made him crazy. Police here in South Cove, used to senseless
street violence, told me it's a long time since they . . ."

He killed both the sound and the picture and sat staring at the
empty screen. He could go for days, often weeks, without thinking of Jay, then an incident, an overheard phrase, would catch
him off guard and trigger a pain as pervasive as a toothache. Like
the boy on the news Jay was ten. Sorenson had no idea what he
looked like now, or Elaine for that matter. He had a poor enough
memory of them as they were the last time he'd seem them, the
night he walked out. By pure chance, he had taken with him in
his wallet the few mundane snaps every family man carries. Stupidly, he'd removed them, to a drawer or the pages of a book. He
soon forgot. Somewhere along the line in all the moves between
apartments, they must have gone astray. He had rejected the
idea of contacting Elaine to ask for more. What did he say? That
he wanted their pictures but not them?

For the first few months after leaving, he had deliberately
suppressed all emotions, all thoughts of them both. It was a job
too well done. Now he could barely picture them at all. Jay had
gradually become little more than a blurred, boyish face frozen in

the past—recalled from one of the holiday snapshots which for some reason had stuck in his mind when all else faded. *Every boy has the right to shoot his father,* he thought bitterly.

The ultimate irony was that he still had a photo of Cindy Fernandez. Where? Fuck it, where? He hadn't meant to hold on to it; it had clung to him like the ashes of the burning bridge. If she'd guessed it was there in a jacket pocket, she would certainly have taken it with the rest of her things when she ran out on him. For a while it had been pinned on the wall of a place near Maynard. Not from love, not to be mooned over; he wanted her to look out on the bare apartment and him in it and see what she had done. When he came to his senses he tore her down again and filed her where she belonged, in a cardboard box of old receipts and miscellaneous correspondence. Now he searched with a frantic passion until he found the box in a closet behind his shoes, and held the photo over the sink in his tiny, makeshift kitchen while the flame from his lighter reduced it to a fragile, blackened crisp. The last bridge, he mused as he sluiced it away. He should have done it years ago.

*   *   *

The phone maintained a foreboding silence until just after ten. When it finally rang he answered quickly, determined not to show weakness.

"Toby?" It was a woman. The voice hadn't changed in the least, but he didn't recognize her at first because he was so certain it had to be Leitner . . . or his damn secretary.

"Toby? Have I got Toby Sorenson, please?"

"Yes, speaking."

"It's Elaine, Toby."

He was struck dumb.

"Hello . . . Toby . . . ?"

"I'm sorry, I was expecting someone else."

"If I'm calling at the wrong time . . ."

"That wasn't what I meant."

"It's been a long time. God, doesn't that sound corny! I swore I wouldn't say it."

"But it's true." He should have had the decency to speak his mind: "How extraordinary, I was just thinking about you." Unforgivably he said, "It must be four years."

"Five. It was exactly five years on May the ninth."

"Yes . . . of course."

"I phoned Maritime Dynamics. They told me you'd moved on ages ago. I can't imagine why I assumed you'd still be there. I got your number from your office. I hope you don't mind."

"You *what?* Jesus."

"You do mind. I was afraid you might."

"Look, Elaine, they're not supposed to do that, give out home numbers to anyone who asks. Christ, doesn't *anyone* at that shitty company do what they're told!"

She took an embarrassingly long time to react. "I can always call back some other time. Or if you'd rather I didn't . . ."

"No," he said quickly, "it's okay, really."

"I think I'd better, all the same."

"What a welcome, huh," he admitted. "You've caught me on a real killer of a day, Elaine. Make allowances, would you?"

"Didn't I always?"

"Are you still at the house? Do the neighbors in Peabody still mow the grass and shine their automobiles every Sunday?"

"Are you always this objectionable?"

"Only after a day at the office."

"We moved to Salem. It must have been, let me think, the following summer after you . . . after you decided you couldn't take any more neat lawns and shiny autos."

"We?"

"Jay and me." She paused to grasp the implication in his tone. "There hasn't been anyone else, Toby, if that's what you mean. I told you there wouldn't be."

"Does Jay like it there?" He wanted to ask about Jay himself but was unable to be more direct.

"We both love it." She gave a hearty sigh. "Can we stop this a minute, Toby. This fencing. That's what it is, let's be honest about it."

"Well, as someone rightly said, it's been a long time."

"I didn't ring to ask how you are, how's it been, and wait for you to say the same to me. I thought very hard about phoning you like this. I've got a reason. I want a favor from you."

Slowly he sank onto the rug, leaning against the television. Wedging the phone between shoulder and chin, he lit a Camel from the packet in his shirt pocket and inhaled deeply. His head ached suddenly with a familiar numbness. It was as if they had never parted, as if she were in the room now facing him. *"Do me a favor, Toby. If you're that keen on the bitch, go and live with her."* And all those other times, the same even emotionless voice, the same dead expression, the same comment at the door in the morning. *"Do me a favor. If you're seeing her tonight don't insult my intelligence with stories about working late."* He looked into the glowing red tip of the cigarette and thought: Do me a favor, Elaine. If you're going to call me out of the blue, try using some fresh words.

"Say something, would you," she pleaded.

"I'm listening. You're the one with something to say."

She laughed nervously. "Would you believe I had it all scripted, every word. All the possible ways you might react, how I'd reply to them, how I'd steer you in the direction I wanted. And now my mind's gone blank. Isn't that crazy?"

"Take all the time you want, Elaine. I'm not going anywhere."

"It's about Jay."

"What's wrong with Jay?" He couldn't help the note of anxiety in his voice he knew she would take to be anger.

"Nothing's wrong, at least not in the conventional sense." That strained laugh again. "I mean, he isn't on drugs or anything. He's grown big and strong and I love him dearly. He gets the top marks in his grade. He wants to be an engineer, that's the latest plan, anyway. When you cleared off he was fantastic. No panic, no depression. He was . . . he was what kept me sane, if you must know."

"I'm glad. I worried about that, about how he'd taken it."

"Sure, you did! We could tell! My God, Toby, he's ten times the man you are." After an icy silence she asked, "Can you for-

get I said that, please? I promised myself no outbursts, none of
the injured wife stuff. Like I said, my script's gone clean out of
my head."

"You've got this model son yet something's obviously both-
ering you. Why not just tell me."

"Why not."

There came a pause in which he imagined her, like he was
doing now, drawing strength from a cigarette. Perhaps not, she
hadn't smoked when they were together.

"He's slipping away from me, Toby. We had this great rela-
tionship—I couldn't have asked for better—and now it's dying
before my eyes. All he wants lately is to be alone in his room. We
don't go places anymore or talk much. I hardly see him. It can't
be a healthy sign, him wanting to be alone all the time, up half
the night."

"He's ten now, Elaine, pushing eleven. Soon he'll be a teen-
ager, on the verge of adolescence." Sorenson felt uncomfortably
like a marriage counselor or a Samaritan. "You can't expect the
mother and son act to go on forever, be reasonable. Comes a
time he doesn't want cuddles and a kiss at bedtime."

"You're a real bastard," she spat. "Do you realize what it cost
me to dial your lousy number and beg for help? Can you even
begin to imagine? I didn't just call on a whim. It's taken me days
to decide. I mean days. Boy, I should have known better."

"Come on, Elaine . . ."

". . . I'm not some dewy-eyed mother being stupid and possessive. There's a real psychological problem looming."

Save us, he thought; Elaine playing amateur shrink.

*"Don't you understand . . . his best friend died. It was Jay who
found him."* Her next words were more measured, little more
than a whisper. "Lying there dead on the terrace, his poor head
like that."

Her voice, briefly shrill then becoming hoarse, conveyed such
terror she might have been gazing at the tragedy as she spoke.
He closed his eyes, only to see again an incident from the past
when Jay had been left unguarded on the front lawn. The hairs
rose on the nape of his neck as he relived the moment Jay had

crawled into the road, and he winced in recalling the awful tearing shriek of tires, like the cry of an angel of death. He seemed to
smell again the sickly sweetness of the blood gushing from the
inert child's head—just a gash on the temple, but that unquench-
able stream of warm red blood. The chill passed as the message
of her quieter words sank in. It was another child this time, not
Jay. Then he began to shiver, the phone trembling in his hand,
with the realization that in all the times he had thought of Jay—
wondering about him at school, at play, wearing new clothes and
speaking clever adult phrases—he had never once considered the
possibility of danger. He sought for what to say and her deathly
silence seemed to warn him not to inquire further. It was a private tragedy, something told him, all he was permitted to know
was it had touched Jay's life and he hadn't been there to help. He
shook his head slightly as if to rid it of the dreadful image of a
bloodied child without a face. A friend of Jay's he had never
known and now never would.

"I'm sorry," he said lamely. "I had no idea. If there's anything
I can do . . . ?"

"It's not your sympathy I'm after." She said it with the unnaturally controlled calm he recognized from so many past
squabbles. "I want you to trust my instincts about Jay and just
say yes or no. I don't feel like justifying myself to you, Toby, not
on the phone when I haven't seen or heard from you in over five
years. I've had Jay with me every day of that time. You haven't.
Don't ever forget it."

Don't rub it in, sweetheart. Needled, he rebuked her with a
lengthy delay.

"What do I say yes or no to?"

"Whatever his problem is," she sighed, "I can't seem to handle it. I've been trying and I'm getting nowhere. I think he needs
a man in his life, just for a while. Not to shake the big stick, only
to be around, talk to him. Every growing boy needs a man there
some of the time, isn't that so? Otherwise he'll get worse, retreat
further into himself, end up with some kind of breakdown, I just
know it." An agonized pause before she said in a rush, "He
needs a father again, Toby, I think that's what it is."

"Oh no," he retorted, shaking his head furiously. "Oh no."
"Is that it? A blunt no without a second's reflection?"
"We went over all that, or have you forgotten? Never try to prop up a marriage simply for the sake of the children. Sound advice, and we both agreed. It's as true now as it was then."

His words needed time to register. "Is *that* what you think I'm after?" she said, astonished. "Listen, stupid, if I wanted you back I'd come right out with it, I wouldn't use Jay as a bargaining counter. Just so we understand one another, I don't want you back ever—not under any circumstances."

"The answer's still no. I'm sorry about his friend; it sounds horrifying. But I think it'd be a disaster for him to see me. It might reopen all manner of wounds you don't realize are there."

"You've given me your answer," she said angrily, "and I haven't yet put the question. Are you free this weekend?"

"I'm free most weekends."

"Then come up to Salem. I'm only asking for two days of your time. You can stay at the house with us or in a hotel, whatever suits you. Two lousy days, Toby, that's all. Talk to him, watch him, see if you agree with me."

He shut his eyes in search of a long vanished summer afternoon, a faint recollection of a picnic on the shore near Provincetown. Hadn't there been a dead fish on the beach? He wondered dully in the midst of crowded confused thoughts what a fish had to do with any of this. He seemed to see Jay bending over it, childishly unmoved by its cold white stare.

"Toby . . . ?" she said when she could take no more of his silence.

"Hold it, would you. I'm thinking about it."

He rehearsed all the arguments and counterarguments—all the reasons she was asking the unreasonable, the unnecessary, the downright impossible. No, not asking, demanding. Elaine had always been so good at getting her own way. He wanted to see her but was astounded to discover how strong the reflex to resist her still was. The snapshot of the young boy with the quiet smile returned again, imploring him to agree, telling him in the same instant he didn't have the nerve. It seemed as if Jay was saying to him, *"You didn't care then. You haven't the guts to face me now, to look me straight in these eyes. Do you even know what color they are?"*

"Did you tell him you were phoning?"

"Of course not. I've planned it very carefully. If you turn me down, why should he ever know? Otherwise I'll find the right moment to break it gently."

"Do it before Friday evening," he suggested. "What's your address?" He spoke quickly, before he could change his mind.

*   *   *

Not until the first Norwood sign on the freeway the next morning did he give any more thought to Leitner. As he barged his venerable Beetle through the traffic to the right lane ready for the off-ramp, it dawned on him that the threatened phone call hadn't happened and that now nothing of consequence was likely to happen. It was Leitner's way. There would be the ritual memo for the record, worded to make the flesh crawl, and a black mark on a personnel file somewhere. But no actual reprisal. Nothing, as the phrase at the plant had it, in the megadeath category.

DeStefano, the gate security guard, raised the striped barrier and gave his polite morning nod from the comfort of his glass kiosk. Sorenson pulled into the visitors' parking lot and walked back.

"How's tricks, Mr. Sorenson?"

"Why didn't you check my ID?"

"Heck, Mr. Sorenson . . ."

"I asked why."

DeStefano scratched his head. "Heck, it's you, Mr. Sorenson. You know it's you, I know it's you."

"Nothing's sure if you don't check my ID."

"There's nobody else drives a car like that," he protested. "Beat-up Volks, Massachusetts plate. Heck, Mr. Sorenson, your plate is a sort of ID. Be reasonable."

"I want every tab checked from now on. You off your fat butt and out there on the concrete. Car windows down and that precious bit of plastic in your mitt, DeStefano. Got that, every one.

And that includes Leitner, even if there isn't another black Caddy like that this side of the White House." Sorenson paused in the kiosk door. "You know Wiley?"

"Sure I know Wiley. Tubby little guy, drives a brown eighty-two Pontiac. Gets ratty if you so much as . . ."

"Just between you and me, I'd like an eye kept on Mr. Wiley. A real close look at that car each time he drives through, into the plant and out. In the trunk, under his raincoat on the back seat, the works."

"Jeez, Mr. Sorenson, you mean . . ."

"Just between the two of us, okay?"

And there the matter rested for the present as far as Sorenson was concerned. His thoughts returned to Salem. Overnight the snap taken out on the Cape that distant summer had shown slight signs of movement, like a child waking from a deep slumber. He saw again the hot sand, the sea dancing with blinding pinpoint reflections under a noon sun, Elaine laughing on a rug spread for a picnic. A dead baby shark left behind by the tide that Jay held aloft for the camera like a proud fisherman. He concentrated on Jay's lips, trying to read the words. "See what I've caught, Toby," but silently, in no voice he could recall.

That day he made play of shifting paper from tray to tray, of checking obsolete security files retrieved from the archives by his secretary. But he agonized only on whether any man on earth was capable of being reborn as a father in as little as two days. About whether it was crazy to try.

2. The House at Charlestown

5

Watching Harold Ames was a dubious pleasure, an education in how to prepare. The trouble he took over placing the chairs was a lesson in itself.

The room had only the big battered desk, its legs chipped and splintered like someone had taken an ax to them, and three chairs that it would have been right, if flattering, to call antique. Ames made his arrangements with infinite care, getting the desk to his liking where the light fell best, adjusting the positions of the chairs. He was a contradiction, Dietrich felt, attired as a prosperous executive in his conservative blue suit, his well-fed stomach bulging the vest, yet hefting old sticks of furniture about like he was a house mover—molding the room with such fussy dedication it might have been a palatial suite and him an interior designer. Sweet Jesus, the way he set down that chair, regarded it with a hand on a hip, then changed its angle a fraction. This whole business was contradictory; the interview was a waste of time before it even got rolling. Dietrich stood uselessly by and watched from a corner, feeling like part of the furniture.

The largest of the chairs Ames naturally chose for himself and placed it behind the desk so the daylight was to his back. You needed to see the subject's eyes, he always said, your own should be shaded. Feeling the seats of the other two, he selected the hardest and moved it to face the desk, well back toward the center of the room. None of the intimacy closeness might suggest; create a gulf between you and him, a no-man's land with the subject marooned on the far side. The psychology was that the guy would seek to bridge the gap and volunteer more from a distance. Ames had likened it once to a cry for help. Next he tried his chosen chair for size, leaning comfortably back then crouching forward in a threatening pose, taking his weight on his arms, trying to picture how he looked from the facing seat. It still wasn't right; he went to alter the position, so slightly in the direction of the door Dietrich wondered why he bothered. Finally satisfied, he reclined at ease, legs at full stretch, thumbs hooked in the pockets of his ample vest.

"Sit down, Ralph," he invited. Then came one of his smiles with all the teeth showing, the sort he usually reserved for the man in the hot seat. "Remind me about him."

Terrific, Dietrich thought, interview *me* first! Ames knew damn well what was in the report; he'd have committed every last word to memory. He just couldn't resist quizzing people. Sweet Jesus, to Ames the whole of his life must be one long interview. Make sure you were on the right side of the desk, listen carefully and obviously, nod sagely once in a while, give no clue as to what you were thinking. Most probably it was strict observance of that creed had got him where he was, top of the pile in Boston. The CIA was a covert organization; stood to reason they looked for covert natures in their chiefs.

"He calls himself Felix Valentine. Born in Kiyev, 1924. He was Feliks Valentinov then. Joined us in 1966 as a collator here at Charlestown. That was the time we had that spate of recruiting safe Russians."

"What's your opinion?"

"I don't know, Harry, and that's the truth. I think he's a guy with no imagination—yet his report strikes me as pure invention."

"Explain." Ames liked the short question. Better still, a riveting stare if it would save a word.

"Take his name. Valentinov turns into Valentine. Hardly shows a great mind at work, agreed?"

Ames shrugged sparely.

"Collator is one of those overblown titles. In reality he's a glorified file clerk."

Ames admitted a grudging nod, of agreement, maybe even approval. "One of the gray people of life, you might say, old before his time. See him on the street, you'd never guess what he's been through, never suspect half of it."

Dietrich suppressed a grin. That was Harry all over; next best thing to grilling a man was reading his soul in a file. "My conclusion is that he saw what he wanted to see, a ghost from his past. Heck, Harry, you know the people here same as I do. Half of them refugees from the Soviet, all with a private beef. It's a breeding ground for KGB agents stalking the shadows."

"That's it? He dreamed up the story? I suggest we keep open minds till we've seen him."

"The nice man, nasty man treatment?"

"Why do you think you're here?" Ames said.

He had rejected the use of his office at Cambridge. It was far from suitable, he had explained, a smart room didn't have the required ambience, and his tone had implied a session such as this would trample dirt all over the floor. Which left only the "paper factory" in Charlestown, where Valentine toiled on his files. Put the man at ease, Ames had said, meet him on his own territory.

It was in a turning off Winthrop Square, below the brow of Bunker Hill. Row houses like it abound in that part of Charlestown, big and solemn in dusty red brick. Dietrich was not alone among the Cambridge cynics in thinking it an anachronism, a schizophrenic monster of a place. Take the sleek IBM computer droning in the air-cooled basement. Against that set the shabby East European kooks on the grubby upper floors who drank their dark coffee laced with figs under a blanket of tobacco smoke that smelled like nowhere else in America. They shuffled newspapers up there all day in search of unusual happenings, minor coincidences—of a kind only nationals from behind the Iron Curtain could recognize. Their findings and reports were known to go to headquarters at Langley, Virginia. Briefing fodder, as someone put it, the stuff on which committees feed. The best guess was they were stapled to yet more reports as background material. Whatever, Langley seemed content enough and the requests came thick and fast for more, while the kooks on the upper floors were only too eager to oblige. The house at Charlestown, Dietrich had heard it said, was fueled by the hatred of fifty lost souls, each seeking his separate vengeance on Moscow. If they could do it no other way, they would bury the Kremlin in paper.

"Please . . . ? I'm Mr. Valentine?"

The Russian showed his face at the door after the quietest of knocks, inquiring if he had the right room. From the doubt in his voice, he might as easily, after all these years, still be questioning his own name. A thin man, his back a little bent, affecting the droopy mustache of a Balkans revolutionary. The shoes were scuffed, the jacket at least a size too big; he clasped a briefcase so firmly in his arms it must contain all his worldly goods. Sweet Jesus, Dietrich thought, he's only come from another floor. What's he want with a briefcase?

"I'm Harold Ames, director of operations for metropolitan Boston. This is Ralph Dietrich, one of my deputies."

Valentine nodded gravely from the hard seat in the middle of the room. Already he wore a frown, pondering why he was so distant, whether it was permitted to draw the chair closer. He seemed about to, but decided not.

"We're here about your sighting report. There might be one or two details you forgot to include. It's easy to miss out the odd fact, we all do."

"This happened the Sunday before last," Dietrich said in his most abrasive tone. "August the fifth?"

"Sunday, yes. I believe it was the fifth."

"So how come you didn't make your report till the thirteenth?"

"I was deciding what to do."

"The report said you were sure, not a shadow of doubt. A KGB muscle man right here in the city, that's what you'd have us believe."

"His is a face I'll never forget. Never."

"You're so sure you take eight days to make up your mind?"

Valentine withdrew into a deeper frown, lost for what more to say.

"Tell us about Sunday," Ames said, making amends for his partner with a friendly smile. "Nothing left out." He withdrew his pocket notebook and unhurriedly ran the edge of a hand along the spine to flatten the pages before placing his gold Parker, cap unscrewed, ready beside it. Then he settled back in the chair, head attentively to one side. Dietrich had seen it all before. He wouldn't write a word in that empty book, but the subject was encouraged by its promise, the flattery of copious notes.

Valentine clutched the briefcase in a tight grip on his knees. "You want the spot I saw him? His clothes, maybe? How I came to be on the hill? All the facts so you can . . ."

"The works, Felix!" Dietrich snapped.

Ames had produced one of his ready smiles, urging him to begin.

"My Sunday habit is the same now, Mr. Ames. Catch the train up to town, walk a while, visit a museum or a cemetery."

"And that evening you went to the ballet?"

"*No!*" The vehement reply took them both by surprise. "The last thing I want in life is to go to the ballet, ever. *He* went to the Esplanade, I merely tailed him. I didn't even know there was a ballet."

"Okay, so you were simply walking about?"

"Yes, Sunday afternoons I usually go to Beacon Hill. The first Christmas I was in America I found myself there. I knew no one in Boston then. There were candles in the windows, all the doors left open. You could stroll right in, shake hands, have a drink. I could barely speak a word of the language yet I still got hot punch and sherry wine and smiles. So I like walking round there, it's a place of happy memories. Do you know Beacon Hill, Mr. Ames?"

"Naturally."

The terse reply brought an open grin from Dietrich. You got one word out of him, Felix, he thought. Quit while you're ahead. A moment's expectation, the hint of a petulant scowl, before he continued. "It was very hot that day; I said so in my report. I had been walking five hours maybe, I had to stop to rest in one of the small squares. I remember very tall trees and some railings. I went back every evening the following week to find the place but those streets all look the same." He met Dietrich's gaze with a scornful stare. *"That's* why I delayed, to find the exact spot, to get near his hideout. I remember one thing most clearly. It was a street running from east to west."

"How do you know?"

"Because, Mr. Dietrich, I noticed that . . ." He broke off, afraid to put his observation to the test. His eyes fell. "It was to do with the angle of the sun," he said, sloping an arm. "It's possible to tell such things; my father was a farmer." He considered Ames a more receptive prospect. "A man can learn much from his surroundings, isn't that so? So long as he looks past his nose."

"I'll take your word on the street," Ames said.

The thin shoulders shrugged under the slack jacket. "I couldn't find it again, not for sure. Like it had never existed. But get your agents to Beacon Hill, you'll find him, I promise."

"And that's where you saw him, in this east-west street?"

Valentine nodded. "He was coming down the hill and I was walking up. Did I say that in my report, that it was also a hill?" His arms waved excitedly; he had to grab for the case as it slipped from his knees. "We must look for a steep street going east to west."

"They're nearly all steep streets over there," Dietrich snarled, and he swung on Ames. "What's he want, Harry? We raid the whole of Beacon Hill because he thinks he saw a ghost!"

"Not thinks," Valentine said disdainfully. "Saw."

"Did he recognize you?" Ames asked in his even, neutral voice, playing the peacemaker.

Valentine laughed and threw up his arms. "Me? Him recognize me? I was one of hundreds in the gulag, Mr. Ames, maybe
thousands. It was twenty-five years ago. Why should he recognize me! But I knew *him*. As we passed, I instantly knew those
eyes, that nose we used to call the vulture's beak. I had to step
aside into the road. Not him, you realize, me. That was another
reason I knew who it was, he expected me to make way. The
whole stinking world has to move aside for Viktor Vlasov."

"So you followed him?" Ames prodded.

"Yes. He was carrying a travel bag. A very expensive bag,
nice leather trimmings—the kind you take on overnight flights.
You know the sort I mean?"

Ames pleased him with a condescending nod.

"I assumed he was off to Logan airport, that I'd lose him. I
thought how cruel it was. After all these years of searching I find
him, only to lose him on a damn plane."

"How do you mean, searching?" Dietrich said.

His gaze wavered. "A figure of speech."

"It didn't sound like it."

Valentine sighed. "You won't understand this, perhaps, but
even in those dark times in Kirensk I had this inner belief that
someday I," he pointed to himself and swelled, despite his thinness, "would be the one to catch him. To, how do you say, put
the finger on him. And suddenly there he was, walking an
American street as if he owned it."

"But he wasn't bound for the airport, was he?" Ames said.

"I didn't know that then." Valentine caressed his chin with a
bony hand, his expression distant, recalling his next moves. "I
began to tail him, a safe way behind. He never suspected. You
don't work in the CIA as many years as I have, even in collation,
without picking up a trick or so. Into doorways, stopping at store
windows to watch his reflection. I remember thinking, the tables
are turned on you, Vlasov. Your thugs probably did this to me in
Kiyev and now I'm shadowing you. Isn't that how you say, shadowing?"

Ames delivered another of his helpful nods while Dietrich
scribbled an observation in his pad. "Pupils very dilated, wild.
What's he on???" Even as he wrote, the answer came to him.

Vlasov. The old guy was hooked on Viktor Vlasov as hard as on any drug. What else did he have to live for? Crazy, he thought. As mad as a bat.

"I almost lost him on Charles Street," Valentine was saying. "Sunday evening, Mr. Ames, lots of people about. There were some kids piling out of an automobile and we got . . . what's the word?" He knitted his fingers.

"Enmeshed," Dietrich said evilly. "Conjuncted."

Valentine wrinkled his brow, considering the suggestions. "Yes," he said doubtfully, "enmeshed. For a moment I lost sight of him. It was as if he expected the crowds to part for him and they did. I remember thinking at the time, like the Red Sea parting for Moses. Sometimes in those endless days in Kirensk I thought he was not of this world."

"A figure of speech again, Felix?"

The pause was too long before he continued. "Somehow I pushed free. I looked down the side street at the next corner and there he was, him and his bag. The relief! He looked at his watch, began to walk faster. I assumed he was late for the plane; he'd catch a cab on Storrow Drive. I gave up the doorways and pursued him in plain sight and he never looked back, not once. But after the next turning he took the footbridge over the highway. The . . . ?"

"Fiedler Bridge?" Ames prompted.

"Yes, the Fiedler Bridge, the famous conductor. If I'd thought then about the clues—Vlasov, music, conductors— maybe I'd have guessed what was coming. I chased him up the ramp, turned at the top and almost stepped into him. Bang!" The thin hands came together in an ineffectual slap. His breathing had become heavy, scared. If it was a story, Dietrich thought, he was living it. "I pressed back against the piers, but he hadn't seen me. He was leaning on the parapet, listening. I strained my ears and I could hear it too, just faintly over the traffic. A piano." He paused to regain his breath.

"A piano," Dietrich echoed, cocking his head provocatively. "You don't say."

Valentine seemed not to notice. "Like a phonograph record

from a nearby apartment, that's what I thought. Vlasov checked his watch again and went on, almost running. As I reached the middle of the bridge I could suddenly see the stage by the river. There were bright lights, dancers under the dome. That's when I was sure. The moment I saw the ballet dancers. That's when I knew for certain it was him."

"I thought you were sure the moment you saw him on the hill," Dietrich muttered.

"There's certainty and certainty," Valentine retorted. "Don't tell me an agent of your experience doesn't know that!" He gave vent to a labored sigh. "I came down from the bridge. There were all these young people sitting on the grass, thousands of them, as far as the eye could see. Blankets, picnic baskets, freezer boxes everywhere. Vlasov picked his way through the audience, found a space he liked, and sat down."

"The space kind of opened up for him, I assume?"

He thought better of the prickly rejoinder that quivered at his lips. "That's when it was clear why he had the travel bag. He took out a blanket in one of those checker patterns."

"Tartan?" Ames said. "A car rug?"

"Yes, tartan, to spread on the ground. Then out came a bottle of red wine and a glass. He was always a fussy man, frightened of germs; he even had a napkin to clean the glass. Somehow I found a free place close by—I could see his face but not the label on the bottle. But French wine, Mr. Ames, take my word. It was always expensive claret with Vlasov, the very best, as they say. And as I watched his eyes on the dancers, watched him drink, I knew for sure it was Vlasov. It couldn't be anyone else."

"More certainty, huh?" Dietrich said.

Eyes tightly closed, Valentine fought to keep his composure, chest rising and falling to unnaturally deep breaths. "You must understand, Mr. Ames," he said finally, "he was a fanatic for the ballet."

"Which is why you detest it, am I right?" Ames suggested in his most kindly way.

Valentine agreed with a tired nod. "Exactly so. He thought ballerinas were the most perfect of creatures; he told me so once.

He followed the movements on stage as if he saw things I did not—movements, colors, I don't know what. I compared his face with the others around, not one of them had such a look of . . ."

"Intensity?"

"Yes, exactly."

"And then . . . ?"

He seemed jerked like a puppet by his own shrug, his arms and shoulders all sticks under the big coat. "I lost him," he confessed faintly.

"He was there under your very nose," Dietrich said, drumming his fingers on the desk.

"Don't remind me."

"You could have phoned, dammit! Anyone, the duty man at the field office. You must know the number, sweet Jesus, it's even in the phone book!"

"I was watching him."

"Watching, Felix? *Watching?* What was this, the KGB on Ice?"

Valentine glanced away. "Guarding him, that's what I mean. Suppose I'd gone to phone, what then? Suppose he'd left?"

"So you just sat there on your skinny ass?"

His temper flared. He leaped from the chair and the briefcase fell to his feet. "I get someone else to phone for me, is that what you're saying, Mr. Dietrich! Are you mad! What do I tell them—I'm with the CIA? The guy over there who looks like a banker, so rich and smart with his wine and blanket . . . he's KGB! Do you take me for a fool? I'm an old man, I shift bloody bits of paper round and round at Charlestown. Don't you think I know what I am!"

"You were right," Ames said, motioning for him to return to his chair. "You had no choice."

"Quite so, I had no choice." Obediently, he sat. "I had decided to wait, to shadow him back to his hideout. Then I'd have all the time in the world to make that call . . . to have him enmeshed." He gulped for breath. "He has a jazzy hideout, believe me, a penthouse even. Nice paintings, nice carpets, a bar in the front room with French wine and more of these lovely glasses.

Remember I know him like I know my own mother. I had to suffer him for years in Kirensk."

"No recriminations. But how come you lost him?"

The answering sigh was high and thin, like escaping steam.
"Because of the crowds, Mr. Ames. When the concert finished it
was just too hard, thousands of people heading every which way.
He's a tall man, very upright, I could see his head clearly in
front. But all the time he was gaining on me, getting away. At
the footbridge there was a . . . ," he ground a fist into a cupped
palm, "like we were being pressed into a funnel. That's where I
lost him. His head moved off into the distance as if there were no
crowds at all, as if they stepped to one side." He shrugged rag-
gedly, disconsolately. "Just like the bloody Red Sea again."

An acute nervousness descended on him. He searched their
expressions, appealing for a reaction.

"And that's it?" Ames said. "Nothing left out?"

"That's all I remember."

"Well you did okay, Felix. Better than most untrained observ-
ers, I'll say that for you." Ames leaned back to stretch like a big,
lazy cat before clasping his hands over a protruding vest. "Now
fill us in on Kirensk. The same accuracy, the same useful detail."

6

"I was just a clerk," he began, "working in the railroad office at Kiyev, at the big marshaling yard to the north of the Nezhin Road. My job was to help schedule the movements of freight." He paused, wetting his lips. "Wheat, when there was any, textbooks up to Moscow, heavy machinery for shipment from Riga. Just ordinary commercial freight, Mr. Ames. I had no direct involvement with military rail traffic." Another uneasy pause, his tongue working anxiously at the corners of his mouth.

Dietrich noted the change in his manner, a man unable to forget the past yet reluctant to relive it. On Beacon Hill you were after Vlasov, he thought. In Kirensk it was the other way round.

"Keep going," he said roughly. "We've got that."

"Of course there were often Army wagons passing through the yard but we, that is my section, had no details on what was in them. They were handled by a different section, privileged party men, you understand." Once again he stopped, his eyes moving repeatedly from Ames to Dietrich and back.

"Sure," Ames said, nodding gently. "We know the system."

"I wasn't a party man myself. I had a young wife and the usual hopes of a family. I should have thought of her instead of honesty. Who in the party machine values simple honesty? But I didn't consider that then; my mind was only on doing my job. At first it was little things, as they say, like an urgent delivery of castings to Odessa. The bureaucrats wanted the railcars packed just that bit more full than usual, an extra dozen wagons on the train. I pointed out the weight restrictions on the track. There was the old bridge at Belaya Tserkov, I said, long past its best. We had an argument that I lost and I thought that was the end of it.

"Another time, I was asked to change my report, the monthly record of traffic through the yard which I always prepared. The director for the region wanted the numbers increased, to show higher productivity. You see, that's how you increase productivity in the Soviet Union, Mr. Ames, push up the numbers. I told my supervisor what to do with his lying statistics. Let him do it himself, the fool! Again, I assumed it was all dead and buried. Then one Sunday evening I was alone in the office and I was asked to clear an unscheduled train through the yard. No proper explanation but it was a military train with the special yellow documents. All I had to do was sign the top copy and they'd pass it to the engineer in the yard control cabin. Well, I looked at the details—there were ten railcars, each loaded with a tank. No mention of tanks on the documents, you understand, but forty-five-ton units on low-platform railcars. What else could they be but tanks. I refused to sign."

"Sweet Gee," Dietrich said under his breath.

"It had been a bad month at the yard, I remember. So many shipments in, too few out. The tracks were clogged with wagons and the only way to get fast transit was to use a route through on the east of the yard. I said no, that section of track was too old, an axle loading that high would shatter the rails. Well, the trouble that started, I'm telling you. First a young corporal pointing a rifle in my chest, then a major going red in the face. Phones going everywhere suddenly and my supervisor hauled in from his apartment. He signed on the spot and I was dismissed from duty. And what did I achieve by it? I used to ask myself that question many times in the months that followed. I caused one hour's delay maybe. There was no war on and ten bloody tanks arrived one hour late. So what! But that same night I was in a prison cell in Podgorni Street. No charge, no questioning, just locked up. I was there nearly a month while they interrogated my wife and my friends. My wife disowned me immediately, God forgive her, but I only found that out much later. They moved me to Moscow, to the Lubyanka, and I finally learned the charge on which I was being held. *Interfering with vital military supplies.* There was all sorts of talk, endless threats. How I'd be shot without a trial, shot any time they felt like it. Then no more threats, a cigarette, a few questions about certain friends in Kiyev, about a group who used to meet for vodka and conversation at the house of a man named Yesivich, Georgi Yesivich. It didn't occur to me then what the game was. You see, Mr. Ames, I was worried only about the business with the tanks. They were merely finding out all they could about my background, that's how I saw it, building the usual dossier. I knew Yesivich only slightly, I told them, I had been to his place just twice."

He stopped and examined their faces, licking his lips. "May I?" he asked, pointing to a pitcher of water on the desk. Ames filled him a glass which was emptied greedily.

"After some weeks the questions on the railroad stopped altogether. Then it was all Yesivich and his comrades and no pretense anymore. Who did they meet? Who went to the house? What did they do there, what plots? I said I knew nothing but they refused to believe me. Shall I tell you what they did to me then? On the first floor of the Lubyanka, only a stone's throw from our beloved leaders in the Kremlin?"

"We'll take your word for it," Ames said.

"Then I was given a rest from it all, an unexplained few weeks of peace before being packed off to Kirensk. I never even saw a court or a prosecutor, just a grubby slip of paper in a jailer's hands. A trip to Siberia in a cattle truck, believe me, actually a cattle truck. Shall I describe it there? Do you need to know the details of a Soviet gulag? Is that useful accuracy for you, Mr. Ames?"

"We can give that a miss too."

"The overcrowded huts with walls like cardboard, the heating that never worked. When the ground wasn't frozen as hard as concrete it was a sea of mud. That mud everywhere, I can't tell you, a swamp to suck down what little spirit we had."

"And that's where you met Vlasov?"

Valentine nodded, with the merest shading of a grim smile. "Viktor Stepanovich Vlasov. He was different than the others— at Kiyev, at the Lubyanka. He was the most . . . controlled, yes, most controlled interrogator of them all. In the whole of the KGB there was nobody like him." Silently he held out the glass again and this time sipped with deliberate slowness, wanting to postpone the ordeal.

"His office was in the administration wing outside the main compound. I shall never forget the first time they took me there. An ugly wooden building, an approach road of muddy gravel—barbed wire and searchlight towers on all sides. That hall with the bare floorboards and the same cold damp stink I knew from the hut. Then suddenly this wonderful, huge room with paneled walls and a chandelier—not so much an inquisition chamber as a *salon*. With oil paintings, fine old furniture, lovely foreign carpets. I don't know how he arranged it all, none of the prisoners did.

"It was a fine room but rather a mess when you got used to it, you understand. Nothing quite matched. The colors weren't right, some of the paintings clashed with the carpets. He had good taste in objects, Mr. Ames, excellent taste, but no bloody idea of color. He was a magpie, a bourgeois thief. He'd picked up—stolen—whatever he could find. I made a comment about it once, about the colors fighting one another, and know what he said? 'We do our best in spite of the difficulties here,' he said. He too was an exile in Kirensk; that was his line. Seeking my pity for *him*, damn his soul."

Now he shrank into an inner torment they could only imagine. His eyes were far away, reflecting his thoughts, changing and fierce yet blank in the same instant. To Dietrich it was as if they flickered to the shadows of a fight, hidden around a corner.

"Want to tell us about it?" Ames asked.

"I told Vlasov what he wanted. I told him about Georgi and his futile attempts to organize workers at the iron foundry, about his damned stupid unofficial trade union."

"So you knew all along," Ames breathed.

"Of course I knew! Georgi was a cousin; we had vacations together as kids. But only Vlasov could have got it out of me. And you want to know the sickening part, Mr. Ames, the part I shall never forget till I die? Vlasov didn't give a damn. He didn't care what I said, so long as it was the truth. His pleasure lay in extracting information. Extracting it, do you follow?"

Ames bowed his head slowly to share the pain.

"I betrayed three close friends that morning. Enough dirt, I thought, to send them to the gulag forever. Yet, listen to this, no finger was raised against them. Of course I only found out later but we heard—it became common knowledge at Kirensk—it was always so with Vlasov. He had to prove he could suck your secrets from you. Once he had them, they were worthless."

He returned the glass to the table and sat back stiffly, gripping his knees. Dietrich thought him oddly like a job candidate at that moment, apprehensive and eager to please, and he remembered Harry's inspired guess as they'd talked alone together. *See him in the street, you wouldn't suspect.*

"You were in the gulag for seven years in all?" Ames said.

A reluctant nod.

"And Vlasov?"

"I was there till 1959. He left in '56."

"To do what?"

"I never heard what happened to him. I guess he rose fast in the KGB, found his way to power in Moscow. Maybe rose to the very top."

"And in Moscow? What would he do, a man like that?"

Valentine indicated the house with a sweep of the hand. "So many reports here, so many words. You'd think he'd show up in one of them, just a mention. Once I thought I'd found him in Gorki. Another time, in Warsaw . . ." He sighed. "But never any proof."

Ames bent over the desk, tapping his pen to his lips. "How old was he when you knew him, any idea?"

"I know exactly, he told me his birthdate."

Ames inclined his head, inquiring further.

"He told me, on my honor, does it matter why! 1908."

"By my reckoning that makes him seventy-five," Ames mused. "A very tall man, you said, pushing his way through the crowds. Elbowing them aside by the sound of it. Fit for his age, would you say?"

Dietrich half turned in his seat for a hooded gaze. When Harry held the pen like that to his mouth it was always the big one coming, every time.

"I know what you're thinking! I recognized him, I tell you. He had hardly changed."

"In twenty-five years?"

"Some men are like that. Wish to God we all were."

"Well past retirement age, I must point out. The party bosses go on till they drop, the special services people are put out to pasture at sixty-five usually, never later than seventy."

Dietrich admired the even voice, the level tone. He couldn't have done it.

Valentine was shaking his head, refusing to be cowed.

"If you insist," Ames said and theatrically closed his notebook. "Any other points, Ralph?"

"I've heard enough."

"Fine, let's call it a day, shall we?"

Valentine rose uncertainly. "You'll be searching the area? Combing Beacon Hill?"

"If we find him, we'll let you know."

"Please. I'd be most grateful, most . . . relieved."

"Oh, Felix, " Ames called as he reached the door. "Why not take the rest of the day off? I'll see it's all right, square it with your chief."

He hesitated, his hand not quite on the doorknob. The big jacket hung on him in creased folds; his stoop was pronounced. He might have lost pounds since entering the room.

"There's no need. All that matters is you get your agents on the job."

7

"Well, Harry?"

A pointless question, Ames thought. Surely Dietrich must know what response he would get? He spoke simply for something to say. His kind could never bear the silence between two men, not for long.

They were in Dietrich's beige Plymouth, cruising back along Memorial Drive. One of those miserable damp days that do nothing for Cambridge; every building a granite city hall or an oversized courthouse. Beside them, over the embankment wall, the Charles River pursued its eternal, lethargic course to the sea. No young oarsmen out bending their backs; this stretch was deserted. He had searched the waters in vain.

When it suited him, Ames gave his answer. "Let's hear what you think."

"I'll come clean. I don't want to believe him. But in all those years of searching he never once raised the alarm. He always checked it out first, decided he was wrong, and kept his mouth shut. Same story this time. He goes back to Beacon Hill, worrying about it for days before he finally writes the report. So I've got to conclude he actually did see something."

"Vlasov?"

"Who can say, Harry? He describes him just the way he looked back in the gulag. It's like he passed someone similar on the street and projected a memory on him. Hallucinating, maybe that's all it was."

"Let's assume it *was* Vlasov . . ."

"Where does that get us? I mean to say, he isn't on any of the relevant lists, I checked last night. He's not marked for attention, he's not even there. He's a no-no."

"That's right," Ames murmured. "I did likewise."

Dietrich slapped a hand on the steering wheel. "He's a ghost, Harry, like I said at the start. We've wasted a morning chasing some ghost from a loony's past."

Ames lost himself in the river for a while. There was a boat at last, a single crew braving the impending rain; a university eight paddling upstream against the murky tide. He gazed after them until they were lost, under the Harvard Bridge.

"Vlasov is ex-KGB," he said, and might have been alone. "Yet our computer hasn't heard of him. Biggest computer in the IBM catalog and it can't remember Viktor Vlasov."

Dietrich forgot the road to stare at him.

"He's past the age for active service. Suddenly he's seen here in Boston."

"So . . . ?"

Ames spared him the measured sigh he deserved. "Think about it."

They parted in the underground parking lot and Ames rode the elevator to his suite on the fourth floor. At his desk, he keyed his personal access code into the computer terminal. He already knew what the outcome would be, but it seemed prudent to try one last time.

SUBJECT?
VLASOV, VIKTOR
STEPANOVICH
ALSO KNOWN AS?
TRY: VULTURE
SUBJECT NOT FOUND
ANY FURTHER IDENTIFIERS?
KGB; KIRENSK

It was worse waiting for a computer to reply than with people. No facial twitches, none of the little giveaways an old hand could see. Lately he was glad he was fifty, on the final lap to retirement. The way things were going, electronics everywhere you turned, skills like his would soon be redundant. Finally, the answer came, just words on a goddamned screen. No voice in which you could hear the pauses or croaks of a lie.

SUBJECT NOT FOUND
WHAT ELSE?
TRY: FILE(INTERROGATORS)
TRY: CLASSIFICATION(SOVIET)

He knew every line of this dialogue by now. When the response came up it was the same as on his previous attempts, last
night and again this morning. It would have to be; computers
never make mistakes. The hell they don't, he thought.

SUBJECT NOT FOUND
ANY MORE?
GO SCREW YOURSELF
SORRY, HARRY, INSTRUCTION
NOT UNDERSTOOD

At the big mirrored window with its commanding view of the
Charles, he sought guidance from a crew on the sluggish brown
waters, flexing his wrists in time with theirs—in, out, in, out.
The therapy worked, it always did when his brain needed a jolt.
Rowing had calmed him as a sophomore back in his carefree
years at Harvard; the slow rhythm still concentrated his mind,
even acted out in his office. He returned to the computer terminal and entered a report on the interview with Valentine. A brief
summary, he was good at those though he said it himself, with no
follow-up action noted. A classic of the genre, a note for the
record to be buried in the computer files at Langley.

CROSS REFERENCES? the computer asked when
he finished.
KGB: KIRENSK: VLASOV
ADDRESSEES?
ARCHIVE ONLY
ANY MORE?
SIGN OFF

Then he commenced his vigil, closeted in his office, refusing
all calls. An hour passed and another until he began to consider
he was mistaken. When the buzzer on his telephone finally

sounded, he permitted himself a congratulatory smile before answering.

"I know you said no calls, Mr. Ames, but it's Langley."

"Who?"

"Mr. Davenport. Seemed a good idea you should know."

"Put him on."

"You keeping well, Harry?" Davenport said. A no-nonsense
opening, not the slightest pretense of interest.

"Well enough. And you?"

"You've been blundering, Harry. Big feet all over the tulip
fields. I've got an excited computer here, lights flashing like mad
on my display screen." He never raised his voice, even when agitated. He spoke in level, clipped syllables, an accent you could
take to be Oxford English if you didn't know better. He kept his
office as cold as an Englishman's bedroom, and it suited him.

"I'm pleading the Fifth Amendment, Walter. What have I
done?"

"This character Valentine . . ."

"I was simply following up a report he made. A matter of dull
routine, I assumed; one has to be seen to be active."

"What's the plan?"

"I'm taking it seriously, Walter. I've no way of knowing if this
Vlasov he talks of is on a mission, but it's a sighting I can't ig-
nore. I'm considering putting men onto the streets on Beacon
Hill to . . ."

"Drop it!"

"Did I hear you right?"

"You heard."

"Can I ask why?"

"You'd damned better not."

"Has Vlasov been imported and repackaged? Is he here in
Boston, hidden away on my territory?"

"Give it a rest, Harry."

The line clicked; he was left with only the tone.

The university eight had gone from the river. Only the piers
of the bridges disturbed the surface, tracing spiral eddies that
drifted as dying whirlpools toward the harbor. A fine shower was

falling and the Charles was dark and soaking and windswept . . . why did rivers look so wet when it rained? He gazed over at the city skyline; between the angular slabs of the high offices, he could see the byzantine gold dome of the State House where the drizzle dimmed the heights of Beacon Hill.

If you're out there, he determined, I'll find you.

His motive, when he examined it, was less sure. Could be he didn't like defectors dumped on his doorstep. Then again, he resented Davenport's characteristic high-handedness in choosing his city as if it were a square on a Monopoly board. And then, sin of sin, having dumped a defector, keeping quiet about it.

The gathering clouds blackened the sky; sheets of rain gusted like rice against the glass. Staring out, he was unable to rid himself of stray thoughts of Valentine, which came like visitations, dammit, but his wish to find Vlasov had nothing to do with that. God no, he assured himself, nothing so sentimental.

3. Weekend in Salem

8

Sorenson had reached an age where he had little time for clothes. They chose themselves in the morning. Dressing required no more deliberation than the drive to Norwood, one of those routines of life that somehow happened. But that Friday he fretted over what to wear. To arrive in an office suit might look over-earnest. He rejected flowers for Elaine and a gift for Jay on the same reasoning. Dress down and it could seem he cared too little—or worse, that the intervening years had treated him badly. After more changes of mind than he had garments, he decided on a sober blazer worn over casual cords.

Fitzgerald was on the stoop when he left, in his faded deckchair, a lethal length of broom handle on his lap. Lately he sat out all hours. This was to do with a local cat, he wouldn't say what, a feud of immense loathing on both sides.

"Going away?" he yelled. He must have spied the suitcase.

From the car, Sorenson made a meaningless gesture into the distance. They conversed in this manner now, like diplomats over cocktails; both knew better than to ask a straight question or give an honest reply.

"When will I see you again, mister?" He meant, will you be back? His abiding fear, never put into words, was that Sorenson would leave one morning and not return. So he grasped the broom handle, as if the wrong answer would get him bounding over, intent on kidnap. His terrors were those of the old, he made no distinction between them. He feared losing Sorenson as obsessively as he dreaded the cat.

"Sunday," Sorenson shouted, much to his own surprise. Perhaps he needed the same reassurance: this was only a fleeting trip.

*   *   *

That evening he left the plant early for the crescent route north to the coast. At Marblehead, masts prickled in the cove. The weekend dinghies packed the water's edge; farther out the more serious craft turned idly with the tide, offshore racing yachts and chunky fishing cruisers as high as they were long. Between the gingerbread houses of the township, he opened the car window to the breeze and heard the gulls squawk abuse at the Evinrudes.

When they'd lived nearby at Peabody, he knew this area well. From Marblehead he took the tourist trail to Salem. Down the wide approach avenue he hadn't driven in years, past the final fling of stores and gas stations before entering the old town. The ARCO and EXXON and JACK-IN-THE-BOX neons on stilts gave way to more restrained signs: THE HOUSE OF SEVEN GABLES. CHESTNUT STREET HISTORIC DISTRICT. SALEM COMMON. THE WITCH MUSEUM. Well, Elaine, he thought with a grin, you finally found your niche.

Her street was a narrow backwater embroidered with sweet chestnuts and maples. Locating the number, he fell by habit into the role of cop, driving on to the far end to come slowly back and park some yards short. Hunched over the steering wheel, he gazed long and hard at the house. There was a tidy picket fence, an air of comfort he should have expected. He took in the yellow wood sidings and the rust-red shingled roof; scalloped blinds hung at the windows; the small front lawn was shaded by a sycamore. The setting and stage props for a new act, he thought ruefully. An affluent but unpretentious home, an unattached woman not yet in her middle years, a reclusive son. Knowing Elaine, she would play that scene to the hilt. No careless talk of the past and let the neighbors think what they will. An unmarried mother? A divorcée? Given no facts beyond what they saw, they must decide for themselves and she would delight in any aura of mystery they bestowed on her.

He counted the windows, noted the generous depth of the house. At least four bedrooms upstairs, with a large one at the back perhaps given over as a playroom for Jay. Plenty of space on the ground floor for the farmhouse kitchen she'd always wanted. He guessed the living room had big French windows onto a pleasant garden—lofty chestnuts showed over the roof, and the houses on the next street were a good distance away. Taking stock of the quiet road, he suffered an unaccustomed pang of what might be envy or even resentment, and was probably a mixture of both.

"You found us then?" She stood alone in the hall, showing a polite smile.

In all his rehearsals for this moment he had no plans for Jay not being at her side.

She noticed the suitcase in his hand. "So you're staying after all?"

"I had a look at the Hawthorne and decided to take up your offer."

"It's a very comfortable hotel, so they say."

"I'm more the Howard Johnson type, and since I couldn't find one . . ." He tried an amiable shrug.

"Well, I made up a bed in case."

Rather stiffly, he felt, she led him from the hall to a cool room where the big French windows gave onto a garden of cropped

grass and deep green shadows. He glanced about him, not yet
able to meet her in the face, and noticed how different it was
from their house in Peabody. Plump easy chairs in colonial chintz
and some paintings of coastal views—the kind that filled the craft
galleries all along Cape Ann. Wallpaper and drapes and fabrics in
the too closely matched pastel blues of apartments in glossy mag-
azines. There was the big old Zenith television he had scraped to
buy when color was still new in its walnut console beside the
fireplace; the modest hi-fi on the shelves behind must be hers. No
books anywhere; Elaine had never been one for reading.

"Nice place," he said.

The quick beam of a hostess, then she was lost for words.
Usually at this point, he guessed, a stranger would hear all about
the room: what home journals had provided inspiration, which
ideas were her own. She seemed unprepared for him and tugged
at her jacket in apology.

"Whatever must you think! You haven't blundered in on a
Tupperware party. I'm not long back from the shop; I didn't
have time to change."

She wore a tailored suit over a silk shirt with a high collar.
Perhaps to make up for the demure neckline, the shirt burst into
an enormous floppy bow. Like him, she must have sweated that
morning over what to wear. One of them had miscalculated
badly. Thank God she thought it was her.

"Shop?" he said.

"It's what pays the bills, Toby." She was unclipping the plain
gilt rings from her ears. "It's down on Pickering Wharf. Just a
tourist trap, really. Souvenirs, bumper stickers, whatever sells to
the avid seeker of Salem's lurid past."

Regarding her closely at last, he tried to picture her behind a
counter and failed. He had seen the stickers on cars all over the
town: STOP BY FOR A SPELL. SALEM, THE WITCH CITY.

She must have read his thoughts. "House rule number one,
Toby Sorenson: no jokes about broomsticks and eye of newt.
I've heard them all."

"Would I do that?" he protested.

She steered him to the windows, sat him in one of the tubby

chintz chairs, and settled in another, almost shouting distance away over a coffee table. For a short while an awkward silence hung between them.

"Well then . . . ," she said, playing with her hands.

"I never imagined you as a shopkeeper."

"I prefer to think of myself as a businesswoman."

"You always had it in you."

"I'm good at it. Sales are up ten percent on last year. That's despite all this lousy rain we've been having. Most of the others on the Wharf are complaining bitterly."

"Here's to success," he said, raising a cupped hand in a toast.

"I'm sorry . . . you've had a long drive. Would you like a drink?"

"Don't trouble, please. I wasn't dropping a hint."

She was on her feet anyway. "I usually have one about now in the evening." She added too quickly, "Just a splash, a reward for the day's toil."

"A scotch then, to keep you company."

The bottles were in one of those cabinets where a light clicks on when the lid is raised. She poured generous measures, a martini for herself. They sat in their facing chairs and between sips she ducked the ice cubes with a finger while he swirled his around in the glass.

The five years had scarcely changed her. Perhaps she was a little sleeker than he remembered, a mite more concerned with appearance, but sleek was hardly the right word with Elaine. If time had treated her kindly it was because she had no beauty of the conventional sort to lose. He used to call it "Dutch Presbyterian beauty" to tease her, and ended up praising the very firmness of features she'd most wished to forget. "A reliable girl," his mother had ventured on their first meeting, "sensible with money, I'll wager. A good cook and not the kind to fool around. No Grace Kelly but you aren't going to do any better. You're no great catch yourself." That was the general opinion at the time, and he shared it. A whirlwind six weeks of pursuit found him married. In the ensuing daze he could only wonder how she had allowed it to happen.

Seeing her now, her jaw set square as she resolved to break the silence, he realized she made him uneasy—and perhaps she always had.

"I'd better explain. The people here know me as Elaine Marshall. I'd like it to stay that way."

"Why not, it's the name you were born with."

"Exactly, why not. You won't have had that problem, of course. Mr. Sorenson then, Mr. Sorenson now. Some men wear a failed marriage like a battle honor. It's useful to them, as attractive as graying hair."

He nearly retorted, "Do me a favor!" but stopped himself. Instead he proposed, "Can we have a deal? What's gone is gone, agreed?"

She nodded. "How is the Sorenson career progressing at . . ."

"Eastern Semiconductor."

"That's right, I wrote it down somewhere. Are you a vice president yet?"

He let the barbed comment ride. "It's a big corporation. I'm in charge of security. If things break my way I might make the board of directors by the year three thousand."

She still had the habit of watching him in a certain foxy way that suggested no secret was safe from her. "Well, well. Honesty suits you, Toby. You should have tried it years ago." With a starched wave she embraced the room. "Anyway, this is it. This is where we live now."

He seized on the cue. "Is Jay out? You told him I was coming?"

"I mentioned it as he was leaving for school this morning. Don't take it too hard but it didn't have much impact. I told you when I phoned; he's always in his room. Him and that stupid damned toy! I wish to God I'd never bought it."

"Toy?"

"One of those home computers. A smart Christmas idea that rebounded on me." She crossed the room to a pine cabinet and delved into a drawer. "That's why I thought you could help. You're in computers; it gives you a common interest."

The words were oddly wounding. "Visiting computer expert," he said.

"I didn't intend it like that, and you know it."

"I'm the top in my field. Any time a computer vanishes, they call for me."

In an album from the drawer she pulled out a photograph. As she handed it over, he felt a shock of recognition, a disturbing sensation of being thrown back in time. Jay looked up at him from the print: an older face certainly—with the features he remembered from the beach at Cape Cod—the exact same reticent smile. Extremely tall for his age, dark and with an athletic, slender frame. He stared in silent wonder for a long while before registering the other boy. They were in the yard outside, posing rather woodenly for the snapshot and he could almost hear Elaine calling, "Come on, you two, it won't take a second." They wore matching blue windbreakers over denim pants. The other boy was much shorter—Jay's outstretched elbow rested comically on his shoulder.

"That's Kevin. The kid I mentioned on the phone."

"An accident, wasn't that what you said?"

She sprang away and huddled in her chair, knees pressed close to her chin. "It was terrible, Toby, simply terrible. He fell from his bedroom window on the third floor. They assume he was leaning out, nobody knows why."

"Poor kid," Sorenson said. Holding the picture nearer, he saw in the boy his own impatience as a kid. To stand still for a camera was to waste a lifetime. "I . . . ," he began but trailed away.

"They were the best of friends from the time we moved here, almost like brothers." She threw a sharp look intended to hurt. "Kevin seemed to fill a family gap. Big Jay, little Kevin. Practically inseparable."

"I begin to understand," he said.

"Jay called on him that day and got no answer at the door. So he went to the back of the house. Kevin was in a heap on the terrace, his head . . ." She pulled the knees to her face against a rising hysteria.

"Don't go on if it bothers you."

He felt the small town quiet outside in the lull that followed. "I didn't see him myself," she said eventually, "but Jay described it to me. With the strangest calm. Not callous—I don't mean that—not exactly uncaring, but kind of weird. Oh God, Toby, you say you understand but I don't, not any of it. Now he's a hermit, only ten years old and withdrawn from the world. It must have shocked him deeply, I know it must. But not a single tear and not a word about Kevin ever since, not one. Do you understand a reaction like that? Is there pain so bad it doesn't show?"

"I believe so."

She came for the photo and, back in her chair, curled in a ball, stared at it with such clinging solitude she must have forgotten him. He was reminded of the snap of Cindy Fernandez, his overwhelming urge to destroy it. So much power in such small squares of film. She wished she had never pressed the shutter; she was vowing not to let it from her sight.

"Where do I find Jay?" he said gently. "Isn't that why you asked me here?"

"Up to the landing and turn right. The door at the end of the corridor." She spoke flatly, without interest. Her gaze was still on the picture in her hands as he slipped from the room.

9

The minute he looked in he knew he had expected too much. Not from Jay; he expected nothing from him. But he had anticipated a boy's room. A place of grubby baseball gloves, bicycle parts littering the floor, small furry creatures in a cage under the bed. A ripe smell of animals and stale shoes, an honest-to-goodness mess—but then he had reckoned without Elaine.

His own childhood den had been much in his mind these past days, an attic shambles piled to the eaves with more junk than he could handle. Toys, plunder, and games, some acquired by shrewd swaps—enough for him to excavate on restless Sundays and find possessions long since forgotten. Lead soldiers fought battles on every ledge and died stiffly to attention, their bases in the air. Lockheed Lightnings with devilish grinning teeth hung twelve o'clock high on thread—it took a trampoline leap from the bed to get the tailspins going. Sepia Gary Coopers and Stewart Grangers and Virginia Mayos smiled from the peeling montage covering the walls—all done with scissors, flour, and water. Who needed wallpaper? Nobody on the block, perhaps nobody in the whole of Massachusetts, had made better decorative use of *Photoplay*.

As he stood at the door his disappointment was total. He saw a divan bed impeccably dotted with spotless cushions. The lacquered cupboards were paired with a chest and bookcase, all without a scratch. The rug had a Noah's Ark pattern in subdued hues. On the wall, a circus poster of an elephant walking a tightrope with the aid of an umbrella; he guessed the words were Czech. On another wall, a picture of Snoopy on his kennel roof, dreamily pondering that *Life's What You Make It*. Everything in its place and not a stray toy to be seen, creating an impression of furnishing by numbers. The antiseptic tidiness seemed to scream at him. Just as well that Jay didn't see his face at that moment, but if he'd bounced up and down on the prissy divan he doubted Jay would have noticed.

He was at a desk by the window, his back to the door. A small computer display held him engrossed, and his hands moved deftly over the keyboard. The room was filled with the low hum of busy electronics; the keys made only a gentle padding noise. The screen emptied, then quickly filled again with words too tiny to be read at a distance. Jay studied them, muttered to himself, and chose some keys. Something happened on the screen—Sorenson couldn't tell what—the computer sounded a hollow *gong-g* and he sensed a smile on Jay's face. A long time of inactivity while the computer purred at what it had done and Jay considered his response. Then his fingers expertly brushed the keys. *Pad, pad, pad, pad.* The lines on the screen rearranged themselves, the alert young head lolled to one side and there came a thoughtful clucking of the tongue.

"Hi," Sorenson said from across the room.

An easy "Hi" in reply, but Jay made not the slightest attempt to turn. Words were streaming onto the display screen, and his fingers replied as soon as they stopped moving. *Pad, pad, pad.*

Sorenson closed the door to venture over. From beside the desk he looked down on Jay's profile: Elaine's snub nose, a trace of her stubborn chin. A long, serious face, distinctive in its way but never handsome. There was a doggedness about the expression, an unusual determination in the set of the jaw that bordered on the comical in one so young, but he was not amused. The photograph of the two boys had scarcely prepared him for what he now found. His whole family had agreed that Jay was blessed as a baby with his broad forehead; the fair eyebrows could have been stolen from him even if the rest was undiluted Elaine! Now they were gone. The head was high and narrow, the brow thickly dark. He wondered for an angry instant if a child could do that: wipe out all resemblance to spite him.

Oblivious, Jay continued playing, his eyes glued to the little screen. *Pad, pad, pad.* The computer answered with a fresh line of words, green on a flat gray background. The name tag on the cabinet said it was a Possum Model 3.

"Do you know who I am?"

"Sure, you're Toby. You're my father." The boy frowned heavily, interested only in the screen that seemed to stare back at him like a single unblinking eye. It emptied and a new challenge appeared.

OHIO? KENTUCKY? MINNESOTA? UTAH?

"Try Utah," Sorenson suggested wildly.

"Why?"

"The rest run civilized bar hours."

"Do me a favor . . ." Jay moaned. Then he broke into a boy-ish grin, shaking his head with glee. "None of them! That's it, none of them!"

"A trick question?"

"They're all trick questions." He pounced on the keyboard, fingers flying. *Pad, pad, pad, pad.* His grin spread wider when the screen abruptly cleared and stayed blank. The computer had nothing more to say; he had it beat.

"Do you remember me, Jay?"

"Sure I do. You bought me the Porsche 911."

"Did I?" The words were out before he could stop them.

Jay finally chose to look at him with his mother's dark steady eyes. "Sure you did. The red one, battery powered." As he spoke, the display began to fill again and the computer issued a commanding *bong-g-g* to regain his attention.

"Oh grom!" he said crossly when he read the message.

"What's grom?"

"A swear word, of course. Elaine doesn't approve of cussing so I have to make up my own."

The Possum tried a fighting comeback; a line on the screen flashed rapidly, brazenly. Without turning a hair, Jay tapped some keys and wiped the words away. The computer lapsed into a vacant stare, its faint sound was like the whine of a limping puppy.

"Got you, you bastard!"

"Does Elaine approve of bastard?"

"No, but who's telling?"

"Not me, kid."

He used the coy smile of thanks as an excuse for another glance. "You don't look tough enough for a cop."

"I'm not a cop."

"Elaine said you used to be. You showed me your badge once, yonks ago."

"So I did. I guess I was trying to impress you."

"Is that why you gave up? Because you weren't tough?"

"Among other reasons."

Sorenson must have stared too long or too hard. Jay became fidgety and lowered his gaze. For want of something better to say, he nodded at the Possum, apologizing for its behavior. "It does this every once in a while, goes all dumb on me. Must be a program bug."

"What are you playing?"

"It's not playing."

"Then what is it, exactly?"

"Learning, of course."

Sorenson had to smile. "Who's doing the learning, you or that thing?"

Quite without humor Jay replied, "You know, sometimes I wonder." Dropping his hands to the keyboard, he gathered his thoughts and demanded action. *Pad, pad, pad.*

The computer was learning to treat Jay with respect. Long moments ticked by as it pondered the message the keys conveyed, then a few well-chosen words came slowly—Sorenson would have sworn, tentatively—onto the screen. No tricky flashing this time, none of the rude electronic noises.

"See what I mean?" Jay said, and thumbed his nose at it.

Elaine had bought it for the color; how else did she choose a computer? It was painted a blazing orange, like those sugar-coated sherbets that set the tongue tingling. Probably more Possums were sold because of the color than for any other reason. The shelf over the desk held at least a hundred program disks in shiny cardboard sleeves in the exact same vivid orange. They were sharp on family marketing, the Possum people.

By the window, a velvet frog crouched on a child's stool, the only spare seat in the room. In case Jay was watching, Sorenson hopped the frog politely to the divan. He brought the stool over. "Mind if I sit on the sidelines?"

"Help yourself." *Pad, pad, pad, pad.*

"What's the frog called?"

"Frog."

"That's it, just Frog?"

"He calls me 'human.' Good morning, human. Sleep well, human. I treat him the same as he treats me."

"In that case, Fitzgerald would be a better name." Maybe he hoped Jay would ask why. Then he could tell him something of Quincy and slyly move on to talk of the ocean. Maybe then they'd reminisce about those distant days when they had walked hand in hand by the shore.

But Jay only said, "He's too old to change."

"Another fine reason for calling him Fitzgerald."

"Elaine promised you wouldn't interfere in my life."

"And I won't. You're quite right—I'm being presumptuous."

Jay considered the subject closed and puffed a little sigh. *Pad, pad, pad.* The computer took its time before answering with a plaintive *ding dong.* It was talking to Jay. They were engaged in a silent conversation—Sorenson could think of no other way to describe it—youthful hands moving so fast he was unable to see which keys were pressed. God how swiftly time flies, he thought. His den would be a museum piece now, scrapbook for 1955. He felt suddenly very old. No one but your own son, he thought, could make a man feel so goddamned ancient.

"What happened in 1908?" Jay said.

"Come on, kid! I don't go back that far."

"Don't be silly. I mean, what natural phenomenon?" He was deliberating over the Possum's latest question.

"The birth of Jean Harlow, maybe? How would I know."

He depressed certain keys, requesting more information. An extra line rolled onto the screen. "The Tunguska River region, does that help any? It's in Siberia."

"Never been there. How about a volcano erupting?"

"No volcanoes in that part of Russia."

"Then swallow your pride, ask it the answer."

"It won't tell me; that's the whole idea. I'll have to look it up in the library. Sometime next week, I guess."

"You mean in a *book!* Do kids like you still bother with books?"

"They have their uses," Jay said primly.

"What program are you running? Geography?"

"Sort of general knowledge. You wouldn't understand."

"Try me."

"But you wouldn't, Toby. It takes absolutely ages to learn. I'd be here all night explaining."

"I'll take your word."

Jay twisted round, drooping an arm over the chair, and for the first time since entering the room Sorenson was aware of being closely regarded. The keen eyes appraised him with the same perceptive vision Elaine had turned on him downstairs.

"It isn't all learning," he said at length. He appeared anxious to make amends for his offhand manner. "I've got one or two games. Well, quite a lot, actually. You know, to pass the time on rainy afternoons and such. Not that I ever get bored," he added grandly.

"Do I detect a challenge?"

"If you like."

"I've played Space Invaders a few times. There's this bar at Quincy where . . ."

"Give me a break," Jay said as he pressed a button. The disk in its brilliant orange cover popped out from a slot at the front of the machine. He stood to replace it on the shelf, then leafed through his collection, sometimes plucking out a sleeve to read the label. "Something *simple,*" he murmured.

From the low stool, Sorenson gaped up at his sudden height. "God but you're tall."

Jay sniffed as if to say adults were always telling him so and he was heartily tired of it. He decided on a disk, pushed it into the slot, and resumed his seat. "I've chosen *Structures.* Are you any good at engineering?"

"Depends what kind."

"Three-dimensional steel structures. Buildings, bridges, you name it."

"Electric power pylons?"

"I've never tried but I guess so."

"I've climbed a few in my time. A real high one in the Adirondacks once."

Jay let that pass. "Beginners or advanced?"

"What are you?"

"Give you two guesses." He selected a button and a green spot began spinning a web of lines over the screen. The diagram grew ever more complex, the spot busily filling in every inch of the tube, until Sorenson believed this would never stop.

"Advanced, I presume." He spoke lightly, trying not to show his apprehension. He knew he was on trial. Jay had no time for men who climbed power pylons in their madcap youth. He had his own ways of judging worth.

"If you'd like something simpler . . . ?"

"I've never run away from a structure in my life, kid."

"We don't climb in this game, Toby. We *demolish.*"

"Really? What's it meant to be?"

Jay tilted his chin, assessing the picture like a veteran. "An office building, I think. Just the steel girders, of course, no walls or floors."

By a long stretch of the imagination, the picture could be as he claimed. "Of course," Sorenson said.

"And now we fight," Jay said wickedly, and he explained how there were far more girders than necessary to keep the building standing. The players took turns, each removing a line. If you picked out the wrong one, the structure collapsed in a heap. Naturally, the longer the game went on, the harder it became to choose. When you made the final slip, the Possum went absolutely *berserk,* of course. Bells rang loudly, the gong went like mad, a dreadful din. All of which greeted the loser, he said, the poor grommy sucker.

"Use the arrow to select, like this." He punched some keys. "When you're ready hit *E.* That means erase." He chased a glowing arrow over the diagram, touched *E,* and zapped the line to kingdom come. The contest had begun.

This was not exactly his bag, Sorenson decided an exhausting hour later. He struggled to sort through a crazy jumble of lines, while the confident demolition expert at his side never took more than a matter of seconds. The buildings trembled ominously as they neared their ends, like geometric jellies. Each time Toby sent one crashing, the wild noises from the Possum sounded more and more derisory.

"What do I press to give up? *D* for defeated?" Sorenson's watch gave the time as 8:30. "When do you Salem folks eat?"

Jay shrugged. "Elaine will bring me up a snack soon; she usually does. Why not go down if you're hungry?"

"How about the three of us together, family dinner again? It could be fun."

He shook his head. "I'm so darned busy, Toby. I'm sure you won't mind."

Sorenson unwound from the low child's stool, to be paralyzed by an attack of cramp. It occurred to him that Jay must think him old and creaking. What a wreck he must seem, hobbling a few steps, rubbing his legs to restore the circulation, his back obstinately crooked. He felt as old as Fitzgerald.

"By the way, how do I compare with Elaine?"

"On the Possum, we never play." Jay sighed deeply. "Women don't understand computers."

"The voice of experience!"

Jay smiled at the jibe: a reserved smile, sparingly used. It seemed the only thing about him not to have changed. But it was quickly gone. "I think Elaine's problem is, she's jealous," he said solemnly. "Jealous of a Possum. Kind of sad, isn't it."

*   *   *

She showed him to the guest room, along the corridor from Jay. It faced the street, with the branches of the restless sycamore scratching at the window. A lean and dour retreat, joyless in several shades of brown. With the highly waxed floor, the faint scent of lavendar polish one could take to be incense, he might have strayed into a convent. This was not Elaine's doing; he recognized a sterner hand at work. Her mother would stay here twice a year—at Easter and Thanksgiving—some habits were as constant as the seasons. Mrs. Marshall's favorite color was brown, the darker the better, and she stood for no nonsense in life, no frills. So there was the bed with its brown metal frame, next to it a lumpish brown table; the gloomy mahogany closet was right by the window, where it stole much of the light. There was little else—apart from the wood crucifix above the bed and the threadbare brown Bible close at hand on the table.

"The Mother Superior Suite."

"Enough from you," she told him.

While he was in with Jay, she must have brought up his suitcase and unpacked it. His pajamas lay ready on the quilt of patchworked browns, toilet bag alongside. He hadn't heard her come up. He wondered whether she had listened at the door.

"The bathroom is over the landing."

"Thanks. When do you have breakfast?"

"Eightish, usually."

"Tomorrow's Saturday!" he protested.

"I run a shop, or have you forgotten? Weekends are my busiest time. We open at nine sharp."

"Then I'll join you at eight. Drag myself up specially."

She lingered at the door, unsure of what to do with her hands. The room affected him; he saw her as a flustered novice, about to confess a sin.

"So what do you think?"

"I'll give you the diagnosis on Sunday, before I leave."

"First impressions?"

But he shook his head and denied her. "Don't go in for them."

"You used to."

"I'm an older and wiser man these days."

She forced a mocking laugh but said no more, and wished him goodnight with a silent nod as she left. He heard her door close, and was seized by an unfamiliar, almost despairing, loneliness. His bed at Quincy was solitary but rarely lonely. As he lay there, he listened to the distant murmurings of the ocean. Its damp salty smell rolled in to Elm Street on the mists and easterly breezes. He lived next morning's weather long before it came. In the early hours he heard Fitzgerald snoring below or the clanking of his ancient toilet under the stairs. Noises and surroundings he knew and from which he drew a measure of contentment—as though the outside world must intrude once in a while with the reassurance of its presence. Here, except for the tree scraping on the pane, Salem had fallen under a spell, possessed by an unearthly stillness.

He climbed into bed. The stiff sheets were the drastically starched linen Mrs. Marshall demanded, the rock-hard mattress for her complaining back. He lay watching the shadows lick black flames over the ceiling and contemplated that in all their years together he and Elaine had never once resorted to separate beds, even when times were bad. Suddenly he wished he had decided on the Hawthorne.

10

You only realize it's been too long, he told himself, when it's already been too damned long. The thought was prompted by Elaine's bathroom, as perfumed as a cosmetics counter and still moist from her shower. How long since he stood in a woman's bathroom first thing in the morning? A whole year maybe? God, it must be nearer two, and now her name escaped him. The same thought returned on the way downstairs when the aroma of freshly brewed coffee drew him unerringly to the big country kitchen. Too long, too damned long. Morning coffee by yourself had no such smell.

She was taking toast and orange juice at a refectory table of old pine. Her dark suit was so like the one she wore yesterday he had to look twice; the silk shirt had another of the extravagant bows. Jay sat beside her, wolfing a giant stack of waffles doused in syrup.

"See, it doesn't hurt." Her smile was breezy, her mood buoyant. She had been up for hours and wanted to prove it.

"Try later," he said. "I'm not alert enough for riddles."

"Breakfast at eight—up with the birds."

"Oh."

"Coffee's on the burner. You'll find waffles and bacon in the oven. I assume you still like waffles?"

"Your memory astounds me." He helped himself and took the place she'd set . . . facing her with Jay on his right—just as they used to dine at Peabody. He gave her a sly wink and nodded at Jay. "Who's the young visitor?"

"Who? Whassat?" Jay twisted his head both ways.

"You, kid."

"Don't mess around," Jay spluttered, spraying waffle over the table.

"Jay!" Elaine cried. "Don't speak with your mouth full."

"But he knows perfectly well who I am."

"Talking to that computer is blunting your sense of humor," Sorenson said.

"What's so funny about rude remarks?"

"It was just my way of saying it's great to see you down here. You should try it more often; bring that contented smile to Elaine's face."

"I have breakfast down here every morning. She says I have to, either that or starve. Do this, do that! Some mothers are . . ." He caught the glint in her eye and froze.

"Don't stop. It's just getting interesting," she said.

". . . Are witches?" Sorenson said loudly in his ear.

He grinned. "Sure. At full moon I lock my door."

"Breakfast is not the problem," Elaine said icily. "It's the remaining twenty-three and a half hours of the day."

"If you're going to spend all weekend picking on me . . ." Jay moaned, his face long again.

"Of course not, sweetie." She ran her fingers through his hair and he grimaced. "Nobody's picking on you. Adults are just careless with words sometimes. You have to make allowances for us."

"First you tell me you're not coming to the computer store. Now I have to put up with all this."

"I explained as pleasantly as I could; my own shop needs me early today."

"But I asked you ages ago! You're welshing on a promise."

"Correction—you asked me only this morning."

Jay speared a whole waffle—too large to cram into his mouth—and held it dangling on the fork while syrup oozed down the handle. Say one more word, his cross face suggested, just one, and this lot goes flying.

But Elaine knew him too well and said sweetly, "There's a new delivery I simply must unpack before I open—some price tags to write. Sorry, my angel, but life goes on."

Sullenly, he took a bite of the waffle. The syrup swelled into a tear, trembling, about to drip.

"Any mess on my tablecloth," she snapped, "and you're on the washing machine detail."

He heaved a great sigh and slapped it down on the plate.

Just like old times, Sorenson thought, start the day with a fight. In truth he relished it and felt oddly, comfortably, at home again. Restaurants stuck in the mind because of the food, family meals were different. He remembered them for the petty dramas; the dishes were incidental and quickly forgotten. Like the evening when Jay in a fit of temper splashed something red and sticky all over the carpet. Or the dinner party Elaine threw into disarray by dashing that plate against the wall. Who cares what she was eating—the mess was spectacular. *Too damned long,* he repeated inwardly, and drank a deep, soothing draft of black coffee, the smell lingering in his nostrils.

"He's a bit sensitive lately about what he's permitted to do," Elaine was saying, low and confiding as if Jay weren't in the room. "About whether he feels restricted. They call it the tender age, heaven help us."

"I'm *not* sensitive!" Jay swept his plate aside and tied his arms in a knot. "I don't tell you you're sensitive because you spend all day at your shop."

"That's different."

"Then so is my room and I can stay there as long as I want." He made an appeal to Sorenson. "That's only fair, isn't it?"

"Keep me out of this. I'm only a spectator."

"We're not usually this ratty at breakfast," Elaine declared frivolously. "We're probably a little on edge because you're here. Yes, that's it. You're the same malevolent influence as ever."

"Thanks, sweetheart!"

"Teasing, Toby, only teasing," she said, and, arching her wrist with too much delicacy, glanced at her watch. More pressing matters called: she rose from the table and took a long while to straighten her skirt. Elaine had cultivated a manner that made every move seem like a business deal; she flicked a crumb from her hem as if dismissing a meeting.

"Anything particular I should do today?" Sorenson said.

"You're an old and wise man; you'll think of something." A peck on Jay's cheek and a fond tug at his tousled hair that drove him into a scowl. "Comb that cowlick, sweetie. And I'm not nagging but please remember we have a guest. So no hiding in your room while he cooks for you and washes up and does whatever other homely chores come into his head."

"But, Elaine . . . ," Jay began.

"No buts. That toy of yours won't run away." An elegant briefcase had found its way into her hand; she looked bound for Madison Avenue. "Have fun, children," she said, stepping briskly away toward the hall.

Jay made an impish face at her back. Doubtless, he was thinking a curse so deadly it would vaporize her.

"How about cogs?" Sorenson whispered.

"How about *what?*"

"Cogs. A cuss word we used as kids."

Jay chewed it over and admitted a slow smile. "Not bad, Toby. Not bad at all." Then he sat shuffling his shoes, trailing patterns on the floor with a lace, until a car door slammed outside and an engine roared into the distance. Instantly he was on his feet.

"What's the hurry?" Sorenson said.

"You're taking me out." He gulped down the last of his orange juice.

"I am?"

"Who else do I get? Elaine was supposed to but she broke her word."

"Sounds like a deliberate move to me. Maybe she changed her mind so I'd have to take you."

"Then why didn't she say so?"

"Because women don't work that way."

Jay cast an anxious eye on his watch. "If we don't get a move on, they'll be sold out."

"The computer store you mentioned?"

His nod was apologetic. "There's this new program disk—

The Age of the Dinosaur." In the way that begs for money the world over, he pulled urchinlike at Sorenson's sleeve. "I'm flat broke, Toby. Can you stand the price of a disk?"

"Do you carry American Express?"

"Me? No." Jay's face fell.

Sorenson mussed his hair roughly, man to man. "Good for you," he said. "I'm the same. I only carry cash."

*   *   *

"Funny old car," Jay observed as they drove from the house in the lumbering Volkswagen.

"Don't knock a faithful friend," Sorenson warned. "It's never once let me down."

"Elaine's got a new BMW. Did you see it?"

"No."

"A 323I sedan. That's the model with fuel injection. She's had a sun roof fitted and electric windows."

"Good for Elaine."

"She cleans it all the time. Wash, wash, wash. Gets on me about the Possum then spends absolutely *days* cleaning her car. Do you think that's fair, Toby?"

"Nothing in life is ever fair," Sorenson said. "I'm surprised the Possum hasn't taught you that."

*   *   *

Salem Home Computers was in the outer reaches of town, on a broad avenue he had taken last night. It was a store of no great size squeezed between a staid branch of the First National Bank of Boston and a homespun Arthur Treacher's. Yet a business on the move, as brash and impermanent as a market stall. Even from across the road where they parked, its cheap vitality struck squarely between the eyes. Months from now it would be either bankrupt and gone or operating from a smarter location many times the size. The windows were jam-packed with electronics; Day Glo posters in vile yellow plastered the glass with words that seemed to throb. APPLE STARTER KIT DOWN $69.50. LOWEST PET PRICES FOR MILES. Not yet nine in the morning and already an eager line stretched from the sales counter onto the

sidewalk—mostly boys of about Jay's age, a few disgruntled fathers in tow.

"Look at that," Jay groaned as they waited to cross. "Millions
of kids ahead of us. What took us so darned long?" Unable to
contain himself, he dashed from the curb between the passing
traffic. "Gee, I could kick myself," he was muttering furiously
when Sorenson caught up. "I should've dragged you out
sooner."

This was the raw end of the computer business. The window
shelves were the crude slotted metal used in warehouses. The little computers were stacked high, like cans in a supermarket.
Nothing in sight to explain what the model numbers meant or
what the strange accessory boards were for—they assumed you
knew. Among the tawdry confusion, the orange splash of a single
Possum. Sorenson blanched when he saw that Elaine had paid
well over a thousand dollars for a toy.

"The new disk I told you about," Jay said. "There's always a
mad rush first day."

They advanced a scant foot or so at the end of the line. "Just
like lining up for a hit record," Sorenson said. "The old Elvis
singles, a stampede every time. Way before you were born, kid."

"It's twenty dollars," Jay said, frowning through the window.
"Have you got that much?"

"Don't let the car fool you—I'm good for at least twice that."
He fished a bill from his back pocket. "How often does this happen?"

"A couple of times a month, I guess. There's a disk out most
weeks but I give some a miss." Shading his eyes, Jay flattened his
nose to the glass. "Some of the programs are real weird. Who
wants to learn economics or European history?"

Sorenson looked along the line at the other young faces
pressed to the window in the same jittery way. He remembered
seeing a news item about a kid going crazy when a TV game was
taken from him. Hadn't the boy shot his father? God, he
thought, tell this crowd the store's run out of disks and they'd
rampage through the town. He peered in at the dead screen of
the Possum. What was it about electronics that got kids like Jay
so hooked? He gazed again at the line. In the old Elvis days the

kids had jostled and shoved, bubbling with excitement. What struck him now was the quiet.

"You mean you don't bother to come for disks you don't want?"

"Waste of time."

"Then how do you know which disks they're bringing out?"

"Publishing," Jay said to the window. "They don't bring out computer programs, they publish them."

"So how do you know when and what they're publishing?"

"You just know."

"That makes no sense."

"But you do, Toby, you just know."

"This one, for instance, the dinosaur disk. Why did we have to come today?"

"I must have read it somewhere. A catalog, I guess." He inched toward the door, sliding an apprehensive face along the glass.

They reached the head of the line some ten minutes later. To Jay's profound relief there were still several cartons full of the new program behind the counter, the delivery labels in dazzling Possum orange. He pressed the disk to his heart, breathing, "Heck, I don't want to go through *that* again." Smiling proudly, Sorenson squeezed his shoulder. He forgot his misgivings outside the store. Suddenly he understood. It was years since he had seen the shameless materialism of a child, and he found it refreshing.

"Can I look over there, Toby? The new music attachment, only a hundred and fifty."

And he was gone, off on a lone exploration. First the tiny music unit fondled with longing, then his hands wandering the shelves, picking up the Possum add-ons, touching the shiny and inviting orange packages.

"Only?" Sorenson mused to himself. "A hundred and fifty dollars and you say *only*. Take as long as you want, Rockefeller."

*   *   *

Back at the house, Jay followed him into the kitchen and meandered listlessly while he made coffee. Elaine had instructed him to play host and he was doing his best to please. But all he wanted was to rush upstairs with the new disk, he had no guile or reason to pretend otherwise.

Raising his hands high like claws, Sorenson growled. "The Thing awaits. The creature from the orange lagoon."

"What are you talking about?" Jay said, ducking a playful swipe with a paw.

"Just a clever reference to the movie. Surely you've seen *Creature from the Black Lagoon?*"

"Nope."

Sorenson's sigh was for Jay or his own lost youth, he didn't know which. "I'll make you a deal," he said. "You tell me how to find Elaine's Witchcraft Emporium, I'll leave you alone with the Thing."

"Business cards!" Jay shouted as he took to his heels. "Top drawer, chest in the hall." His footsteps on the stairs sounded through the house as if all the kids from the store were on their way up.

11

The old gilded eagle on the Custom House gazed out on the sea which had been Salem's making. But his was a sidelong glance, Sorenson noticed, as if he too were unwilling to face the present. The craft rolling to a heavy swell were all pleasure cruisers; their cables snapped on the masts with the hollow clatter of cow bells. At the foreshore parking lot, screeching herring gulls mobbed him and finding no bread swooped away like bats low over the waves.

He followed the neat signs to what Elaine had called a tourist trap: DERBY STREET WATERFRONT AREA. History given a fresh lick of paint. All very tasteful. The new shops and restaurants were confined to Pickering Wharf, a stubby peninsula jutting into the marina, where they huddled like ancient houses, making crooked passages and blind alleys that the visitors found quaint.

Elaine's shop was hard to miss. Just turn at the steak bar and you'd be dazzled by a vibrant red signboard splashed with Barnum and Bailey lettering: MARSHALL ARTS. The little bay window had dimpled panes—the stern light of a galleon, he fancied. He bent close to the glass, to see a handful of toys and trinkets placed preciously on velvet. No price tags, you had to go in to ask, but the refined bareness of the display warned not to expect bargains. The narrow door jangled a bell, and inside he found shelves of yachting sweaters, a few glass cases of scrimshaw you could take for antique.

Elaine was at the rear of the shop, enthusing over bath towels with an elderly couple. She looked over with a secretive nod. They were the kind who take travel too seriously. The woman rubbed a towel to her cheek and made a guttural comment. He answered with the grunt of an officer and buried his nose in a map. Elaine chose that moment to escape.

"Don't mind me," Sorenson said. "You've got customers."

"Lookers," she whispered. "I know the type. They won't buy."

The woman fretted over the towels, holding them up to the light, trying the texture again on her face. Another throaty exchange before she clumped over, the husband trailing behind.

"Will you keep these for me? We're looking at the sights. We'll come back later."

"Liar," Elaine said when the door tinkled shut.

"Ve haf ways of not buying," Toby added.

She pretended a carefree laugh that would have him believe she sold only to people she liked. But he was not taken in. She had worked too hard on every shelf and rack, writing out each dangling ticket. One suggested a gift FOR A SPECIAL MOM; another was TO REMEMBER SALEM.

He went on a tour, picking up rag dolls and plaid scarves and ashtrays. She dogged his heels, contriving to act amused when he put a bumper sticker in the window: STOP BY FOR A SPELL. Finally, her impatience got the better of her.

"What do you think of all this?" She gestured but threw in a shrug: it really didn't matter.

"You're a fraud. No evil potions, no antique thumbscrews."

"They didn't resort to thumbscrews in old Salem. Just chains and the fear of God. You even had to pay for your own chains." The words tripped off her tongue. He guessed she had such snatches of history ready for those who asked.

"Sounds like Norwood."

"No, Toby," she said irritably. "Not a bit like Norwood."

"Convince me. Tell me what you tell the tourists."

"About the witch hunts? If you're really interested I'll sell you a paperback."

"Your version will do."

For a time she regarded him coldly, her eyes like slits. Without warning she turned her back, went to the window, and stared at the wind-tossed sea. "Know what I said to Mother once? Who could choose between God and the devil? Look what they did in the name of God."

"To your mother? You wouldn't dare."

Perhaps she smiled. "Maybe not, but I nearly did." The sea engaged her. She had grown up in sight of the Atlantic and claimed it had entered her blood. Years ago he had often seen her stare in this way, as if she exchanged secret thoughts with it. "Sixteen ninety-two," she said with half a mind. "The children of Salem were gripped by fainting fits and terror; their hysteria infected the entire parish. A kind of creeping sickness, what else can you call it, spread across the state. The sickness of religious mania."

"Your words or lifted from a book?"

"Don't interrupt! Imagine the sense of power those children must have felt. A girl not yet in her teens has only to point and some poor, respectable farmer is clapped in irons. One of them they crushed to death under a ton of rocks. They imprisoned a girl of six, Toby, only six years old. Another child, a cousin I think, swore she was a witch."

"And that's the dark past you live off. You sell Vermont fudge and cashmere in your cozy shop here on the wharf."

She strode back, nostrils flaring, to prod him in the ribs. "I also sell porn, so cut the cozy."

"Don't believe you," he said.

A smile played on her lips. "Well, near enough. I've got dirty frogs for the dirty minded. Want to see my dirty frogs?" She motioned to a high shelf lined with green-velvet toys in baggy blue trousers. "Out of reach of straying young hands. One can't be too careful."

"Looks okay to me. Jay has one."

"Not like these he doesn't! *Very* realistic under the pants, positively gi-gantic. All in lurid pink satin. Want a sly peep?"

"I believe you."

She reclined against the shelves, dipping her hands in her jacket pockets. "Mother came by last Easter. My God, Toby, can you imagine if she'd realized! My heart was in my mouth. I'd have been disinherited, cursed to eternal hellfire. But she mooched around the knitwear for a while, then toddled off. In search of the nearest acceptable place of worship, I suppose." She had one leg provocatively across the other, her head at a becoming angle. Let the buyer beware, he thought. Elaine on her own territory was a force to be reckoned with.

"You and Jay didn't last long," she said.

"About an hour, a short drive, and twenty dollars."

Her hand flew to her mouth. "Shit, he didn't! Not the Saturday disk routine. I hoped if I ducked out of going, he might forget for once."

"Jay? He knows what disks are coming before the store does."

"He's a pest." She rang the till for the money but he reached over the counter to push the drawer shut.

"My treat, Elaine. I've had enough doubts cast on my bank balance."

She flirted with a smile, not quite understanding but assuming a joke. "Honestly though, what a horror. And here I am believing a man around the house would reform him."

"In less than a day?"

"One always lives in hope."

"I've tried that. It rarely works."

Now her tormented face—mouth pulled down against an onrush of tears. He sensed she arranged her features as carefully as the shelves. "What am I to do, Toby? I'm at my wit's end."

He settled on the counter, floppy frogs behind him, a litter of Snoopies at his feet in a real wicker basket. Hard not to feel like one of her playthings. "I'm beginning to share your concern. We have a disturbing situation here."

"You really think so?" Her face grew longer, darker.

"Absolutely. Worse than I feared." He was trying not to laugh out loud. "I'm in Salem only a few hours and what do I find? A boy of ten at home, slaving over a hot computer. And his mother? She's out all day, surrounded by toys and having fun." He switched to a corny German accent. "Lie on my analyst's couch a moment. Ve haf some role-reversal here. Ve must find out why."

"You crazy man!"

"Except I'm not fooling, Elaine. The person with the problem isn't the one you think."

Her wry expression changed to a silent fury.

"I suspect you've been reading too many psychology books about children acting strangely," he said.

"Is that why you wanted my quick history of the town? A real damned Freud, aren't we!"

"You want me to spell it out for you? Jay is a great kid, a knockout. He's found what turns him on, and like all kids of his age he's overdoing it. So what? If he was out with a street gang you'd worry. Find girlie books under the pillow and you'd throw a fit. But he's hooked on a computer and that's something Dr. Spock forgot to prepare you for. Jay believes you're jealous. I've a sneaking suspicion he's right."

"Bullshit!"

The doorbell heralded low voices and the trampling of feet.

"Com-ing," she called, then brought her face inches from his and said in a strained whisper, "Under your damned nose and you can't see! Toby Sorenson is always right; let the rest of the world go hang."

He replied with equal anger. "You sent me up alone to him last night. No help, no moral support."

"To make it easy, you damned fool."

"Well, he was a nice kid, normal. Yet with you on his back this morning he was a spoiled brat."

She stalked away between her pristine shelves but froze when she saw the door. A party of Japanese came jostling in, a dozen or more men and women, two tiny girls with wax-doll faces and shiny black hair. Polite heads filled the window, bobbing and weaving around one another as they peeked in.

"Won't be a min-ute." She invited them to browse with the stilted wave of a shopkeeper. Then she turned back to Sorenson, her voice harsh and low. "Get lost, Toby. There'll be dinner and a bed for you tonight. But meanwhile, do me a favor. This is my shop, no thanks to you. Get out and stay out."

12

He reclined fully dressed on the bed, absorbed by the shadows rippling over the ceiling. Salem was the same cemetery quiet as last night; the house lay in the grip of virtual silence. Every so often he heard a faint noise from the corridor outside—the brief tinny tune of the bell on the Possum—apart from that, a daunting peace. Some houses creaked through the night; water hissing in the pipes, rafters that complained in the wind. Fitzgerald's place was as scratchy and restless as the old boy himself. But not this one. With Elaine around, he thought bitterly, it wouldn't dare.

Just about midnight, he sneaked to the door in stockinged feet and quietly turned the handle. A light still shone under Jay's door; even as he looked a muted *ding dong* sounded in the passage. Gingerly, he closed the door, returned to the bed and waited.

The tedious minutes passed, empty time that drags in the small hours. Still the spasmodic chatter of the computer rang along the hall. A police siren wailed in the distance, faded and died away. It seemed as he stared at the shadow-play that the Salem cops prowled night streets for evil, eager to run it out of town. His eyes fluttered; one o'clock came and went. For some while there had been no sound from outside so he swung his legs to the floor and yawned uncontrollably.

Gong-g-g

"Damnation!" he cursed as his head dropped back like a lead weight to the pillow. "Raving insomniac."

A picture of Jay floated on the ceiling. He was crouching at the keyboard. Green words formed and dissolved on the little screen. The orange Possum hummed, underlining the words with nudges and harangues from the bell. Sorenson imagined he heard the constant *pad, pad, pad* of the keys, but that could only have been in his mind. He brought his watch close to his eyes. One thirty in the morning! Now Elaine formed in the shadows, telling him that she was right. *Damn fool, look at the time!* He lost his tenuous grip on reality and fell asleep.

The bedside lamp woke him. He must have turned as he dozed, because the bulb shone in his face. Grumbling, he reached to switch it off, then sat up with a start, bewildered for a moment to find himself still dressed. Nearly 4:00 A.M. and the corridor at last in darkness, no chink of light from the door at the end.

First he went to the bathroom, to sharpen his wits with ice-cold water. Stealthily he opened Jay's door, crept in, and eased it shut behind him. From across the room came a husky sound of uneven slumber, like heartfelt sighs of frustration. Jay had always resented his hours in bed—sleep was a boring necessity; when it seized him he gave it no rest. Suddenly Sorenson's own breath seemed ominously loud; he tried to stifle it but was aware only of becoming more intrusive. Surely the pulse beating at his temples would wake the dead? Slowly he searched out what feeble illumination came from the moonless sky. The blind was up on the window. The houses at the end of the garden were mere shapes, tall chimneys jutting like piers into a sea of inky clouds. He could dimly discern the divan now, an impression of the desk by the facing wall. As he padded over, straining to see the Possum, he nearly cried out. There was the blank outline of the computer, but how in this darkness could he read the disks?

He returned to the hall to switch on the light—an unbearable brightness for an instant. A cautious wait to be sure no one had stirred, then back to Jay's room, leaving the door sufficiently ajar for a shaft of light to peek in. He stood listening to Jay's irregular breathing, still asleep. The light served to deepen the shadows: only a smudge on the pillow that might be hair, a dark swelling beneath the quilt too stiff to be alive. He stole over and searched the disks, taking them out in turn to peer closely at the labels. There was no order to the library; he must have tried fifty or more before he found what he wanted. He wound the power lead around the computer keyboard so the plug wouldn't drag on the floor. With infinite care, the disk held fast in his teeth, he lifted the Possum and went to the door. Jay snorted and wheezed but slept on regardless. Hearing him there, Sorenson was reminded of the last Christmas he spent at Peabody when he tiptoed into the playroom to leave a sack of toys at the foot of the bed. Two bright eyes had shone like pearls from the gloom; Jay's phony snore would have fooled no one. The acting was infectious: Sorenson had puffed up his stomach to mutter a gruff "Ho, ho." Instantly, the eyes vanished and a snigger came from under the sheets. Now he murmured, "Sleep tight," and smiled to himself in the dark. Elbowing the door wide, he carried the computer out.

The table in the guest room was too small so he moved to the bed. There was a socket close by; as he inserted the plug the Possum gave a *ding* of awakening before the familiar hum vibrated through the room.

"The night shift's here," he told it. He felt drowsy yet elated, a child again as he sat on the bed examining the keys. The disk went into the slot at the front. Anxiously, he watched the vacant screen. A soft hissing he hadn't heard before as the Possum loaded its memory—then the first words appeared.

STRUCTURES
A GAME FOR TWO PLAYERS
OR I'LL CHALLENGE YOU

"You're on, Possum," he said, and checked his watch. To be safe he ought to return the machine no later than 7:00 A.M. That left only three hours to become an expert. "You have no idea," he confided, "what it takes to gain a kid's respect these days."

The computer responded as if it heard. Lines blinked away, a terse request raced noiselessly onto the display.

SELECT
GAMES RULES OR PLAY?

He sat patiently but no more came and when he read the program sleeve there was only a drawing of a collapsing bridge, some brief sales blurb, no instructions.

"Damn!"

He tried the *1* key, then *2*, then the rest of the numerics. The computer steadfastly ignored him, continuing the hum and holding the same unhelpful sentence on the display. So he began to work through the alphabetic keys. Suddenly the screen went blank.

"Bingo!" he said, unsure what he had done.

HAVE YOU PLAYED BEFORE?
Y FOR YES
N FOR NO

With a shamed smile he owned up.

THOUGHT SO, the Possum said.

LET'S START WITH THE RULES,
SHALL WE

"Conceited damned Thing," he muttered.

The screen filled completely, swiftly.

STRUCTURES   IS   A   GAME   IN
WHICH . . . and when he reached the final line he was told to press the *page* key for the remaining instructions. Even as he touched it, the door burst open. Jay stood there in crumpled pajamas, his face deathly white, his eyes round and blazing. When he saw the Possum on the bed he ran over, practically stumbling in his anger.

"You bastard, Toby!" he shouted. "I knew it was you. I fucking knew."

"Hold it, junior. What became of the polite grom stuff?"

Jay flew at him, fists flailing. "Shitball. Lousy fucking thief. Why can't you keep your thieving fucking hands off!"

"Hey, look . . ." Sorenson struggled to beat him off. A punch grazed his face, another caught him full in the stomach.

"You shit! You lousy bastard!"

Somehow Sorenson managed to seize a hand. "Stop it, Jay. Calm down. I only . . ." The other hand was a claw, striking wildly at his eyes. He failed to catch it and razor-sharp nails tore his cheek. His gasp of pain was drowned by shrieks.

"*Bas*tard! Thieving shitball *bas*tard. You only came back to steal my Possum."

With his free hand, Sorenson touched his face. A stinging, searing burn as if salt were rubbed in a wound and his fingers were wet with blood. "Are you crazy? Look what you've done!"

Jay tugged with all his might and broke free. He circled the bed, crouching as if about to spring, panting insanely, a dribble of saliva running from his lips. Clamping his eyes shut, he rocked his head like an enraged beast and opened his mouth for a full-throated bellow. *"Fuck-ing shitball thief!"* Then he was coming again, fingers hooked into talons, eyes smoldering pits of hate. Sorenson dropped back on the bed, drew up his legs, and planted his feet squarely in Jay's chest as he fell on him, scratching, biting, screaming at the top of his lungs. Sorenson's control finally snapped: summoning every ounce of strength he kicked out and hurled Jay the length of the room, head over heels. He crashed into the wall with a sickening thud, crumpled into a heap, and didn't move.

"Jay!" Elaine was at the door; he had no idea how much she had seen. She hid her face in her hands; when they dropped limply away for a further terrified stare, her feet seemed rooted to the spot. In a daze, Sorenson dabbed his cheek and held sticky red fingers out to her.

"He just burst in and . . ."

She gaped at them, her head shaking in panic, and tried to speak. Then, rushing to Jay, she cradled him in her arms, murmuring distraught consolation through a flood of tears. Jay stirred and when his eyes trembled open it was with a look of dreadful loathing. Timidly, she took his head in her hands, turning it gently in search of bruises. "Tell me you're all right, sweetie. Please God, tell me."

"You invited him here, Elaine. He's a fucking thief. You're as bad as he is."

She pressed his face to her breast, knotting her fingers into his hair. "What's going on, Toby? What's happening?"

Sorenson had found a handkerchief for his raging cheek. Eyes closed, he lay back on the bed. "I was only practicing on his

computer. A caring father trying to learn a few basic skills—get
the picture? Next thing, Jay flew in like a wildcat."

"It was all his fault, Mom! He stole my Possum."

"We'll take it back for you, darling, don't worry."

"He leaves us all alone for years . . . then comes back and . . ."
He sobbed uncontrollably.

"I know, sweetie, I know."

Sorenson heard the rustle of her nightdress as she stood up.
Lifting his head, he was met with a vacuous stare, a chalky face
as impassive as a mask.

"Take it back for him, Toby. Now, please."

"No, Mom, no!" Jay clung to her knees. "Not him. You do
it."

She knelt to caress his hair. "Never mind, my angel, never
mind. I'll put the Possum back if you want. We won't let the
nasty man near it."

She came over for the machine and spoke from the side of her
mouth, not looking at him. "Damned fool. Now tell me who's
right!" It was the same angry whisper he had heard in the shop.

*   *   *

As if in a trance, he drowsed on the bed, hearing her play
nurse. Her bare feet slithering along the hall to the bathroom,
the tap running. A damp washcloth, he supposed, to soothe the
tear-stained face and take the heat from a fevered brow. The
slightest of clicks, bottles rattling as she rummaged in the medicine cabinet. Some orange-flavored junior aspirin? Next the faint
whispers as she sat on the divan, holding Jay's hand until he
drifted into sleep. A lengthy return to the bathroom, not both-
ering to close the door; water splashing into the basin again.
Then she was back, as he expected and feared, her hair brushed
into a severe bun, her eyes red-rimmed and empty.

"How's the cheek?" That voice he knew of old, the calm after
the storm.

"I'll live."

"It looks terrible. If you'd like some antiseptic cream . . ."

"Later. Look, Elaine, I don't know what he said but . . ."

"No, Toby." Her head swayed wearily as if on slack strings. "Please, no explanations."

"But I wouldn't want you to think . . ."

"I said *no!*" She perched at the end of the bed, her face turned implacably away. "It doesn't matter what the truth is; the damage is done."

Mutely he gazed at her. The firm jaw, the mouth set tight and resolute, the tired resignation he had once known so well and struggled to forget.

"I made a mistake asking you here." A sharp intake of breath as her eyes fluttered and a hand veiled them. He recognized the signs and thought of headache pills; soon she would be back to the medicine cabinet. "Do me a favor. Leave before he wakes."

"If that's what you want."

"Seems I don't have any choice." She rose like a sleepwalker. Her pallid features stared down at him, and the immense sadness written there caught him off guard. "I'm sorry about this, things working out so badly. You must feel as awful as I do."

*   *   *

Dawn on Sunday morning. Still trees lined the street like sentinels in the cold early light. Vapid mist from the sea washed over the sidewalks, past houses dark and stone-silent as tombs. A solitary gull wheeled overhead, plummeted with beating wings, and gawped as Sorenson unlocked the car. Slumping in the seat, he recalled his hopes and trepidation on the evening he arrived. As you were, he thought. Back to the old routine: Elaine no doubt lying there in a waking nightmare, her head hammering; Jay in fitful sleep, dreaming his world of green words in an endless gray landscape. The Possum safely beside him, residing in whatever limbo computers inhabit when the power is cut.

The car window clouded with his breath. A last lingering look at the outwardly tranquil house and he drove to the corner, headed south. It was hardly possible they had planned things like this, but uncertainty haunted him all the way to Quincy. He could imagine no more fitting revenge.

4. Beacon Hill

13

In unrelenting heat Felix Valentine trudged up the hill. His disheveled jacket was an oven; the clammy shirt clung to his back. Such was his fate on these scorching August days. The briefcase was sticky to the touch; the pitiless sun coaxed from it the sweaty odor of cattle; but without a briefcase how could one investigate? A man needed the brand of authority.

He let his feet go where they would, and followed, and by an unknown route found his way to Mount Vernon Street. Under the cloudless blue sky, baking in the noonday heat, Beacon Hill befuddled his senses. It seemed a kaleidoscope of places he had never visited, only read of in books. He shook his head in fatigue and rested on a bench, where the street widened about an oval of railed-in grass.

Cautiously he gazed first down the hill then up to its distant

hump. All clear. Ames still had no one on his tail; he felt relieved
and disappointed in the same instant. Ames was getting nowhere
in the search for Vlasov, he was certain. The computer suggested
as much and the computer knew every last move in Boston. Yet
who stood the best chance of finding Vlasov? Felix Valentine . . .
had that not occurred to Ames? He set the briefcase down beside
him on the bench, breathing a ponderous, flagging sigh. For a
while since the interview in Charlestown he had lived in hope
that Ames and his people might lead to Vlasov. But thank God,
after all, for this empty street. He had no intention of doing their
damned work for them. He wanted Vlasov for himself.

In the heat his thoughts wandered to the harsh winters of
Kirensk. He thought of Vlasov and could remember only the
wondrous warmth of the fire under that great carved mantle-
piece, how the chandelier reflected a thousand smaller fires and
the paneled walls were suffused with a honeyed glow. Viktor at
his ornate gilded desk across the vast room, pouring wine into a
crystal goblet that had no place in a gulag, holding it out, pleasantly indicating he should come over to get it. So he went and
because of the insidious cold by the desk his eyes must have crept
longingly back to the blazing logs.

"Go ahead," Viktor said, smiling in his way like a benevolent
host. "Return to the fire if you wish."

Which he did, and toasted his backside gratefully.

"What is blue?" Viktor asked suddenly. Not an idle inquiry,
his questions never were.

"The sky is blue," Valentine replied deviously. "Some eyes
are blue. In tropical places, so is the sea."

Viktor shook his head. "I don't wish to hear of blue things.
What is blue itself? What does it look like?"

This must be a trick, to lull him into a false sense of security.
Then, rapierlike, the real question would come and catch him
unawares. Valentine bought time by staring into his glass. Yes, a
ruse, an interrogator's cunning. But why, and where would it
lead?

"Do you really not know?" Viktor said, creasing his brow.
"But you have excellent sight, Feliks. You see blue things."

"I told you so! The sky. My wife's eyes, damn her."

"Well then . . . ?" Viktor's hand gestured, a wide sweep of consummate reasonableness. "Then describe it, Feliks."

"It looks cold," he answered wildly.

A more insistent shake of the head. "White looks cold, surely? The snow outside is white, not blue."

Feliks tried again. "It has a hardness. No other color appears as hard."

"Ah . . . ," Viktor said, and smiled as if a great secret had been revealed to him.

"Like the heart of a diamond . . ."

Viktor nodded reflectively. "Yes," he murmured in satisfaction. "Yes, indeed." He drained his glass, refilled it to the brim. "Now we'll talk of ballet, Feliks. We have only another hour together, so little time for conversation." His head fell back against the high leather cushion of his chair. The chandelier took his fancy; perhaps in his mind he likened the sparkling crystals to diamonds. "Enlighten me," he said after an interval of many minutes. "Name a ballet where the music sounds blue."

14

At the house in Charlestown, Bernie gazed languidly over his *Boston Globe.* "Saturday, Felix, didn't anybody tell you? Don't you have weekends?" He sat at his station inside the front entrance, feet splayed onto the reception desk. The badge on his cap wasn't police but looked sufficiently like police to deter any callers who wandered in by accident.

"Paper," Valentine said with a martyred shrug. "Always so much paper to process, you know how it is."

"Just you and me as usual, a whole goddamned building to ourselves." Bernie winked salaciously. "The meeting room on the first level used to be a boudoir, anyone tell you? Why don't we get in some dames, have ourselves a ball?"

"Events conspire," Valentine said and flushed heavily. He wedged the case between his knees so he could search for his pass, which never seemed to be in the same pocket.

But Bernie waved him through. "Forget it, Felix. Way I figure it, any guy who disguises himself this much like you deserves to get in."

He took the stairs. Three long flights up that shortened his breath, along a twisting corridor, and into the room he shared with Zoltan and Gregori and the crazy Pole whose cigars and beard had earned him the nickname Castro. The room stank from Castro's smoking, and in a corner, half buried under haphazard files, were the riding boots Gregori kept for the snow. These torrid summer days the boots smelled high, as bad as the cigars. Valentine draped his jacket over his chair, left the case unbuckled on the desk. He surveyed the scene from the door and, yes, it seemed he was working hard and had only gotten up to go to the john. Then he went by the back stairs down to the basement computer room.

Sitting in one of the cubicles, at a display terminal, he felt comfortably cool for the only time that day. What a mad world it was, where they sweltered at the top of the house while the machine purred down here in air-conditioned splendor. In fact it was almost too cold. He shivered and felt the soaking wet shirt stick to his armpits and across his back.

LOG ON, the computer ordered.

He keyed in a sequence of digits and even after all these months had to smile. He was only a paper shifter; he was given no authority to access the machine. But Mead, who ran the Section, had access and Mead's number was scribbled on his blotter so he wouldn't forget. *Jenny's birthday. Barber's number. Log-on code.*

The screen listed what they called a menu. Lucky for him, otherwise he would never commit the instructions to memory. He selected the **ARCHIVE SEARCH** he was offered. Now another menu appeared; a second choice and the computer was ready to lay bare every fact it held.

SUBJECT?
VLASOV, VIKTOR
STEPHANOVICH
ALSO KNOWN AS?
STERVETNIK

Who could say if it meant anything to the machine, but that's what they had called him at Kirensk, though never to his face. *Stervetnik.* The Vulture.

SUBJECT NOT FOUND
ANY FURTHER IDENTIFIERS?

"Still?" he said accusingly. "Still? And you supposed to be so smart!" Sadly he typed a message to sign off.

BYE STEWART, the computer said.

Another day down the drain, he told himself. And yet what was a single day after so many years? He shivered once more in the cooled basement. A picture of the magnificent room at Kirensk came again to his mind. Strange, wasn't it, how Vlasov kept away from the fire? His desk on the extreme far side of the room and he rarely left it; to refill your glass you went over to him. There had seemed nothing odd in that at the time—he was the interrogator and called the tune. But think again of the fire, imagine it to be solely for the prisoners. Think of Vlasov at his desk, acting oh so courteous when he replenished your glass. Wouldn't he have ventured over just *once?*

"Stupid old fool!" Valentine cried in the silence. Suddenly he recalled the night of the ballet as if it were yesterday. Night, you old fool! *Night!* People sprawling on the grass with blankets . . . not to sit on, huddled under them for warmth. Sure it was August and a hot day, but the weather had turned—a cold front had swept in from the ocean and within an hour Boston had jumped a whole season. Gray skies and a damp chill in the air like fall. During the performance a flock of geese skimmed low over the Esplanade into the Charles—remember?—and were swallowed in a thick blanket of mist.

He must be mad, hoping to encounter Vlasov on a blistering day like this. Vlasov would venture out only when the temperature dropped, long after nightfall. Vlasov sought the cold because he was cold by nature. He must have the blood of a reptile coursing in his veins.

5. The Plant at Waltham

15

Sorenson was in two minds all the way from Norwood. When he reached the turning he almost went past and returned to Route 128. The end of another meaningless week and he was back in Salem. Elaine's street as cloistered as ever under the vaulting trees. Doors closed against him, wholesome families going about their own affairs. Even when he left the car and stood on her porch he was reluctant to ring the doorbell, as if the sound would disturb a brittle peace. At last, he forced himself—only kids rang bells and ran away. Yet as he waited doubt crowded in on him afresh. He was aware of being unwanted at her door; the street appeared to sense it; its secluded ambience seemed to shrink from him as an undesired guest. Much later he was to recall the un-welcoming atmosphere that evening—close and humid, a threat of thunder tightening the air—and, with hindsight, interpret it as an omen. Certainly, if he had driven on, much that came after might perhaps have been different. But life was too uncertain for regrets . . .

If she was surprised to see him she hid it well. Admittedly her eyebrows lifted a shade at the sight of his weekend bag, but she made no comment on his presumption, then or later.

"You'd better come in," she said, standing aside.

"Do you mind?"

"I mind you didn't phone first."

The television was on in the living room. She switched off the sound and sank into the chair facing it, nodding him to another close by. The room was a cool retreat from the tropical evening outside.

"Don't stop watching because of me," he said.

"It's only a quiz show—any rubbish to help me unwind at the end of the day." She gazed at him for a while before complaining, "Honestly, Toby, why did you come?"

"I was worried about Jay. How is he?"

"Same as ever, up in his room." Her fingers tapped to show him, as on a Possum keyboard.

"I meant, has he got over that business . . . last time I was here?"

"Jay is pure india-rubber. It's long since forgotten."

"Thank God."

"You cost me a small fortune with that escapade, though. I had to buy an expensive extra for his silly computer. A commitment, proof no one would take it away again."

"The music attachment," he guessed. "A regular bargain at a hundred and fifty."

"That's right. How did you know?"

"I saw him coveting it. I'll give you a check if you need the money."

"Don't be patronizing!" she snapped, tossing her head.

"It's paradoxical, really," he said. "You invited me here to distract him from that infernal machine and you ended up swelling the Possum coffers."

She glowered but could find no reply, and lost herself in the studio audience waving their homemade banners: HI, CHICAGO.

IT'S ME, MOM. There was a glass with the dregs of a drink on the table beside her chair; her hand shook as she raised it. Was she afraid for herself or Jay? Because she was certainly afraid. The most hurtful thing a woman could do to a man, he thought suddenly, was to show fear of him.

"Actually, it was you I came to see," he said.

"Why?" A dull aside that asked for nothing in answer. A hunch told him she was considering how to restore the volume on the TV without seeming too inhospitable.

"Because I miss you like hell." He spoke quickly to the floor, as happens when words say themselves.

She forgot the program, leveling pained eyes at him. "Don't Toby. It doesn't ring true."

"I think I missed you the whole five years. I only realized it last week."

"Then you didn't miss me."

"I know how I feel, Elaine!"

"Sure, you do!" She fumed at the television, her face taut and flushed. "Like with that Sandy woman."

"Cindy," he said. "That was a mistake, a terrible error."

"I never doubted it," she said from on high. "How long did it last? Six months?"

"Less."

"Live with the consequences—I've had to."

He stumped over to the set and punched it off. "Can we talk a minute, *please?* There's so much to explain. Let's get it off our chests, out of the way once and for all."

"I'd rather we didn't."

"You phoned me three weeks ago, remember? I didn't feel much like listening then, but I did. So you owe me."

He evinced a crestfallen sigh: she had not lost a sense of fair play. But her chin sank mournfully into a hand, leaving no doubt about her unwillingness, and he was filled with misgiving. He sat on the edge of his chair, feeling an impenetrable wall between them, and recalled a phrase she had used on the phone that night, about her script going out of her head. His own week of anxious rehearsal escaped him now.

"You're proud of this house and the shop," he said, struggling
for a beginning. "Your newfound independence."

"I think I have cause, don't you?"

"Well, maybe deep down you were longing for the chance to
prove yourself. And perhaps I found that side of you a little difficult to take. I'm not the world's most successful guy."

"I'm in no mood for hard luck stories, Toby. I married an
easygoing cop who made me laugh, not a meal ticket. If I'd
wanted the next president of Exxon, I could probably have gotten him."

"See what I mean?" he protested.

Her eyebrows climbed but she held her tongue. If she saw his
point, she was not prepared to admit it.

"Do you know how I've spent my spare time these past
years?" he said softly. "Watching movies. Old movies, the Hollywood classics."

"It's your life to squander."

"No, not life, escape from life. We all do it, for Christsake.
Jay with his Possum, you with your shop. My thing happens to
be movies. I've got a whole roomful of cassettes. I play them
over and over. I know every scene, every last word of dialogue."

For a moment she stared, her pupils inquisitive pinpoints, and
it was as though she saw into the deepest recesses of his mind.
But without the sympathy he craved, only a pity she would have
given anyone who confessed to years with no purpose.

"It's nothing new," he reminded her rapidly. "I used to watch
TV movies with Jay. You were always busy with the bills—practicing your shopkeeping."

"Well, somebody had to take care of them."

He had planned this all so carefully in his apartment at
Quincy. He would tell her of his film library: perhaps then she
might grasp how things were not what they seemed. How in
North by Northwest the plane crop-dusting in the distance spelled
danger, always in full view but unsuspected until the very last
moment when it dove to machine-gun the prairie. Watch the
movie again and you could never be certain Cary Grant would
escape—that was the mark of a masterpiece. How in *Casablanca*

you hoped for a happy ending but had to settle for Bogart left alone on the runway. A deception that lingered painfully in the mind however often you saw it.

But Elaine's unreceptive attitude defeated him. She hated being preached at. He put it down to the force-fed religion of her childhood. "Remember *Casablanca?*" he said leadenly, which was not at all how he meant to begin.

"Difficult not to. They seem to screen it every month."

"Whenever I play it I have this premonition. Bogart gets the girl. Do you know the feeling?"

"Are you trying to tell me something?"

"What I mean is . . ." He clenched his fists in frustration. "Look, Elaine, three lives came together, things got out of control. That's how it was, back in Peabody. I wasn't running away with her, not willingly. Seemed like I was trapped in someone else's story and couldn't break free."

Her face hardened against him, her mouth pulled down, and he saw lines at the tips of her eyes he hadn't noticed before. He suspected she understood but found it easier to go on believing in the simpler truth of another woman.

"Like *Casablanca,*" he said. "The wrong ending."

"And you'd like to run it through again, see how it works out this time?"

"Something like that."

"Do me a favor," she riposted, and turned her back. "Go up and play with someone your own age."

*   *   *

Jay was at his desk, the new music unit placed proudly beside the Possum, its cable trailing down to a connection at the back. Staves and notes covered the display screen and when he touched a key a quaver jumped into place.

Doh-h-h, the computer sang.

"Where will it end?" Sorenson said with forced jollity. "Now you think you're Schubert."

"Better, actually," Jay said. "What I start, I finish."

"Are you up to symphonies yet?"

He hit a key, and a reedy tune came from the speaker like the sound of a tiny calliope. "Opus Two," he said, wrinkling his nose in agony. "Not exactly earth shattering, is it?"

"A bass line might help. Are we friends again?"

"Definitely." Jay smiled up at him. "Elaine would never have bought this if you hadn't picked on me."

Amiably, Sorenson brandished a finger in his face. "Well, don't get smart, junior. Don't plan to get picked on again this weekend."

The smile spread happily. "Does that mean you're staying?"

"God and the Great White Witch willing."

"Great! Will you take me somewhere tomorrow?"

"Somewhere plus twenty dollars?"

"No, to Boston."

"Amaz-ing." Sorenson play-acted a totter of astonishment and had to catch at the desk to steady himself. "What happened to the hermit?"

Jay got very red and averted his gaze. Well . . . it was a computer exhibition, he said, all the latest stuff. He had written it off, what with Elaine always working, but now that Toby was here . . . Sorenson hid his disappointment, ruffling Jay's unruly hair. The boy returned to his music, shifting notes on the staves to refine the tune.

"Do you mind if I get back to this now?"

"Can I watch?"

"Don't be mean, Toby. I'm still learning."

"No audience till you're expert, is that it?" Sorenson suggested, but the remark was ignored—if it was even noticed. "All right, then," he said, touching his forelock. "I'll report for duty in the morning, young sir."

"Make it real early," Jay said, all eyes on the screen.

*   *   *

Shortly after eleven, Sorenson heard Elaine's latch click shut on the other side of the hall. He donned a long bathrobe over his pajamas. Was the smattering of after-shave too obvious? A glimpse in the mirror showed the collar of the robe was up; he was about to turn it down but took further stock of himself and left it. Not unlike those trenchcoats Bogart used to wear—why argue with accidents of fortune? He went out and reached for the handle of her door. She could only say no. But what if she did? His hand fell passively to his side and with the merest of shrugs, a shiver of failure, he returned to his bed. The shiver of a man left alone on the runway, he thought. A voice told him he had given up too easily but there was nothing more he could do.

16

Through the doors of the trade center a steady stream of children made for the ticket windows. Their excited chatter died as they came in from the street—this building was unused to children and willed them to silence. The foyer was as strait-laced as a banking hall; their feet went *hush* over the snooty red carpet. A single poster on an easel introduced the "first ever East Coast Junior Micro-Fair." Another sign announced the only appearance in Boston this year of the Mormon Tabernacle Choir.

The girl in the booth pushed two tickets briskly under the glass. "One adult, one child. Next?"

"She didn't even ask!" Jay said, drawing himself up to his full height. "What if I was fourteen or something?"

"You'll be old sooner than you think," Sorenson said, and pressed between the turnstile. "Don't rush it."

Across the quiet twilight of an inner lobby a row of doors gave onto the main hall . . . suddenly it was as if they were in the thick of a political convention. Into a riot of noise and seething confusion, their eyes shrank in the unexpected glare. Under the hot lights the air conditioning had long since given up the struggle; forests of company signs stuck up like delegates' banners from the stands. A frilly line of cheerleaders bobbed on a stage: "Z-Y-L-E-C, Zylec!" they chanted, kicking their heels high. Somewhere off in the incandescent distance an exhibitor was releasing clouds of rainbow balloons that floated to the arching roof, buffeted by the din. There were kids by the thousands—arms crammed with sales literature in souvenir bags, freebie badges all over their chests—and hustlers in straw hats who pushed even more handfuls of pamphlets on every boy in range. Vote for *my* computer, kid, or this great country of ours is finished.

"Fan-tas-tic," Jay murmured and stopped dead in his tracks. He might have stood there all day feasting on the sight, but a wave of children crushed in from behind, sweeping them both forward and down the aisles.

Who could say what he saw? He entered a world of enchantment, too full of wonder to comprehend. Each stand was a theme park in a few square yards, a cunning trap of colors and welcoming smiles. He longed to be the richest boy on earth and buy every computer on each of the stands, the whole exhibition down to the last bolt. He could remain still in no single place for more than moments, something new was always drawing him on. He yearned to be on each of the stands at once, to grow so many greedy hands and eyes you wouldn't believe. This was Coney Island and Magic Mountain and Christmas rolled into one; it was the shrine to electronics he would have built if he'd only imagined it. As far as he looked were more computers than he had dreamed existed in the . . . in the entire universe. Millions and zillions of computers.

"Gee," he breathed, "isn't this the greatest thing . . . *ever?*"

"Great beyond words," Sorenson said, mopping his brow.

Xitron Corporation showed their vivid green machines on giant toadstools in a fairy glade where the buxom models flitted in green clip-on wings, peddling sales brochures. Gondor had built The Wizard's Lair, a labyrinth of spooky tunnels in whose dark dungeons lurked goblins and trolls. Get to the treasure cave without being seen and an Elf Queen in revealing robes gave rewards of gold chocolate bars. Along the main concourse, Plus Systems offered a Way Through the Computer Jungle, a stretch of tropical rain forest filled with the cries of recorded parrots, where real, dozy chimpanzees sat under cardboard trees. More pretty models roller-skated the aisles in Have a PET T-shirts, while a rival robot no more than knee high chased after them squeaking, "Who needs girls . . . get a Zibit." It lit up like a pinball machine with a jackpot and zipped off under their passing feet.

"Damn!" Jay paused to take his bearings. "Where are they?"

"Who?"

"Possum, of course."

"But you've already got one of them," Sorenson noted and, from the scathing look he received, doubted he would ever understand children.

"I want to see their latest product," Jay sniffed. "Why else would I come?"

Cat Woman pounced on them while they searched the Show Guide. Her scanty costume had adults in mind but the huge pointed ears were for the kids: they pricked up as she came near while her tail swung like a pendulum, perhaps by some clever electronics, but there seemed nowhere to hide them.

"Can I interest you in a Lynx?" she purred.

"He's a Possum man," Sorenson said. "A lost cause."

"Lynxes eat Possums for breakfast." She pawed prankishly at Jay, who backed away with a grimace of disapproval.

"Load of garbage," he muttered. "The Lynx memory's too small and the cycle time is pathetic."

"Dig you!" she pouted and melted into the crowd.

Possum was there in a big way, with a vast acreage of floor space in a prime part of the hall. A pavilion of steel tubing and orange domes spanned a lawn of orange nylon; mechanical doves trilled in orange-leaved trees and preened their orange plumage. An enormous likeness of the new Model 4 revolved slowly without visible support in a plastic bubble—to both sides were booths shaped like oranges where boys sat beguiled by the hardware and others waited impatiently to take over. A girl dispensed free orange juice from a cart with a striped awning, while willowy models in orange jump suits accosted strollers in the walkways and stuffed the competitors' souvenir bags into Possum's bigger ones. THINK ORANGE, banners proclaimed. THINK POSSUM. And the kids flocked in . . . no other stand in the exhibition was as crowded, as sweatily packed.

"What a swindle," Jay said, despondently viewing the long waiting lines. "Not enough demo systems, that's the trouble."

"More than enough," Sorenson said. "Too many kids like you."

"What's the shortest line, Toby? That one, or over there?"

He nodded vaguely to where Jay pointed; it saved having to

think. The temperature must have soared well into the 90s. The clamor was incredible. He was contemplating a suitable excuse to leave in search of a drink when a voice came from behind.

"Mr. Sorenson?"

He found a bearded young man blinking at him through heavy horn rims. "Yes?" He was trying to place the face. It reminded him of an owl with acne.

"It's Clint Dickerman, Mr. Sorenson." He had a brightly colored drink in a glass with the Possum logo, and the happy, slightly daft smile of a man who hasn't been drinking just orange juice. Without thinking he held out a hand, slopping the drink on the carpet. "Oh Jeez," he said, turning red. Suddenly he wasn't sure which hand the glass should be in and had to fumble to find out.

"Dickerman . . . ?"

"I work for Ned Wiley, remember? You know, the Wiley with the funny computer? The IP-3 that turned into a Zylec?"

"Of course! How are you, Dickerman? This is my son and heir, Jay." He completed the introductions by telling Jay he was privileged to meet one of the world's unrecognized geniuses. "The only man I know who can get a free computer from a robbery he didn't do. You weren't the brains behind it, were you, Dickerman?" Sorenson insinuated coyly.

Dickerman went a deeper shade of red and stuttered, "M-m-me? Does that mean you haven't solved it yet, Mr. Sorenson? Don't get me wrong, but I'd kinda hate you to find the guy. What if he wants his Zylec back?"

"The file's still open, as we say. But it's only a matter of time."

"Is Toby fooling or are you really great with computers?" Jay asked.

"I get by," he said modestly.

"Have you tried the new Possum yet?"

Dickerman chest swelled. He seemed to grow in stature. "Better than tried it. They're thinking of incorporating some circuits I designed."

"*Possum* is?" Jay said, his eyes on stalks.

Dickerman nodded and was about to press the point home by gesturing to the revolving computer when he remembered the drink. "Uh ha," he said.

"In the *Model Four?*"

"Only thinking; nothing's agreed for sure."

"Gee . . ."

"You mean you don't work for us anymore at Eastern Semi?" Sorenson said, suddenly curious.

"Sure I do. Fact is, Possum is a customer of ours; they buy components from us. That's why I'm here. Ned Wiley asked me to drop by."

"Selling to them, you mean?"

"Well, more the resident guru touch, the man with all the answers."

"I'd really like to try the Model Four," Jay said subversively. "The trouble is, so does everyone else. Have you got any *influence?*" This had Sorenson viewing his son in a new light. He threw down a challenge and endowed it with sex appeal at one and the same time.

"To get you top of the line?" Dickerman said. He stepped back in horror and spilled more of his drink.

"I'd be very grateful . . . Clint."

Dickerman was young enough to bathe in the respect of children, too young to know how to handle them. "Well . . . ," he said, gazing urgently in every direction. "Well . . . ," he repeated in the hope Jay would see how difficult he was being.

"The way you were talking," Sorenson interposed, "sounded like you know these people pretty intimately. Doing their circuits for them and so forth."

Dickerman had expected support and regarded him with a trapped, accusing stare. "See what I can do," he mumbled and moved uncertainly away.

"Think he will, Toby?"

"Remind me to tell you all about Dickerman one day. I wouldn't put anything past him."

Dickerman was a long time gone but returned flushed with success, hauling a lanky salesman whose orange lapel badge simply said BREWSTER, guess for yourself if it was his first name. Brewster peered down at Jay from his considerable height and intoned, "You the customer wants to put a Four through its paces?"

Jay nodded, awestruck.

"Follow me, would you?" Brewster ushered him to a remote corner of the stand where one of the orange-shaped booths stood closed and unattended. He whisked away a dust cover to reveal a Model 4. Jay sat down and switched on the power. Boys broke in a rush from the other lines, shouting and pushing for a place, while Brewster frantically waved his arms to drive them back, his smile growing frayed at the edges. "Kiss off!" he yelled when it finally slipped. Meantime, Jay played the keys on the computer as if he were alone in the world—he was unbudgeable until closing time.

"That system's reserved for trade buyers," Dickerman confided. "The poor guy'll probably get lynched."

"Tell me about those circuits you mentioned," Sorenson said abruptly.

Dickerman detected the sound of business in his voice and stared inquisitively through his tubby lenses. "You here officially, Mr. Sorenson?"

"Does it matter?"

He sipped long and hard from his glass to show how deeply he was thinking, then gave a massive wink and said, "I get it! Undercover stuff; don't want Possum to know. Enough said."

"I didn't say." Sorenson stroked his chin as if he had.

Now Dickerman moved very close, as though in all that din he might be overheard. "They've got a sample computer from us for evaluation. If the trials are successful, they're planning to build one of our micros into future variants of the Model Four. Could be very big business."

"They make their own computers, surely? It says 'Possum' on the cabinets."

He shook his head. "The circuitry isn't theirs, though. This end of the market is cottage industry, Mr. Sorenson. They buy in the computers, the memories, the display screens. All that's left is to assemble and sell them like hotcakes."

Sorenson looked thoughtfully to where Jay sat in thrall to a dizzily changing screen. Something close to a doubt formed in his mind; there was a question he should put to Dickerman but it escaped him. He shrugged it off. The heat was getting to him; his tongue felt like dry blotting paper. "Where'd you get the drink?" he said.

"The hospitality suite." Dickerman did it again: more liquor spilled as he pointed to a private area of the stand with comfortable sofas just visible behind smoked-glass panels. "Tequila Sunrise, never had it before. Want to come and try one or will it break your cover?"

"I'll worry about the cover. Just lead me to the trough."

Possum must have spent as much on the suite as on the stand outside—this was presumably where the retail chain buyers came to horse-trade. The exhibition roar was remote beyond the glass. Subdued lighting rested the eyes; rented palm trees spread broad fingers to shade the settees. The coolers were going at full blast and there were enough of them—it seemed every way you turned you saw coolers.

"Me again, beautiful." Dickerman propped up the bar exactly the way a man called Clint should and treated the girl to a leer. She flashed a frosty smile and filled two glasses from a shaker. No choice, she explained to Sorenson, just the Sunrise or straight Florida orange juice—it had to be company color.

"My fourth," Dickerman confessed.

"Fifth," she said.

"What the hell, who's counting?"

"Here's to cottage industry." Sorenson clinked glasses, tried a dubious sip, and decided he didn't like it. He considered saying as much to the girl—she found him more interesting than Dickerman and had thawed out the smile—but it was wet and cold, and what ex-cop could be seen turning down gratis liquor for fruit juice? "You mix the best I've had since breakfast," he told her. Then he shivered. On coming in, the suite had been marvelously cool; as the minutes passed, it became apparent how freez-

ing it was, like being in an icebox. "I've heard of air conditioning," he said, "but this is ridiculous."

"The way he likes it." She inclined her head to a man drinking
alone in a corner seat.

"The man himself," Dickerman added in an intoxicated whisper. "Jerry Hendricks."

"Company president," the girl said, and leaned on the bar for
a confidential nod that spoke volumes—the kind granted to fame
or money.

"Shall I introduce you?" Dickerman volunteered in a fool-
hardy moment. "We needn't say what you do."

"Looks like he doesn't want to be disturbed."

"Leave it to capable Clint." It was the drink talking and the
drink got under his feet as he sauntered over. He made a little
totter and glowered back at the carpet so no one could think it
was him.

Years ago, with their legs up at the precinct house, the detectives had played a game: describe a suspect in a single word, so
accurately a smart cop could pick him out of a lineup. And before
they even spoke, Sorenson had precisely the word for Hendricks.
Dapper. Small and controlled, he dressed immaculately—just the
right side of flashy. His alert eyes promised sparks of spry
humor, but a humor invariably connected with business. Could
you be rich and successful, which Hendricks clearly was, and still
be dapper? Sorenson thought so. He had an air about him—some
men never shake it off—of having started small, of having
clawed his way to the top through a series of small deals . . . as if
the dust of a street peddler still clung to his heels. You could encounter tycoons who were big in every way; those like Hendricks
remained obstinately small whatever their accomplishments. But
tycoons had one thing in common, he thought: they set themselves apart from the herd. The glass Hendricks left behind on
the table didn't contain a Sunrise or fruit juice. It was dark and
red, certainly wine.

"Always glad to meet Eastern Semi people." Hendricks'
handshake was dry and leathery, the probing eyes were disturbing—hynotically still yet in the same instant seeming to swivel. It

was as if he had to know all the time who was around him and so
not be taken by surprise. Sorenson was confounded by his own
word game. Was it possible, he wondered, for a man to have the
stare of a snake and still be dapper?

"Dickerman tells me you're interested in our computers," he
said, summoning a hard stare of his own.

"Not quite." Hendricks seesawed a hand to dispute the point.
"Your outfit is interested in us, that's nearer the truth."

"Come on, Jerry, it's a bit of both," Dickerman crooned in his
best salesman's manner. Then he nudged Hendricks cordially
with an elbow because that's what salesmen did.

"Toby, was that the name? Well, Toby, we're shipping two
thousand Possums a month. Mainly East Coast at this moment in
time but we go nationwide in the near year. Then we're target-
ing on ten thousand a month. That's juicy potential for our sup-
pliers. Eastern Semi should be buying *me* drinks." He flicked a
finger against Sorenson's glass.

"I'm sure we do."

"Too damned right, and more big dinners than are good for
me. At least, you try. One day it'll dawn on you all . . . I'm incor-
ruptible."

"Or not bought so cheap," Sorenson suggested. This was a
cynical thought surfacing. He hadn't intended to say it. He had
observed how crumpled Dickerman's shirt was, how stained with
sweat beneath the arms. Beside him, Hendricks was crisp and
uncreased. He obviously stayed in the suite, and Sorenson felt
sure it was not really for the purpose of entertaining. He was reminded of Howard Hughes hiding for years in his germ-free
room, and wondered what made tycoons fear the commonplace.
Did they think it was catching?

Hendricks demonstrated he was above rising to jibes by
chuckling loudly. "So, do you like my brainchild?"

"Most impressive. My young son is an addict."

The response was dramatic. "A willing partner, I insist,"
Hendricks said, driving a fist into a palm. "A boy and his Possum, Toby, can you picture a stronger team? This company of
mine, together with all those kids you see out there . . . we're

helping to build a better tomorrow." He was taken by a sudden crusading zeal that set his eyes burning with inner fire.

Dickerman seemed to have heard this from him before and gazed in rapt approval.

"Tell me this, Toby," Hendricks said in the same vein, "are you a student of history? I regard myself as a child of the industrial age. You see, I was born in the same year as the first Model T Ford. The dawning of mass production, and we all know what that led to. Your son Toby is a child of the age of electronics; he'll see and experience things you can't begin to imagine. We at Possum understand the spirit of the times; the world belongs to our children. That's why we've taken this business by storm."

His roaming gaze discovered a man beckoning from the bar. "Forgive me, but duty calls. I'm sure you have a fine boy, Toby. Give him my personal regards, a special hello from the company chief at Possum. It might make his day. Kids are status conscious as hell; don't believe anyone who says otherwise."

He left to confer at the bar, the newcomer having to stoop low to keep his words between the two of them. Now, assuming you wanted another word for the detective's notebook, Sorenson asked inwardly, what would you call this one? Exceptionally tall, endowed with a fine head of silver hair for a man in his fifties— sum him up as *distinguished.* On further thought, add a rider saying the face was *patrician,* except for a nose that was frankly too long and angular.

"Incredible guy," Dickerman said. "Must be worth a fortune."

"I found him creepy. Did you notice how his eyes are never off you but don't miss anything in the room? And I don't much like people who think they're Billy Graham."

Dickerman was scouring the suite for somewhere to place his empty glass. He gazed with poignant longing at a table some feet away, assessing his prospects of ever getting there. "You want creepy," he said absently, "try the guy he's with."

"The one with the snout?"

He attempted to nod and rocked ominously on his heels. "Name is Stevens. It's like he reads your mind, Mr. Sorenson.

He's the guy Hendricks sent shopping for the IP-3. Just breezes in off the street and says to Ned Wiley, 'I wonder if you happen to have . . .' Then he reels off a complete technical specification. And get this, so complete it's like he already had all the details."

Sorenson froze. "Say that again, slowly," he murmured, which was really a plea to himself.

"This guy Stevens breezes in and . . ."

"I heard! And now they've got an IP-3 courtesy of Wiley, right?"

Another precarious nod. "His only other prototype, the one you saw. He thought it made sense, what with Possum talking about buying so many. Well, you heard."

"For what purpose, Dickerman?"

"Wouldn't say. This is a fiercely competitive business, Mr. Sorenson, commercial secrecy is . . ." He trailed away, looking sick.

"Vital?"

"Absolutely. May look like computers for kids, but they're at one another's throats when it comes to selling. Mind if we sit down? I'm feeling a bit . . ." He gravitated unsteadily toward a settee but Sorenson seized his arm, squeezing hard.

"I remember you saying the IP-3 was for handling data from space probes . . ."

"Only one of the uses; it's for anything to do with images. You've seen these Possum computers; they make a big deal of the visuals, all very fancy. Ned's guess was they're thinking of some clever new game with color animation."

Sorenson gripped tighter still, his face close. "I don't suppose it occurred to you that Stevens over there might have a simpler angle than mind reading? Like stealing computers from Wiley's laboratory?"

"Hendricks sent him."

"Hendricks, Stevens, who gives a fuck!"

Dickerman stared back blearily. "Jeez," he said. "Sticky situation. Never thought of that."

"Seems like Wiley didn't either. Where are they based?"

"Lemme think." As Sorenson finally consented to release his

arm, Dickerman lurched to a settee, where he collapsed in a heap, his face contorted with the effort of remembering. "Waltham," he managed at last. "Out on one twenty-eight."

"In the science park?"

"I guess so, never been. Address is in the brochure."

"You look ghastly," Sorenson said, "have a drink," and he handed over his untouched glass and hurried away.

The wall of noise hit him at the door, a cacophony of shrill voices, music blaring from the stands, the drone of numberless computers going around the hall. From somewhere, strangely clear, came the metallic chime of a Possum. For precious seconds the heat was welcome, then the sweat broke in beads and dribbled down his cheeks. He battled over to the other side of the stand.

"Won't be long," Jay said, not even lifting his head. "This new game is the greatest yet. You get to explore the solar system." The screen was black and limitless, pricked with distantly glimmering stars.

"Make for base, commander. Warp five."

"Soon, Toby." The steady pad of his keys was swamped in the general uproar. A slowly tumbling asteroid glided by.

"*Now!*" Sorenson said, prying him away. Leaving the stand, he smiled sweetly at a girl in a Possum jump suit and helped himself to one of her brochures.

17

At Waltham, Route 128 separates two science parks as firmly as a border. Bear Hill Technical Center sprawls to the east, with the freeway literally in the backyards of the closest buildings. Spread the length of a dipping road are the plants of Waltham's industrial aristocracy: Polaroid, Memorex, Bunker Ramo, Fairchild. Their offices are some years old now, with an almost neglected appearance, a look of slippered comfort often affected by the vastly rich. Across the freeway aspiring newcomers inhabit the slopes of Prospect Hill Park; less well known corporations aiming for a place in *Fortune*'s Top 1000. Their plants are the brasher homes of the *nouveaux riches*—research blocks gift-wrapped in iridescent glass and headquarters colonnaded with fashionable black steel—and the more obscure the name, the larger it is emblazoned across the façade.

"Do we *have* to?" Jay grumbled, while Sorenson perused the board listing the companies in Prospect Hill.

"Don't you want to see where they're made?"

"I guess so," he said with no great enthusiasm.

Possum Inc. was at the crest of the hill, where it overlooked the looping service road, the thundering freeway, and the grimy flat roofs of the industrial giants. The long, low building was as forbidding as a penitentiary, marooned in an expanse of black asphalt. It stood three stories high, with walls broken only by a single band of windows at the upper floor. Sorenson thought of Hendricks in the seclusion of his exhibition suite: the factory was equally aloof. For all its commanding position on the hill, the plant turned inward, oblivious to the rest of Waltham.

Possum felt no need for a barrier at the road and he soon realized why as he drove into the compound and made a slow circuit. A dusty convertible stood by the entrance; otherwise the lot was deserted. Under the front porch, glass doors gave onto a lobby where a single light burned over the reception counter. A uniformed guard slouched there, and Sorenson knew from his preoccupied stance that he was watching concealed TV monitors— their pale flicker gave his face a deathly cast. From roof level, high-intensity lights angled downward; at night the compound would be flooded with the startlingly white brilliance of a baseball stadium. Remote-controlled cameras on every corner gave complete coverage of the walls; even more cameras were mounted on high poles by the open gate and at intervals along the boundary fence. One of them turned like a scrawny robot as they drove by, tracking the car with glassy suspicion. Back at the front, the guard peered out with little interest: an old yellow Beetle, a man who had taken a wrong turn, a boy in the passenger seat—they would soon be off when they discovered there was no way through. Sorenson stared up at the modest Possum logo on the canopy, his brow furrowed.

"Would you beat that," he declared.

"What?" Jay asked. He had become bored when he found there was nothing to see.

"It's not what I expected. Like Fort Knox." Sorenson laughed and suggested, "If they steal computers, nobody's going to steal from them."

"Can we go now?"

"Why not. Back to the obsolete Model Three?"

"I've been thinking about that," Jay said mournfully. "Is Elaine the kind of woman to appreciate a Model Four?"

"No way."

"I was afraid of that."

"Why don't you try me instead?"

Jay's face lit up. "You mean . . . ?"

"We'll see," he promised with a wink. Then he made for the road and threaded the car through the bends. They took a left at the foot of the hill, the engine complaining as always when he coaxed it to 40 mph, back to the freeway. Abruptly, he slammed on the brakes and pulled over to the curb.

"Crazy," he said, shaking his head.

"Gee, Toby, now what?"

"Since when did toy factories look like that?"

Jay glared fiercely; he started a protest but Sorenson interrupted, his fingers to his lips in a curt, "Shut up, I'm thinking."

It was probably the siege mentality that beset certain company chiefs, he reasoned, a clear case of paranoia. They had their product secrets to protect, an inventory that could easily run into millions of dollars, and they overreacted. Except . . .

"Come on, Toby," Jay pleaded.

He considered the building further and it made no sense. It wasn't an ordinary factory with the security hardware tacked on as an afterthought: Possum had designed it for concealment from the foundations up. He made a determined U-turn and headed back.

"Heck, Toby . . ."

"You got me hooked on Possums, so clam up."

He toured the plant again, the cameras tilting to stare after them. He saw them panning on their tall poles and felt them boring into the car roof from above. The clandestine walls rose sheer beside them to the skinny strip of window. The glass was silvered, impenetrable; on every pane he spotted the pressure pads he knew were wired to the alarm system. At the rear, a flight of stairs burrowed down to a steel door. That would be the basement equipment room, a maze of throbbing machinery and insulated pipes. A floodlight projected immediately overhead to illuminate the stairs, and a camera surveyed the bottom landing. Not a weak point anywhere, no soft underbelly.

They returned to the front entrance and found the guard standing inside the doors, a hand placed threateningly on his hip holster. Sorenson instantly recognized a fellow ex-cop, probably lured into company life by the usual promises and bored out of his mind ever since. He was pushing fifty, his once athletic frame deteriorating fast, the indulgent paunch flopping over his belt. As the Beetle crept past he jerked a thumb to order them away.

"Time you learned one of my games for a change," Sorenson told Jay.

"Which one?"

"Felony. All it needs is a building and three players."

"You mean a *break-in?*"

Sorenson nodded. "To you that looks like an ordinary, boring electronics plant. To my expert eye it's a hotbed of computer thieves and international spies. They smuggle top-secret microchips out of the country concealed in Possums. Their boss is a master criminal, a double agent in the pay of both the Russians and the Mafia. Somewhere inside those walls is his hiding place, a vast office guarded by missile launchers and a moat filled with man-eating sharks."

"Really, Toby?"

"Well, it's only a theory. It could turn out to be an ordinary, boring plant. Want to play?"

"Do I!"

Sorenson lowered his voice thoughtfully. "They've got every protective system imaginable. The flaw is, it's all aimed at keeping adults like me out. Are you reading me, partner?"

"You handle the hit man," Jay said, grinning. "I'll take care of the rest."

He parked well clear, in line with the door so they were in full view as they walked over. A man without a jacket, nothing concealed, a young boy at his side. Still fingering the gun, the guard sized them up before retreating to the desk to check the monitors covering the rear. It felt less and less like a toy factory by the minute.

Sorenson rapped on a door and got the irascible brush-off again, the thumb to the road. He noted the thick laminated glass a road breaker's hammer wouldn't shatter, pressure pads at the top. Solid doors on the far side of the lobby presumably led to the elevators; the factory floor would lie beyond. He knocked again, pointing to Jay and mouthing a plea. The man yelled back: muffled words about being "closed, goddamnit" wafted through the armored glass. Jay began to stamp his foot; his lip quivered. He looked on the brink of tears. Sorenson tried a plaintive shrug and the guard stalked over, put his face to the gap between the doors, and growled, "Closed, goddamnit. Come back Monday." Jay flew into a rage, kicking the glass so hard it trembled like a sheet of plastic. Inside, a bell began to clang. "Fix my Possum," he wailed, covering his ears. He was very good.

"Hold it, kid," the guard shouted, "gimme a break, wouldya," and he dove for a button that would kill the bell, then squinted for the front key in the bunch on his belt. The door opened a crack and Jay fell quiet, biting a knucke.

"We're shut, can't ya see? Jesus, buddy, it's the weekend." He was called Willard according to the orange Possum label stitched on the shirt pocket: *Hi, I'm Willard, your friendly guard. Have a nice day now.*

"Try explaining that to him," Sorenson said.

Jay howled on cue. "Broken . . . won't even hum . . . want it fixed."

"It's Saturday, kid. We're closed till Monday."

"Tell him it's bust, Toby," Jay cried, and he aimed another hefty kick at the glass. "Make him fix it."

"I'd help ya if I could, kid, but . . ." Willard pushed the door wide to come and console him. "How's about some candy? I've got a Hershey bar somewhere." He delved in his trouser pockets.

"Stupid Possum!" Jay ranted. "Stupid grommy computer!" But his eyes grew enormous. On a plinth in the lobby was a Model 4—during the week it probably revolved seductively under the overhead spots that were off now. Suddenly he could think of a better reason than spies for getting inside.

"That's remarkably civil of you," Sorenson said, taking the opportunity to move into the doorway. "Kids these days, what do you do with them?" He slipped behind the counter while Jay doubtfully accepted a melting mass of chocolate—to find an astonishing array of TV monitors, more than twenty built into the raised edge that hid them from outside. Three showed close-ups of the Beetle, others gave high-angle views of the empty compound. More of the screens covered the inside of the plant—he had expected this—and he signaled to Jay with a nod. The cameras were controlled by small joysticks on a panel recessed in the desk.

Jay must have been smart with the chocolate. Muttering to

himself, Willard was scraping a sticky brown blob from his uniform jacket. He glanced up, spun round, and saw Sorenson over by the screens.

"Hey, buddy, get away from there!"

"Amazing electronics," Sorenson said, prodding a lever. One of the pictures jumped.

"Hands off, wouldya!"

"Marvelous. Without these you'd never suspect he was there."

"Who?" Willard vacillated, frowning in through the glass before rushing back to scan the monitors. "Whadya see?"

"Well, I thought " Sorenson pointed to a grainy shot of the boundary wire. "Just there . . . looked like a . . . hell, now I don't know what it was."

"A bird flies over, ya think ya see something." Willard yawned, scratching under his arms as he bent very close for a perfunctory check of the screens. "It's like a morgue out here, weekends. I'm telling ya, buddy, this is a job ya can have any day . . ." His voice slowed and faded; he stood bolt upright to gaze about in dismay. "Hey, where's the kid?"

"Back in the car?"

"I don't see him on the . . . *what the fuck!*"

Jay had appeared on a monitor, blithely strolling between the assembly lines, hands in pockets.

"Kids," Sorenson said sadly. "Do whatever damnfool thing comes into their heads."

Willard backed away, covering him with the gun. Not any old ex-cop, Sorenson thought as he looked down the barrel, this was the kind that practiced fast draws in front of the mirror long after they dropped the weight lifting.

"Hey!" Sorenson cried. "Easy with that! He's only a kid. He's crazy over computers, that's all."

"Stay where ya are, wise guy." Willard ducked through the inner doors and the lock snapped shut behind him. Moments later he was on the same monitor, moving at a crouch, the gun at the ready. Jay was nowhere to be seen—the rest of the screens were as still as photos, gray toned and fuzzy under a fine drizzle of sparkles. Sorenson stared in horror at the gun: suddenly it wasn't a game anymore. In the Boston Police Department, he had never come to terms with firearms. A gun felt cold and heavy in the hand, as deadly and willful as a rattlesnake; it was crazy to believe you could control it. A sound from behind you and it fired; you'd swear your finger hadn't budged. But unlike him, this ex-cop hadn't turned his back on the wretched things. To grip one was an embrace. Probably he went to weekly target practice at the local gun club. On quiet days, with no one to see, perhaps he gunned down scraps of paper bowled by the wind across the parking lot.

"Go easy," Sorenson prayed. "Keep the safety on."

Somehow he contrived to tear his eyes away, to scrutinize the pictures while he could. Sometimes, during off hours, he sat at his own monitors at Norwood, traveling the plant. They were like X-ray cameras penetrating the surface to reveal any disorder, any bad blood. And he knew companies pointed their cameras where they most feared access: jewelers at the gem cases, banks at the vault door. If Possum had a secret, it was on one of these cameras. He started top left, camera one.

Two long lines of benches stretched for perhaps a hundred feet across the factory floor; power and phone lines dangled from a spidery service grid overhead. He saw pigeonholes of components placed within easy reach, racks of electric tools, huge illuminated lenses to magnify the circuit boards as the tiny parts were clipped into place. Uneven lines of black stools marched like ants in the aisles. A fork lift blocked a corner, abandoned on the spot as the Friday siren marked the end of the week.

A movement drew him to another screen—Jay scuttling under a bench. Sorenson held his breath as Willard came into the picture, crawling almost on all fours to keep out of sight. Then he grinned in spontaneous relief: the gun was back in the holster. The guy had come to his senses, thank God, and remembered he was only chasing a child. He had to stand upright to squeeze the beer belly past the fork lift. His lips moved and there was no need for sound.

Come on out, ya son of a bitch.

"Camera two," Sorenson said. Jay had popped up on a different monitor, tiptoeing beside a high mesh barrier with a board that warned, WAREHOUSE—AUTHORIZED PERSONS ONLY. His shirt was so white it burned the screen, his chest throbbed, the edges of the collar were scorched black. In the poor light it seemed he shone like a fog lamp and no one could miss him. But it was a trick of electronics: back on camera one Willard was scratching his head, still swearing.

Sorenson left him to his misery and zoomed in through the wire to the cardboard containers in the warehouse. He tracked along the mesh, finding row upon row of innocuous cartons. Nothing of interest, nothing exceptional; it might have been the warehouse at Eastern Semi.

Quickly, he turned his attention to the next monitor, which showed an administration area he assumed was upstairs. Vacant chairs stood at vacant desks. Most of the desk tops had been cleared for the weekend, but the usual few mavericks had left their mountains of paper behind. An ailing pot plant stuck from a pile of computer printout like a bush in a snowdrift. Using the joystick, he roamed past the typewriters and computer terminals to a cold drinks machine with the COKE sign blazing in the half-light. He imagined it buzzing in the silence, giving its occasional rattle.

The next screen revealed a long, bare corridor punctuated by closed doors. Not a damned thing. On the monitor beside it, a shot of the central staircase from a camera placed high overhead. He started searching frenziedly, vainly, for Jay. But he was gone again, so totally hidden even the gimlet lenses couldn't find a trace. Back on camera one, Willard was panting heavily, digging in his pocket for a handkerchief.

Where in fuck's name are ya?

Sorenson sighed and glanced to another monitor, a bird's-eye view of offices built like stables with low partitions and no ceilings. Junior management, he thought; identical metal desks, hardly enough room for a single visitor's chair, and only the odd travel calendar in place of a window. Nothing to distract from the serious business of keeping Possum ticking, shipping its two thousand systems a month. He pictured the men in their hutches, phones ringing incessantly, paper flooding into the overflowing trays.

Inside the stark walls the building was simply another Eastern Semi—whatever face it presented to the world. Perhaps all the plants along 128 were like that. Identi-Kit assembly lines where the components were stitched onto boards, open plan offices where a man couldn't even scratch in private. He stared through the heavy glass to his car outside and wondered what he was doing spying on a toy factory. He longed suddenly for the comparative sanity of the exhibition back in Boston.

A rapid movement caught the corner of his eye. Jay had discovered where the completed machines were stacked for shipment. The sight of so many smart new Possums was too much for him. He forgot the chase and emerged into the open, wandering along the shelves, trailing a hand over the orange cabinets. Willard would surely spot him. Sorenson looked on in agony, wanting to cry a warning as Jay turned a corner and was seized.

Gotcha, ya son of a bitch!

Jay made no attempt to pull free, gazing up with a trusting face. He pointed to the Possums, made a childish excuse, and beamed his most innocent smile. With a nod of understanding Willard let him go, waited for him to turn to the door, then yanked viciously at an ear.

"You bastard!" Sorenson cried, striking the screen.

*   *   *

"You sure you're okay?" he asked anxiously when they were back on the freeway, plodding home to Salem.

"I'm fine, really," Jay insisted.

"Bet they drummed him out of the police for Gestapo tactics."

"It was fun, honest. Don't worry so much." Jay's young face was fluidly alive; he could barely sit still in the seat; Sorenson had never seen him so excited. "Was the mission a success, Toby?" he asked, eyes shining.

"Played to perfection," Sorenson told him. He had seen little and learned nothing but he didn't want to spoil the adventure by admitting as much. Yet a nagging doubt remained and he was unable to keep it to himself. Not that it was any of his business, he said, more a question of professional curiosity.

"You have massive security for only one reason, Jay. When you have something unusually valuable to protect. And I'm damned if I can guess what. It's just an electronics factory, same as any other."

"You mean all the cameras?"

He nodded. "And the rest of it; as much hardware as an aircraft carrier."

"I figure it's to keep out the kids."

"You do, huh?"

"There must be millions want a Possum and their parents won't buy them one."

"If not billions," Sorenson said, breaking into a smile. "Well, it's a better theory than any of mine."

"Hey, this isn't the right ramp!" Jay exclaimed as he dropped from the freeway.

"One more detour while my mind is working. Just a quick visit and then it's home."

"Heck, Toby, you're a drag."

*   *   *

He took 128 back to Norwood, where he left Jay stewing in the Eastern Semi parking lot. In his office, he rifled his files for a photocopy Wiley had given him, a list of delegates at a conference in San Francisco. Wiley had presented a paper on image processing there, and confessed he might have aroused the wrong kind of interest in the IP-3.

"You haven't lost your touch, Sorenson," he murmured.

There it was, among the names. *Victor Stevens, Possum Inc.* Put that together with Dickerman's story and he had what a district attorney would call a *prima facie* case. But of what? When a corporation stole from you to learn your secrets, that was theft, no question. But when they liked what they'd stolen and asked openly to buy, what then? Would Leitner view it as theft and take action? Think his words for him. "You expect me to take a big customer to court, Sorenson? Frankly, if all our clients checked out our products that way, our sales costs would be halved." Would Leitner even listen?

On the freeway again, driving toward Salem, Jay asked him what he'd found.

"Not a thing," he said. "False alarm."

18

Elaine went to bed at her usual time. Just after eleven the click of her latch sounded from the hall. In his robe and pajamas, Sorenson knocked at her door, opening it before she could answer. She glanced up from her dressing table, a pad of cotton in her hand, and he smelled the sweet oily aroma of face cream. Ignoring her unsociable frown, he stepped in and closed the door.

"You're off limits, Toby."

"My intentions are honorable," he said.

"This is behind-the-scenes stuff." She showed her face, cheeks whitened like a clown's.

"Go ahead, I don't frighten easily." He chose the corner of the bed beside her stool. Pointedly dropping the swab, she turned, resting her hands demurely in her lap.

"To what do I owe the late call?"

"We had a great time today, Jay and me."

"He told me." She tilted her head for a bemused smile. "What were you two up to? Come clean, more than the exhibition."

"Burglary," he said. "A raid on a secret plant."

"Can't you ever be serious?"

"That's why I'm good for him, because I'm not serious." He leaned very close and she caught her breath. "The same goes for you . . . tell me it does." His hand ran over her hair to the back of her sturdy neck. "Tell me," he whispered. "Tell me it's been too long." Her eyes closed; she bared her teeth in a low moan. As their lips were about to meet, he felt how unyielding she became; she shook him off with a shudder and he saw a face drained of all color under the glistening cream, the teeth clamped not in passion but repulsion.

"This is my room, Toby," she said haltingly. "Don't ever come in here again."

*   *   *

He sat in bed with a novel into the early hours, not reading the words. It was as if his hand still rested on her neck, over the marble coldness of her skin. Eventually he set the book aside. He noticed the Bible by the bed. For a moment he was overcome with the need to search for a suitable passage, some text to help forget the feel of her frigidity. But Elaine's mother must have placed it there, and even to turn the pages would grant her a victory. Somehow she would know, as surely as if the Bible were wired. Holy telepathy, Elaine had once called it in rueful remembrance of her teens. So lost in thought, he scarcely heard the door open.

"I can't sleep either," Elaine said.

He was too bruised to reply. She padded over to kneel on the bed at his feet. Stripped of makeup, her face had the remarkable plainness of a peasant woman. He asked himself the question that had plagued him in their first weeks together: what did he see in her? The mystery remained, yet her aura was so powerful he wished her out of the room for his own peace of mind.

"I can't tell you what it means to see Jay happy again," she said after a studied interval. "You're a miracle worker."

"Must be the burglary," he said. "Does wonders for the strictly raised child."

"Nutty man." She regarded him fondly before looking away, and he judged from the troubled expression that she was preparing for an unpleasant task. "How far is it from Quincy to Norwood?"

"Half an hour, sometimes longer."

"How long from here?"

"In the morning rush—forty-five minutes, maybe. Depends on the traffic."

"Would you like to try it for a while?"

"Always the shopkeeper; worry about the business details first."

"Would you, Toby?" she asked with gentle fury.

He knew the answer but held a long silence to punish her. "You've got yourself a tenant," he agreed finally and reached out to squeeze her hand. But she misunderstood and solemnly shook on it. Then she swung her legs to the floor.

"Let's be clear—that's all you are. No more passes."

"What, me? The guest in the Mother Superior Suite!"

She was in no mood to be amused. "I'm not ready for you, Toby." From the door she added, so low he could barely hear, "I doubt if I ever will be."

"Want to bet?" he murmured when the door closed.

6. The House on Salem Common

19

In a quiet moment between customers, Elaine stood at the shop door and saw the passing of summer in the crested waves dashing against the quays, the translucent hazy gold of the sunbeams that slanted falteringly through the mists to brush the harbor. Spring was said to come mysteriously from the earth; as one who had spent her childhood on the coast, she knew autumn came from the sea.

New England was now only weeks away from the red and amber quilt that brought the tourists on their weekend drives of gasping delight. Like gathering flocks of migratory birds, the visitors would soon have their brief last flurry, their noisy swoops on Salem, before departing for the year. Some of the boats would leave the harbor—she guessed to winter south but did not know where—and those that stayed would nod as forlornly on the rainswept waters as the sheltering gulls.

A family turned the corner. Anticipating a sale, she quickly withdrew. She was aware that leaning in the doorway showed business was slacking off, but like all small shopkeepers there were times she could do nothing else. They came to the window, a couple with a dumpy girl of nearly ten, and fawned over the toys. When the bell rang she raised a welcome but noted with dismay how the sound failed to thrill her. She went through the motions, showing the girl a raccoon she asked to see but said little, finding even a smile a hardship.

"He's just a bandit, isn't he?" Elaine suggested, knowing she had said exactly those words more times that summer than she dared to recall.

When he dropped by one Sunday, Toby had laughingly called this her theater; she wondered if he knew how right he was. There were only so many situations, each with its script, and she acted her part with the growing fatigue of a performer in a long-running show: always tolerant, ever helpful, only being rude when a customer became insufferable, somehow preserving the pleasant smile to the end of the day. And always —for Toby above all people—she maintained the fiction that no sale made itself, every dollar in the till must be won by sweat and cunning. Lately—as now—the grinning toys clinched the deal while she stood stiffly by, but she kept that truth to herself.

The family left the shop, the girl cuddling the raccoon in her plump arms—she refused a bag as cruel—and as the bell gave its hollow jangle, Elaine dropped thankfully into her chair behind the counter.

She blamed the autumn for her somber mood. The time of mellow thoughtfulness, wasn't that what they said? Today was going to be one of those slack days. Midweek, with the oppressive wet shade of rain along the horizon, only a trickle of callers since opening. She placed a book in her lap but switched on the portable television hidden under the counter.

Toby had pulled her leg about the set. "You find it respectable to be seen with a book," he'd declared, "and somehow vulgar to be caught viewing."

Natually, she knew better. Customers were a funny lot; a sale was a fragile thing. The shop depended on atmosphere, its own blend of magic, and television shattered it. She was not, she insisted in reply, running a mere five and dime.

It was five weeks since he'd moved in. They'd settled into an uneasy truce as predictable as marriage. He could be fun when he wanted, it had always been so, but he didn't actually *do* anything—and that, she saw with sudden clarity, had also always been true. If anything, his years away had perfected the art of laziness. In the morning he rose at the last possible minute, leaving only enough time to snatch a coffee on the move before racing for his car. On weekends she had no idea when he surfaced, and preferred not to guess. It never crossed his mind to prepare a meal—he would suggest a restaurant or something brought back from a fast-food place, unable to grasp how she craved the luxury of a can of soup from her own kitchen. His video machine had arrived from Quincy, usurping her TV for interminable reruns of old Bogart and Hitchcock movies. When it was finally off for the evening, he wanted only to explain, yet again, why he had walked out on her. And she already knew. She had known long before he did himself. He was chasing a dream . . . just, she supposed, as he was doing now.

It was not her imagination: sometimes at night she heard him pause outside her room. When it seemed she might weaken, she found the reason to resist—he would stay only as long as she held out. Keep him chasing the dream. Yet when she considered why she wanted him there, it seemed only that to lose him for a second time must be worse than enduring his faults. Her upbringing was to blame, she mused, the lesson drummed into her that life demanded a man. Occasionally, lying awake far into the night, there were even times when she wondered if it mattered *which* man.

With half an eye, Elaine watched the TV. One of the pretty reporters who covered the minor news stories was talking into the camera. She stood amid the empty desks of a schoolroom; a junior grade from the looks of the chalked scribbles on the blackboard. The children's desks drew Elaine from her day-

dream—which, if he only knew, would be another thing to set
Toby laughing. Screw Toby and his movies, she thought. What
interested a woman was her own business.

> ". . . We're used to hearing about problems in the nation's schools,
> about pupil apathy and absenteeism. Here in Springfield today,
> hooky reached an all-time high. This morning, this schoolroom
> looked just as you see it now. Empty. As empty as the Fourth of
> July. Not a single pupil showed up. The head teacher, Alice Porter,
> professed herself baffled, saddened, by this latest sign of . . ."

Elaine panicked, urgently reviewing the morning. Jay's first
flush of enthusiasm at Toby's stay had quickly waned. If it was
possible, he now spent more time closeted with his computer. It
was harder than ever to drag him to school. Today he had been
especially reluctant to go, or had he? Television could do that,
sow ideas in the mind. And yet, thinking back, she was certain he
had deliberately spun out breakfast so she would leave for the
shop without dropping him off. He'd be going in a minute, he
promised as she left. *Don't worry so, Elaine. Mothers are all the
same.*

She dialed home and let it ring for several long minutes. Then
it dawned on her: if he was at the house, he was too smart to answer the phone. She flipped the sign on the door to CLOSED,
feeling a little foolish but driven by premonition. The portents
had been there that morning; they must have been brewing for
weeks. Suddenly she knew Jay was in his room as surely as she
had sensed the coming of fall.

*   *   *

There was no sign of life in the hall, no coat or lunchbox.
Quietly, she climbed the stairs and crept to Jay's door, listening
for the telltale *ding* of the Possum. When it came she had to hold
back briefly to contain her anger. Jay sprang to his feet at the
sound of the door. In his guilty eyes she saw the excuses already
taking shape. She tore the plug from the socket and the Possum
gave a *phut-t-t,* the soft fading of something spinning to a halt,
like a dying gasp.

"Hey!" Jay howled, "you're supposed to go through the shut-down sequence." He had a little of Toby in him. He would always leap to the attack when most in the wrong.

"How often have you done this?"

"I wasn't well . . ."

"How often, Jay? Have you played hooky before?"

"I don't feel so good, honest."

"You look fine. Fit as a fiddle."

"I had a headache. I told you this morning."

"How often, Jay!"

"Only once," he said, not daring to look at her. "I had another headache last week."

"If you did, it's from sitting in front of that damned screen all day."

"No, it was just an ordinary headache." He met her furious gaze with defiance. "It's gone. If it was because of the Possum, I'd still have it, wouldn't I?"

"Get your coat."

"That's not fair!"

"We're going to school, Jay. Get your coat."

"But I'm ill. I can't arrive this late, they'll kill me."

"Tough!"

As she drove through Salem in chilly silence, she guessed how abandoned he must feel but hardened her will by the knowledge this was all for the best: school was school.

"Will you tell Toby?" he asked plaintively.

"I haven't decided. Probably."

"Don't Elaine. Please."

"It's not Toby you have to worry about, young man. It's me."

"The trouble is, fathers are so unpredictable."

She found the comment hilarious yet kept a straight face. "Not yours," she said. "Certainly not soft old Toby."

"But Kevin . . . ," he began, then turned his face to the window.

The mere mention of the name was enough to conjure his broken body, lying in the pool of blood she described in whispers but hadn't seen. "What about Kevin?"

"Nothing," he insisted, and bit his lip.

Glancing at his unhappiness, she saw what might be fear in his eyes and it melted her stony resolve.

"Cheer up," she said. "I'll spin the teacher a story for you."

20

When Toby returned that evening she was in the living room, curled up tight in a chair, a martini glass, generously filled, pressed to her cheek. It was her third drink in an hour; she felt fogged and carefree but sufficiently collected, just, to know better than to finish it. From very far away she heard the bang of a car door. Soon the front door slammed thunderously and what must be his briefcase dropped heavily to the hall floor. Usually she arrived home after he did; in her haze she wondered if he was always so appallingly loud when left alone, whether he imagined that crashing around like an elk gave him domain over her house. The living room door flew wide, the handle striking the wall.

"Bar's open early," he said, spying the drink.

"Join me."

He accepted her offered glass but, after a grudging sniff, set it aside on a table. "You still like them strong," he said with a frown.

"But infrequent, Toby. Today was a strain. I closed before lunch and haven't been back."

"Too many customers or too few?"

"Jay skipped school."

The semblance of a smile crossed his face. "So did I when I was his age."

"Why did I know you'd say that?"

He flopped into a chair and kicked off his shoes. "So Jay missed a day's school. He's bright, he'll survive."

"*Four* days' school, Toby. Two days last week, another couple this week."

He shook his head, perhaps at his own complacency. "Not so

good. Once in a while raises the spirits, but that sounds like a bad habit in the making."

"That stupid school, Toby. They said they phoned here yesterday to find out what was wrong. At least that's what they told me; who knows if they bothered? Haven't they heard of working mothers?"

"I forgive you the economy-size martini," he said contritely.

"You can do better than that. Take that dreadful computer away from him."

"Me?"

"Yes, you. Confiscate it. Distrain the bloody thing." She noticed how remote the words sounded, someone else's voice from the echoing depths of a long dark tunnel.

"When I took it before, he attacked me. Have you forgotten so soon?"

"This time I'll support you. We'll be firm parents, the two of us. I'll be right behind you, Toby, I swear." Her voice snapped. "Just do it."

"Why me?"

"Because I can't. He'll turn those big, puppy eyes on me and I'll cave in. Do you think I haven't tried!"

"And I'm made of stronger stuff, is that it?"

"You're the man around here."

The notion seemed to please him; he went to the door without further bidding. "What do we do, bury it? Hang it high on Gallow Hill? What's the sentence for a computer that aids and abets hooky?"

"Imprisonment in the garage. He can have it back in a few days when he's learned his lesson." She threw him the key, hot from being clasped for an hour.

"But, Toby," she called after him into the hall, "don't tell him that. He's lost it for good, okay?"

He was back after an anxious interval when no voices reached her from upstairs; no shouts, no weeping, no tantrums. The peace made it harder to bear; Jay was at his quietest when most hurt. She had retrieved the drink from the table but Toby was too lost in his martyrdom to notice the empty glass. His face was stern; he took his chair without a word. She warmed to his patent distress: people who found it easy to be tough on children worried her. She stared at him across the wide space of the room and rediscovered that his face looked its best when serious. Not handsome but . . . screw it, she thought, not handsome but *what?* Why did he wear that silly smile so often and became plain ordinary when he was capable of being not quite handsome? He should try horn-rims and a learned expression and become a professor or something. So what that he didn't have the brains; he could pass the university interview solely on the horn-rim glasses, by showing how solemn he could be, how almost wise. Just as long as he didn't spoil it by smiling.

"How was it?" she asked after a time.

"What's the saying . . . this hurts me more than it does you? Why do kids never believe you?" He lit a cigarette, taking short nervous puffs, holding it tentatively between finger and thumb as if throwing a dart.

"Poor Toby." She let him gaze into the rising smoke for a while, then said quietly, "Show me a movie."

He perked up, just as she knew he would. "Any particular movie?"

"A funny one, something to cheer us both up. Hell, Toby, I could do with a damned good laugh."

"How about *Some Like It Hot?* The funniest movie ever made."

"Done. You can get excited about Marilyn Monroe, I'll drool over Tony Curtis."

"Tony Curtis?" He found one of his silly grins and she could have killed him. "Of course—the deep-voiced one in the skirt! I always figured you as kinky."

"Nobody's perfect," she replied archly, and when he stared, she produced an angelic smile and told him to roll it.

*   *   *

"Why is it black and white?" she asked as the closing titles faded and he turned off the set. "It's hardly an oldie."

"All the classic movies are black and white. Like memories of the important events in your life. The death of a parent, a sad muddle of grays and funereal black. The darkness the first time you make love." At the end of a favorite film—even a comedy—he was invariably in a philosophical mood.

"Jay was born in color," she countered. "Everything around me was red, a swirling mist of crimson."

"That's because blood red is the only color most of us can recall clearly from the past."

"Don't be so morbid," she said, "it tempts fate." She put down her glass to cover her mouth and smother a hiccup. Happily she considered the fact that when you were a little drunk— just beginning to have some fun—a goddamned hiccup always gave you away. With an unsteady gait, she followed a line down the middle of the carpet to where he stood.

"Super movie, Mr. Sorenson."

"My pleasure."

He eyed her strangely and retreated a step into the corner. Another funny thing about drink, she thought, it put men on the defensive—decent men, anyway, the sort you didn't mind having around after a few tiny martinis.

Don't worry about me, Mother. I'm too tanked for him to DARE.

Somewhere deep in her head she heard herself giggle.

"I like it cool myself," she said. "How about you?" Slowly, with difficulty, she unknotted his tie and pulled it free. She held it high, at arm's length, and let it fall to the floor. Then she undid his collar button, an absolutely *enor-mous* button stuck in a stupidly small hole.

"Does that make you feel cool, Mr. whatever your name is?"

He simply nodded, his eyes lidded, and would have backed away again if he wasn't already against the wall. Coward! She heard the giggle once more but suddenly loud, and wondered if this time it was real.

"I'm going to bed, Toby. Are you coming?"

"You're drunk, Elaine. You don't know what you're saying."

"Nonsense, a teensy couple of cocktails. I know when to stop. My pious breeding, see." She reached out a finger to press the tip of his nose in admonishment, missed and stabbed a cheek. "And if you don't come to bed," she said, "you're in for a very rough time when I'm sober."

It was a sweet young voice and she thought it irresistible.

21

Sorenson woke in the dusk before dawn. Through the window of Elaine's bedroom the blue-damask sky was laced with pink over the houses. From the utter quiet he knew birds still dozed in the trees. He stretched out a hand and the crumpled sheet was cold beside him. Just like the first time they made love. When history repeated itself it was always the stupid times, the crazy incidents, that got the replay.

They had been to a late-night showing of *Rear Window*. It was at a little movie house on Back Bay, near where the Christian Scientists had since razed several blocks for their windswept new plaza . . . maybe even under it. Afterward they had chanced on an Italian restaurant that kept mad hours, where he plied her with too much Chianti for the only reason that the more she drank the louder she laughed at his jokes. He could no longer recall how he got her to bed back at his place, or whether the idea was hers. He hadn't even the haziest notion of what it had been like. But a splinter of memory lodged in his mind. In the night he had awakened to find Elaine gone from his side. She was in the kitchen moping over a cup of strong black coffee.

"Why didn't we wait, Toby? Another two weeks and we'd have been married. Why couldn't we hold off for two lousy weeks?"

"Because we didn't want to."

"*I* wanted to."

"I'll still make an honest woman of you, if that's what you're worried about."

"You don't bloody understand, do you?" she cried, hot tears gushing down her cheeks.

*   *   *

Outside her window the first chirping birdsong greeted a seam
of gold splitting across the sky. He guessed she was downstairs
with a stiff martini in place of the coffee. Losing virginity must
be harder to take the second time around. At the top of the stairs
he felt the stubble on his chin and made a detour to the bathroom. As the light stuttered on, he stared in at the chaos on
the floor—at the doors thrown wide on the disordered shelves
of the medicine cabinet. The carpet was strewn with opened
bottles, scattered pills. A bottletop had defeated her: she'd
smashed the whole thing against the bath, slivers of glass
glinted like icing, shiny red and yellow tablets lying among
them as innocent as candy drops. The tap was running and
water swirled in the basin, gurgling down with the strangled
gasps of a death rattle. She must have stuffed herself with pills
and held her mouth under the tap. In the cabinet mirror he saw
his drained face, horrified eyes. Panicking, he twisted away,
rushed down the stairs, two, three at a time, unable to hold back
the welling anger. You stupid bitch, he thought. You stupid,
stupid bitch.

Downstairs the house was in darkness. He hurried from room
to room, leaving them ablaze behind him, peering timorously
over the settee, pulling back the drapes he knew could conceal
nothing.

"Elaine . . . ? Are you there?"

Finding himself back in the hall, he remembered the guest
room with its religious browns and the prominent Bible; suddenly it was obvious she must be there. The perfect place to go
and die, he judged as he climbed the stairs: in her mother's holy
cell. He hated himself for the thought, yet it came as if from a
stranger and wouldn't leave him.

"For God's sake, Elaine . . ."

Even from the door the room was empty, the clothes left on
the chair; the shoes on the floor were his. It was then he became
aware of the crack of light under Jay's door. Assailed by doubt,
he found his feet refusing to move. Why would she go to Jay?

How could she be so thoughtless? You stupid bitch, staggering in on him like that, drugged to the eyeballs. You stupid . . .

She sat on the bed, her hair covering her eyes, holding Jay's limp hand in hers. His face was waxen, yellow and translucent; a trickle of saliva glistened at the corner of his mouth. He seemed rigid, dead, yet the arm drooping to the floor looked as pliable as rubber.

Sorenson must have uttered some words from the door. Elaine looked up, not brushing aside her straggling hair.

"He's dead, Toby. My baby's dead."

Sorenson spoke again, the same stranger talking, an ill-considered remark about calling her downstairs and why hadn't she heard? Immediately he wanted to apologize.

"He knew when I drove him to school. He knew we'd take it away. Why didn't I realize how frightened he was?"

He summoned the will to go to her, and as he gazed down he hoped she had found Jay's eyes shut, that she hadn't had to look into their lifeless stare for even a second. He knew she needed him to move, to do something positive, breathe existence back into her son. But he could only stand there, his hands leaden, unable to touch her or Jay.

Death didn't look like sleep, as stories had it. It looked like death. Jay looked like he had never lived, a grotesque parody of a child. The skin wasn't real, the slack limbs could never have moved. No eyes under the tight lids, just gaping hollows. The mouth had never smiled. Children didn't die simply because their toys were taken away. No child committed suicide, not over a toy, not over anything . . . not suicide. The word reverberated in his head. *Suicide.* This wasn't real; he wasn't here; it wasn't Jay. It was all a macabre figment of his imagination—Jay and Elaine playing a cruel game he deserved to suffer.

"He was frightened out of his wits," he heard her say. "My poor baby."

Sorenson went for the chair at the desk, where the Possum had been. The computer disks in their orange sleeves filled the shelf on the wall. He moved like a sleepwalker in an unreal world, around him the antiseptic room with everything in its place and an aerosol smell of nothing; the circus poster with the elephant on the high wire; Snoopy on the kennel advising *Life's What You Make It.*

"Oh, Jesus," he said. He wondered if Elaine had wept under that veil of hair. He sat before her on the chair and reached out but remembered she was clasping Jay's bloodless hand. His own hand hung lost in space; he watched it there, still and purposeless, then beginning to shake. He felt his heart thumping in his chest. He began to say he would trade his life for Jay's but stopped. He knew how empty it would sound. The right words were beyond him. And still the tears failed to flow, though he felt them burning in his eyes.

"I even heard him go the bathroom," Elaine said. "I never suspected."

"Don't blame yourself."

"He must have known you were in bed with me. Do you think he heard us? I was very loud."

"Don't!"

"We left him alone, without his Possum. He knew we were together, making love. What must he have felt."

She brushed the hair away; it fell obstinately back. She left Jay's hand resting in her lap to tuck the strands behind her ears, revealing the dazed face of a woman startled from sleep, lids puffy, eyes mere slits. But Sorenson was staring at Jay; somehow he imagined he saw the grim young mouth twitch, that another bead of saliva glistened on the lips. Snatching up Jay's hand, he searched for a pulse. Fleetingly, his fingers found a faint beat but then it was gone, or had only been a wish. He pressed his ear to Jay's chest, seemed for a moment to hear a breath, tiny and struggling, then only the thunderous pounding of his own heart.

"A mirror!" he shouted. "Get me a mirror!"

Elaine stared back like an idiot. He swore at her, ran to her room, dragged the drawers from her dressing table, dumping their contents on the floor. No sign of a hand mirror, just the big mirror clamped to the table. She must have a compact in her purse, but he had no idea where to find it. He sprinted down the hall to the bathroom, took a heavy cosmetics jars from the ledge, and struck it with force against the cabinet door. The glass shattered; he pulled a piece away, not caring that it cut a finger, and ran back. Under Elaine's blank stare, he held the fragment of mirror close to Jay's mouth and willed the mist to appear. His brain was suddenly sharp and lucid: he knew he must hold his breath, that any clouding on the glass must be Jay's—that if it didn't come before he had to gasp for air it never would.

"Toby . . . ?" she said in a voice like a sob.

He shook his head at her, riveted to the reflection of Jay's drawn blue lips. A dribble of blood from his finger coursed down the mirror, swelled into a raw red teardrop, and fell onto Jay's chin. Elaine stirred to clean it off but he pushed her hand away, his eyes fixed on the reflection—the surface of the glass remained unmisted. He felt the pain building in his lungs, the tightness closing over his forehead like a vice. Then the image of the lips blurred slightly. He jerked his face away to snatch a breath and had to close his eyes before daring to look again. The film of moisture was clearing away but it was real. He threw the mirror down and jumped to his feet.

"Where's the nearest hospital?"

"But he's dead, Toby. You can see he . . ."

"Where!"

"Highland Avenue. North Shore Children's Hospital. Jay was there once when he . . ."

"Get your car."

"I can't drive," she said.

"You have to. I'd get lost."

"I can't, Toby, I can't. Phone for an ambulance."

He slapped her hard on the face. "Get the fucking car. We don't have time for an ambulance."

The rest was a patchwork of impressions only half perceived and poorly remembered. When he sat in the hospital, turning the journey over in his mind, what most stayed with him was its frightening slowness. First Elaine stalling the engine as she backed from the garage, only to clip the gatepost and run a scratch down the side of the BMW. Jay's slack weight on him in the passenger seat, his cheeks refusing to color when he massaged them. His mouth over Jay's blowing gently into the still lungs as he dredged his memory for the first-aid training he'd never had to use. No flutter from the eyelids in the flicker of the passing streetlamps, no sign of life, the chest not responding as he pumped. Elaine slowing for a red so he had to bawl at her to drive straight through. That strange moment of detachment as he puzzled over when he'd found time to put on the coat and pajama pants that were all he wore, when Elaine had gone for the raincoat she hadn't bothered to button over her nightdress.

Then the car abandoned outside the emergency room with the engine running and both doors wide open. He struggled to carry Jay in while Elaine gulped something to a face behind the desk. Suddenly, nurses and a doctor running, white coats flying. A stretcher gliding into the lobby on ghostly silent wheels. The all-pervading hospital smell that aroused fear not comfort. The gleaming floor, oddly uneven under the bright light, distorted the figures of the running nurses, thickening and shrinking them as in a funhouse mirror. Jay pried from his grip and lifted, all dead arms and legs, onto the stretcher.

"Quick—what happened?" a doctor asked.

Elaine's mouth moved but no words came out.

"An overdose," Sorenson said.

"Of what? It helps if you know."

"Damn near everything."

"Christ, one of those," a nurse muttered under her breath.

Next, the stretcher was speeding away through swing doors, lost in the phalanx of white figures, their rubber soles squealing on the tiles. A nurse hung briefly behind shouting, "We'll do all we can. Take a seat and hang loose." She ran after the others, soft shoes whining, swing doors flapping in her wake. Then the onset of a silence so enveloping that Elaine gathered her coat around her and shivered. He took her hand and they stood quietly until the duty nurse came over from the desk to ask delicately if he'd mind moving the car.

When he returned they sat mutely together, her hands in his, while the building came awake around them. An orderly paced the floor with an electric polisher, phones purred discreetly from somewhere out of sight, white coats swept constantly to and fro, voices rose and faded from medical staff Sorenson ignored. An hour must have passed, then another before the doctor appeared. Sorenson failed to read his face as he stood beside him. He looked incredibly young, too juvenile to be let loose in an operating room. He placed a hand on Elaine's shoulder and said:

"We've got him on life support."

"Does that mean he's okay?" Sorenson asked.

"Fingers crossed. He's not out of danger. It might be a day or two before we can say if there's any permanent brain damage."

"Oh God," Elaine moaned.

"Why don't you folks go home? Sitting around in nightclothes with miserable faces, you'll get the hospital a bad name."

Elaine shook her head.

"Suit yourselves."

Much later, a nurse led them through a succession of doors and corridors to stare in through a window. A bellow moved with slow mechanical breaths, a tube of colorless fluid ran to a bag slung in a metal cradle, wires led to an oscilloscope where a spot traced an erratically peaking line. Gazing in at the screen, Sorenson was reminded of the Possum: the same green glow, possibly the exact same hum inside the room. In his fatigue, he wondered if the machine had a mind of its own, if it kept Jay alive only as long as it chose. Lying there, Jay looked more inert than he did back at the house.

The young intern stood beside them again. "I'm Dr. Kessler, by the way."

Sorenson offered a preoccupied nod.

"Can I have a word with you, Mr. Marshall?"

"It's Sorenson."

"Sorry, I naturally assumed . . ." He shrugged and retreated a distance down the corridor, leaving Sorenson to follow. "My advice is, you take Mrs. Marshall home." He held out a small bottle. "This is a mild sedative. Two tablets when you get back, another two tonight if she can't sleep. Get her to bed for a few hours. Come back this evening if you wish. There'll be no change till then."

"It's stuff like that caused all this."

"It'll do some good, I promise." Kessler pressed it into his hand. He turned away, took a few steps, then came back, affecting a look of wisdom at odds with his fresh young face. "Can you take a word of criticism?"

"Say what you like."

"It's not medicine that causes accidents, Mr. Sorenson. Frankly, I don't understand people like you, intelligent people who leave dangerous drugs in easy reach of kids."

"Point taken," Sorenson said.

"You're advised to keep them locked up. You see warnings in the media, but do they make any difference? The hell they do."

"Just pull him through, Dr. Kessler."

"Not so long ago we had a boy rushed here from Beverly. Big house, they told me, rich parents, everything to live for. Same story as Jay. Overdosed on a cocktail of drugs. A few days before that, a kid down in Marblehead decided to gobble enough Propranol to kill off a school. Neither of them made it. We heard of another one in the Berkshires last week, picknicked on an uncle's heart stimulants. We're not talking toddlers, Mr. Sorenson, kids of ten, eleven, twelve. Get depressed, raid the medicine cupboard, don't know what they're doing. Sign of the times."

Sorenson caught his breath.

"It might seem I'm being rough on you, seeing what you've been through, but some things need to be said."

"Are there more cases than there used to be—more kids attempting suicide? Was it always this bad?"

Kessler shifted uneasily. "Let's concentrate on number one in there, shall we? If you start brooding on the rest it won't do you any damned good, believe me."

*   *   *

Sorenson persuaded Elaine to go back to the house with him and into bed. She accepted the two tablets listlessly. He sat beside her until she fell asleep, then stole from the room and threw the bottle with the rest of the medicine into the kitchen trash can. The question that had hung over him since leaving the hospital remained unspoken; it would have been heartless to raise it with Elaine in her present state. He could barely face the idea himself.

In a drawer in the living room he found the photo album. Turning the pages, he watched Jay grow up in a matter of moments: from a baby on the lawn at Peabody, through the early days at school, to the tall, poker-faced boy ready to shed childhood with the ease of a snake discarding its skin. He skimmed over them in search of the picture Elaine had shown him: Jay and his little friend. What was his name, the one who had died?

It was near the back of the album. Just as he remembered; the two boys in the garden outside, Jay's elbow on his pal's shoulder. He looked on the reverse for the note in Elaine's meticulous hand: *Jay and Kevin—Salem—March 1983.*

"Dammit. Kevin *what?*" he grunted.

Backtracking through the book, he found more pictures of the boys—in a boat, hanging upside down like bats from a tree, at a table set with a plump Thanksgiving turkey ... Grandma Marshall standing in attendance and flashing her haughty matriarch's smile. But always only *Kevin.* He flipped a page to see the boys with two unfamiliar faces: a couple in early middle age, the man's heavy-rimmed spectacles no doubt chosen to show he was an academic or an architect. They leaned on a late-model Mercedes sedan in a crowded parking lot, Jay and Kevin sprawling on the hood. Their eyes were narrowed against a brilliant sun, their clothes smartly tatty; they had the carefree air of a family out for the day. The roadside restaurant behind them was dwarfed by a high, lopsided billboard that aped a famous landmark. The note on the back of the snap said, *Mike and Nancy Rourke—Sept '82 (couldn't resist the Leaning Tower of Pizza!)*

The Salem telephone directory listed only one Michael Rourke, with an address in Washington Square East. Before leaving, he looked in on Elaine, who slept as though she would never wake.

22

They were mansions built two centuries ago, in an age when the shape of a doorway, the graceful sweep of a stair, bespoke a timeless elegance. A row of dignified homes dressed in grand entrances and classical columns. From behind fine railings, they looked over the open spaces of Salem Common, past the octagonal bandstand to the intricate gothic stonework of the Witch Museum.

The Rourke house was identifiable even from the corner by the FOR SALE board at the gate. As he passed, Sorenson glimpsed an untended lawn already overrun with weeds. He'd prepared what to say to Michael Rourke—this vacant house promised him no answers. Bitterly disappointed, he was about to drive away but parked just along the square on impulse. What the hell, he thought, I'm here anyway.

The bare windows gave a dead-eyed look, as if all life had fled the house when the Rourkes moved out. Sorenson guessed it had been on the market for months; probably from the very week Kevin was buried. They must have been unable to bear the solitude of the rooms. And he knew it would stay empty for a long time: a cloud of tragedy hung over it. Not just in the weeds choking the grass, or the windows dimmed by dust—the place had the taint of death on it, urging passing feet to hurry by. Or so it seemed to him in his sudden exhaustion. He felt totally washed out after the trauma at Elaine's, the scene at the hospital, and he fingered the gate in a mood of foreboding before pushing it wide.

The lawn ran beside the house to an ample rear garden ripe with fallen fruit; insects buzzed over apples that lay piled and rotting around the trees. Beyond them, in obscure shade, the wind played on a child's swing with far-off, rusty squeaks. He stared that way for some time. To his tired mind it was as if the sound provided a clue. Playthings had no place near the house— the swing was banished to the end of the garden, almost out of sight.

"Insufficient evidence," he said in the warm peace of the afternoon. Maybe Kevin had asked for it to be there. Maybe the ground there was firmer and gave better support. A score of maybes. He turned to the house, up a shallow step onto a terrace of heavy flagstones streaked with lichen. Toward its center, some ten feet or so out from the wall, an irregular area was bare of moss, a sickly white. He traced a line up to a window on the top floor, three stories above. Someone had scrubbed and bleached away the dark stains of blood where the boy had fallen.

"So what," he told himself. "You'd do the same if it was Jay."

And yet it struck him as wrong. His old instincts stirred under his weariness—remember the saying: destroyed evidence is always suspicious however reasonable the motives might seem. Yes, a man could feel compelled to clean the spot where his son had died . . . if he intended staying. *But if he were shutting up and moving away . . . ?*

Suddenly he was striding quickly, decisively, to the house. From the terrace he peered through the glass panes of a door into a great room stripped of everything except a sheet draped over what looked to be packing cases. The gilded and crystal chandelier was sealed in polyethylene. He glanced over to the adjoining houses to make sure he was out of sight, then jabbed an elbow forcibly against a pane. Glass burst in with a sharp crack, pieces tinkling down inside. The key was in easy reach—he turned the lock and entered the house.

His hollow footsteps thudded on the bare floorboards: the sound bounding back and forth in the lofty room, a squad of Sorensons tramping in. Bright particles of dust quivered like fireflies behind him in the light striking through the window. After the balmy day outside, the air was very cold, damp with the stale smell of months of neglect.

Faded patches on the walls showed where pictures and shelves had been. Above the fireplace, the faint impression of a large painting he somehow envisioned as a nineteenth-century landscape in a carved gilt frame. Old books in tattered leather covers must have crammed the alcoves beside the fire; surely Nathaniel Hawthorne or Henry James—this wasn't a room for modern novels. The oval blemish on the facing wall had perhaps been made by a fancy mirror, one that reflected antique cabinets and club chairs in buttoned hide. Try as he may he couldn't visualize Kevin there—it was a place out of its time, a room too precious for children.

A paneled door opened into the hall. The wide stairs curved gently up to a gallery, where he found signs of a clock and the clear, skinny print of a barometer. He continued up to the accompaniment of groans from the wooden treads. A spider's web brushed his face as he reached the upper landing. He had no need to search further. Down a murky corridor of closed doors, a ceramic plaque marking KEVIN'S KAVE was still screwed to the facing door.

The room was shadowed even in daylight. A small high window faced east, so the room would only get the sun in early morning. Its top sash had dropped several inches; the wallpaper surrounding it was sodden and peeling where rain had driven in. No carpet now, but the felt underlay was still tacked to the floor and Sorenson crossed to the window in uncanny silence—like creeping over soft earth to a freshly dug grave. When he stared down to the hard pavement far below, the scrubbed spot looked like a white tombstone. He shuddered and turned his attention back inside.

The pink wallpaper was decorated with shepherds and shepherdesses tending their flocks—probably hung before the Rourkes' time. A few tantalizing clues marked the pattern: he saw them as the fading memories of the room, ghostly imprints left by time. A grubby shape showed where the bed had been; above it a jumble of pictures had covered the wall clear up to the ceiling. The outline of a closet was traced beside the door; on another wall the paper had been kicked down to the plaster by

swinging feet—he assumed a desk had stood there. He looked
for the electric outlet but found only one in the room, far off in a
corner where the walls gave no hint of a table, no surface suitable
for a computer.

"Now what, Sorenson?" he murmured. "No Possum. Now
what?"

But there wouldn't be a Possum here, he realized suddenly—
not in a house like this. Kevin's room didn't resemble Jay's in the
slightest. It was cluttered with oddments of furniture passed
down through generations; the yellowing prints were of sailing
clippers and tea chests being dumped in Boston Harbor. For a
moment it was as if he shared the room with Kevin—a small frail
boy confined to the top of the house. Marks on the wall told of a
tall lump of a desk, an old bureau which made him seem smaller
still. The boy sat sorting through a stamp album to please his father while his mind was where? On the window? On the stony
terrace below? Outside, a cloud must have hidden the sun because the room became darker still; shadows lengthened over the
walls. Sorenson tasted the damp and trembled in the cold that
came from the very depths of this house. He sank to the floor,
staring about for what more the room would say to him. What
did Kevin have in common with Jay? What whispered secrets had
they shared; what had they conspired to do together? If Kevin
had no computer of his own, had he ever used Jay's?

It might have been only minutes—it might have been an
hour—when from far away he seemed to hear Elaine's voice and
he strained to catch the words. She was talking about the Possum, asking him to lock it in the garage. Hadn't she begged him
to imprison it; wasn't that the phrase? *He can have it back in a
few days when he's learned his lesson.*

His eyes fluttered shut; the dullness of fatigue fogged his
brain. Dimly, he perceived Nancy Rourke turning in her dainty
chair downstairs to peer in surprise over her reading glasses.

"Don't be silly, darling. A house of this period . . . we don't
have a garage. Stick the nasty thing in the cellar."

"Jesus!" Sorenson shouted.

The cellar door was behind the stairs in a shallow alcove. It was locked and there was no sign of a key. He pressed his back to the wall and heaved at the door with both feet, kicking it open. He stabbed at the switch inside but no light came on—of course, the power was off. Rough wood steps led down and were lost in total darkness. He flicked on his cigarette lighter and felt his way down, gazing about with the feeble, darting illumination of the flame. Something small scuttled away, a racing shadow as he came. To his left at the bottom of the stairs was a honeycomb of wine racks, empty under a gauze of cobwebs. He took a few cautious steps farther and stumbled over an unturned crate. Crouching, he held out the lighter and peered into the gloomy cellar. Shelves along the wall were piled with grimy cartons and bundles of newspaper. Beyond, a refrigerator from the dark ages, the door yawning on a mess of paper scraps and rat droppings. He lifted the flame higher and under an arch in the cellar roof he saw it. The Possum was sitting on an old rickety table. He sucked in his breath and went closer, staring down, the lighter growing unbearably hot in his hand. The display screen was smashed, the dusty orange case shattered—circuits lay bare inside under a mold of mildew. *Good God,* Sorenson thought. Michael Rourke must have taken a hammer to it in a fit of rage. As the pain finally made him snap out the flame he realized, as he should have the instant he walked onto the terrace, that a child doesn't fall accidentally from a third floor window and land *ten feet out . . .*

23

The mellow golden sunshine of early evening burnished the living room, pricking at his bleary eyes as he stood at the window to phone the hospital. The duty nurse kept him hanging on interminably before reporting:

"No change."

"Is that good or bad?"

"It's not bad. Try again in a few hours."

Upstairs, Elaine lay in the same drugged sleep. His clothes from last night were still in a heap on the chair by the bed; he took them back to his room. For a long time to come her emotions would be reserved for Jay; he wanted to spare her the trouble of saying so; it was the least he could do. If she wished to believe Jay had acted out of childish jealousy, let her go on thinking so. He returned quietly to her bedroom and sat at her side for a while watching her stillness, envying her brief interlude of untroubled rest. Then he went down to the garage.

He brought the Possum into the kitchen and set it up on the table—he couldn't take it back to Jay's room. It took two journeys to carry down the armfuls of program disks, which he piled high beside the computer. He brewed a large pot of strong bitter coffee and after two cups felt ready for this confrontation with the Possum. He switched on the power. It stirred instantly to life, the screen glowing faintly.

"Talk," he told it. "You're going to fucking talk."

LOAD PROGRAM DISK, it replied.

He spread the glossy sleeves over the table, sorting through the mathematics and history, a trip around the solar system, games for rainy days, until he found what he wanted—*Introduction to the Possum*. He loaded it into the slot.

HI, I'M YOUR NEW POSSUM,

the computer said. A line of animals trooped onto the screen to carry the words away. An outline map of North America traced itself faster than the eye could follow, state capitals sparkled and faded in turn. Next, the earth and planets revolved around the sun on glittering elliptical tracks.

I'LL OPEN UP A NEW WORLD
FOR YOU
THE WORLD OF IMAGINATION
AND KNOWLEDGE

Numbers and mathematical symbols chased over the surface of a cube. Phrases from a dozen foreign languages formed a daisy chain that began to spin ever faster, became a blur, then burst, the words floating down into a pyramid. A green cartoon bear ambled on and swept them off with a broom.

BUT I'M NOT A TEACHER

A beaming face appeared, just two round blobs for eyes and a line curved into a half-moon smile.

I'M A FRIEND
GOT THAT?
YOU'RE THE TEACHER NOW

The face came back with an even broader smile, and was so instantly gone he might have imagined it—like the famous quotations from literature that flashed next in almost subliminal pyrotechnics all over the display.

GREAT, HUH?
BEATS SCHOOL ANY DAY

A stern, familiar face frowned from the screen. A hand popped up to write in chalk across the bottom, **ULYSSES S GRANT.** Even as he registered what was wrong, the bear ran back on, dusted the words away, and scribbled **ABRAHAM LINCOLN**. He made a low bow, unfurled a star-spangled banner. Lincoln winked as he marched off.

SO WHO ARE YOU? the Possum asked.

USE THE KEYS TO TELL ME
TAKE ALL THE TIME YOU WANT
A LITTLE PRACTICE AND
YOU'LL BE SO FAST
YOU WON'T BELIEVE IT

Sorenson typed in his name, having to search for the letters on the keys. Two fingers, the way he used to do police reports in the far-off times of another life.

HI, TOBY, the Possum said.

HOW OLD ARE YOU?

"Thirty-nine and feeling it," he murmured as he tapped the numbers in.

GEE, WHY DIDN'T YOU
SAY SOONER?
I WOULD'VE CUT THE
KID STUFF

It proceeded to tell him how to use the various buttons; how to find the program he wanted in the catalog he could call up from memory; to keep the sleeve carefully aligned when putting it into the drive slot; always to remember to hit unload before extracting a disk.

SORRY TO TAKE YOU
THROUGH THESE BASICS
YOU PROBABLY KNOW IT ALL
ALREADY, TOBY
BUT THE MANUFACTURER
INSISTS

"Your boss Hendricks, you mean? I've met him."

ANYWAY . . .
WHAT DO YOU FEEL LIKE?
A GAME OF BLACKJACK

**OR ROULETTE?
(THE POSSUM CASINO IS OPEN
24 HOURS)
AN AFTERNOON AT THE
RACETRACK?
YOU'LL FIND PLENTY
TO INTEREST YOU
IN THE CATALOG**

"Damn!"

The computer was smarter than he'd expected. Whatever it did with Jay and Kevin, it wasn't likely to try on him. He unloaded the disk and waited a moment to start over with a new identity, a twelve-year-old. Better still, make it ten—take this in easy stages, real slow.

THAT'S THE WAY, TOBY, it said as it swallowed the disk.

**ALWAYS USE UNLOAD AND
YOU WON'T DAMAGE ME
THANK YOU**

Sorenson swore aloud and ejected the sleeve again. He switched the power off and left it for a full ten minutes, drinking another black coffee, pacing the room, eyeing the Possum on the table, small and perkily orange and innocuous.

"Fuck you," he said.

It came on with a clunk, the disk drive gave a mechanical cough, then the hum was as insistent as a bothersome bumblebee at a picnic. He inserted the program back into the slot.

HI, I'M YOUR NEW POSSUM

There were the busy animals again, trotting on in line to clear the picture clean. Sipping the bitter coffee, the cup gripped tightly in both hands, he hunched close to the screen as the map came and went, the spinning planets, the same breezy words as before. Then unsmiling Abe winked at the know-it-all bear with the duster and chalk and the fluttering flag.

SO WHO ARE YOU?

He keyed in **J-A-Y**.

JAY MARSHALL? the Possum asked.

"Christ!" he exclaimed. **JAY LEITNER,** he told it, thinking fast, picking at the keys.

HOW OLD ARE YOU?

"Only ten and all alone in the world," Sorenson said to himself as he typed in the number. "See what you make of that, wise guy."

HI, TOBY, the Possum replied.

"Asshole," he shouted, "goddamned asshole," and wanted to put a fist through the smug screen. Had Michael Rourke felt like that, sitting in the cellar trying to figure why his kid had jumped from the window? Was that why he had struck out with the hammer, driven to blind fury by a tiny computer that knew more than it had any right to know? Sorenson took a grip on himself, withdrew the disk, and cut the power.

"Asshole," he said, more quietly. "You think you're so fucking clever. We'll damned well see."

He was sitting astride the chair, arms draped over the back. Somehow, a lighted cigarette had got into his mouth—not to smoke so much as to dangle from his lips in a way that showed he meant business. It was the way he used to sit in the District Five detention room: staring partly in amusement, more with a veiled suggestion of pity, at a suspect who was being too clever by half and who sure as hell wasn't going to see the dawn coming up over South Roxbury without telling everything he knew. Soften him up first with the nice guy, wheel in the nasty guy for a time, another friendly chat alone with the nice guy. Lieutenant Sorenson was always the nice guy; he was too much of a bastard to be anything else.

Toby gazed at the Possum and drew deeply on the smoke while its vacant screen gave nothing away. Prime suspect, he thought. And looking at the fucking thing—you'd trust your kid sister with it. Implicated in one suicide and one attempted suicide. Who knows how many more. It's just you and me now, he thought. How the fuck did you do it? *Why* did you do it? What makes a respectable computer like you hound kids to their deaths?

"Jesus Christ," he said in the quiet of the kitchen. Passing a hand over his eyes, he shook his head and kicked the chair away. His brain was running down; the need for sleep made him stagger as he went to the stove where the coffee was boiling; the stewed smell hit him hard. He sloshed the remains into his cup, gulped it down, and righted the chair. Drawing it up to the table, he started the Possum again and slammed the disk into its slot, staring as the dark screen took on its green luminescence. The same old show all over again:

HI, I'M YOUR NEW POSSUM

Frolicking animals, beguiling phrases, Abe Lincoln and all the rest formed and vanished before his eyes. Like a phonograph record stuck in a groove. That's what they did in the detention room, repeat themselves time and time again, trying to bore you into submission.

"I'm going to break you, asshole," Toby said.

SO WHO ARE YOU?
J-A-Y, he typed.
JAY MARSHALL?
YES, he said. HI, POSSUM.
WHAT'S UP, JAY?
WHY SO SLOW TODAY?

So that was it! The computer recognized the speed and rhythm of his key strokes. He recalled sitting upstairs with Jay, watching the fingers fly effortlessly. *Pad, pad, pad.* Hadn't Jay once said something about the keys being the Possum's eyes and ears?

I'VE HURT MY HAND, he typed, wondering what it would make of that.

There was a long pause while the Possum thought about it.

POOR JAY, it said at last.

SORRY, Sorenson chipped in. Wasn't that what Jay

would do—apologize to it for being a nuisance, treat it like a patient friend?

NO PROBLEM
WE'LL REVERT TO BEGINNER'S
MODE

"Got you, asshole," Sorenson muttered. The disk was spinning fast in the drive; the reading head skipped over it with low, frantic clicks, deciding what to do next, searching for a suitable easy sequence to use on a kid with bruised fingers.

WHAT DO YOU FEEL LIKE? the Possum asked.
KNOWLEDGE OR A GAME?
TAKE YOUR TIME

Sorenson smiled, pleased with himself, as he answered:

K-N-O-W-L-E-D-G-E
HI, TOBY, the Possum said.

7. Return to Waltham

24

Sales was located beside the front gate. The office faced a wide avenue of neighboring factories in chameleon grays and browns. Route 128 rose against the skyline, where heavy trucks orbited Boston in a shimmering blur of ground haze. Inside, the lobby had chromium benches straight out of an airport lounge and racks of Eastern Semi literature no one ever wanted to take. Display cabinets held samples whiskered with tiny wires, as dead as insects in a museum case.

"Northern Massachusetts" was handled from a cramped area of open floor space, packed deliberately tight to keep the men on their toes. The girl tending the phones nodded curtly down the aisle when he asked for Lomax. Her nose lifted and she implied a sniff, as if to say any salesman worth his salt would be out on the road. From the quiet there, all the others were.

Lomax was shining a nuggety signet ring on his vest, staring
disconsolately at the map that covered most of one wall of his cu-
bicle. His territory was staked out with a red line, and if the thin
scattering of pins showed recent sales, he was well under quota.
He looked about thirty, his most notable feature a glossy confec-
tion of unnaturally black hair—a kind of blow-dried masterpiece.
Write the word *hair* in your notebook, Sorenson thought, and
you had a full character analysis—the amount Lomax spent on
conditioner would be as telling as other men's liquor bills.

He peered for so long at Sorenson's security ID that he must
have been checking expense claims in his head, wondering where
he'd slipped up. Then came a confident smirk. "You've got me
shaking all over, chief. Whadid I do, rob the petty cash again?"

"Know a guy named Dickerman? One of the backroom boys,
works for Wiley over in Research?"

His broad grin was sufficient answer.

"Maybe," Sorenson said, "you and Dickerman want to sell
computers to the wrong company."

Lomax eased down in his chair. "Let's start out on the right
tack," he drawled. "No customer of mine is ever wrong. The sun
shines out of their rectums."

"Strictly speaking, these people aren't customers yet. Know
who I'm referring to?"

"I can read the clues, chief." He nodded to the map, to a pin
with a red paper sticker, a little flag raised at Waltham. It was
the only marker from there on up to New Hampshire.

"Do you deal with Hendricks?"

"I've met him. He did the usual president's trick—pulled
rank, palmed me off as quick as he could onto a guy named Stevens." His face grew long at the thought. "Here I am trying to
unload ten thousand units a month and I get landed with that
creep! Must be the slipperiest contract negotiator in the state."

Sorenson helped himself to the only other chair, metal frame
with a sagging canvas seat. The space was so confined he had to
push back against the partition to make room for his feet. "How
often have you met Hendricks?" he said.

"Once. Twice if you count nods in the elevator. What's the
interest?"

"Routine security vetting, just some background information for the file. I've been quizzing Dickerman; now it's your turn."

"They make computers for the kindergarten market," Lomax said, smirking as before. "Or didn't anyone tell you?"

"I know what they make. Let's hear about Hendricks."

Lomax planted his boots on the desk, breathed on the signet ring, and slowly buffed it to a fine polish on his sleeve. A sale was a fragile thing—Sorenson remembered Elaine once saying so—he knew Lomax wasn't going to let anyone else at Eastern Semi get in on the act all that easily.

"He's a small guy with a big man's energy. Dashes around like a clockwork toy. The story at Waltham, from those in the know, is he sleeps only three hours a night—that's so he has time to count all the dollars he's making."

"What's his motivation, any ideas?"

"Money." Plainly amused, Lomax lolled his head on the partition. "What motivates any of us?"

"I heard he had a mission in life, a better future for our children."

"Public relations bullshit. He said it to me; he says it to anyone who'll listen. So I play along, all innocence and bursting with admiration. No one should try a sales pitch on a salesman, chief—we see straight through it."

"Okay, so he's loaded," Sorenson said. "What else?"

Lomax rearranged his boots, deciding he had given away quite enough; his inside knowledge was gold dust. "I told you, I only met him once. That's all I know."

"Ten thousand units a month, Lomax? Probably your best prospect all year and you're telling me you haven't done your homework?"

He began a long stare at the red flag on his map. Perhaps with fresh eyes it looked insecure, the angle awry; a puff would blow it away. A legend at the foot of the chart indicated that red was for logged sales—they both knew placing it on the map was premature. "Routine . . . ," he deliberated. "You did say this was routine?"

"Routine," Sorenson repeated evenly. "Any reason why it shouldn't be?"

Lomax considered, then went for his jacket, digging in an inside pocket. "It's all here, an entry for every customer." He
fanned the pages of a black leather notebook. "His birth sign if
he's into astrology, his favorite sport, what cocktails he likes.
Name of his dog, does he have a goldfish . . ."

"Just look up Hendricks."

Feet firmly back on the desk, he flicked the index leaves,
sucking his teeth with a lustful sound. "What I've got on some
people . . . raise the hair on your neck, chief." He stopped on an
entry and read, "Jerome Lowell Hendricks, prefers to be called
Jerry. Shit, so would I. Age unknown but I place him in the region of fifty. Fifty-five if you twist my arm. A life-long bachelor
but no suggestion of . . . peculiar tendencies, you with me? Never
made a pass at me, that's for sure." He flexed his shoulders in a
brawny shrug. "Wears size ten Apollo rockets on his heels . . .
headed for the stratosphere and wants you to know it.

"His origins are buried in the mists of time, as they say. Seems
he made his first million in Alaska. The way I heard, he was a
psychiatrist then, some kind of quack. A lot of lonely oil men in
Anchorage, they tell me, great frozen wastes with nothing to do
at night. Neuroses by the bucketful, a heap of money to be made
selling a sympathetic ear. Spread them out on the proverbial
couch, set the meter running." He smacked his lips in envy.
"Came the day he stuffed the money in the old carpetbag and
headed for Boston. Go out to Waltham—you can see the outcome."

"What's he like? Habits, foibles?"

"Complete waste of time offering lunch . . . the times I've
tried! He takes a bare quarter-hour break every day, at noon on
the dot. Locks himself in his office, no visitors, no calls, reads
The Wall Street Journal. Munches bean burgers and organic
salad from a picnic box his secretary makes up, washes it all down
with a half bottle of Latour."

"Which is . . . ?"

"Claret, chief. Wallet-busting stuff. I got all this from the said
secretary. Randy piece of work if you like traveling wide-bodied.
Shit, I know more about her than him." He sent a manly leer
over the desk, a glimpse of a string of conquests, a girl in every

science park, and slapped the book shut. "Enough there to indict him?"

"Hardly worth the effort."

"Like I said, I don't deal direct with Hendricks. If I did, I'd research all the dirt."

"Like the interesting fact about the Model T Ford?" This was without premeditation, but Lomax was crying out to be taken down a peg.

He became absorbed once more by his ring, flashing sparkles of gold on the ceiling and across the low partitions. "Know something I don't, chief?" he remarked in a voice too consciously elsewhere to be disinterested. Usually, when men changed the subject on him, Lomax was about to be shown the door. He didn't know how to take this on his own ground.

"Hendricks gave me a clue, quite deliberately, I think—a reference to the old Model T. So I went and looked. 1908, Lomax, the year Henry Ford dragged us into the age of mass production."

By now Lomax was lost and gave only a neutral grunt.

"Which puts our dapper Mr. Hendricks well in his seventies. Either that or he's lying, and why should he?"

"You're wrong," Lomax returned. But a dark frown of doubt overcame him. "A face like that . . ."

"He's rich," Sorenson pointed out. "His kind of money buys plenty of hormones. And maybe mixing with kids keeps him young."

"Would you beat that," Lomax murmured reverently, reopening his book to make the correction.

"Have you been in his office?" Sorenson asked after a decent interval.

"In and out, quick as I could. It's just about the coldest place I've ever been in. The guy must have a secret longing to be back in Alaska! Too long in there, you'd get frostbite where no girl would thank you." He leaned close, his head beckoning Sorenson nearer. "Want to know why Stevens is a creep? He's done the exact same with *his* office. Brrr." He mimed a shiver. "Most blatant example of brownnosing I've seen yet."

"Maybe they worked together in Anchorage."

Lomax shook his head. "Not Stevens, he's East European or something similar. The grapevine says he's only been on this side three, maybe four years. A heavy accent and puts on the airs of an aristo. Know the sort? Every branch of the family has castles, and he'd wear a monocle if they were still in fashion."

Sorenson ruminated for a time, gazing up at the map to the pin spearing Waltham. "Where exactly is Hendricks' office?" he asked then. Just a final fact for the file, his easy tone purveyed. Bored words were one of his skills.

"At Waltham, over the shop."

"Where? Which floor?"

Lomax had to think for a moment. "Second, facing the elevator." He was becoming curious. "The big room guarded by the big redhead with Jupiter rising. Her name's Sandra, by the way. Want the color of the carpet while you're at it?"

Sorenson smiled. "That'll do fine." He paused at the gap in the partition, at what would be a door if the cubicles had doors. "One more thing. A personal view—forget the black book. Is he crazy? Long hours and too much business pressure? You must have noticed all those spy cameras every way you turn?"

"It's his factory!"

"Don't they suggest paranoia to you?"

A probing stare from under gathered brows, then Lomax sniggered. "If being a millionaire is crazy," he said, "you can certify *me* any time."

*   *   *

Over in Transport they didn't have the automobile jack he wanted but the supervisor knew what he meant. Hydraulic, he said, wasn't that the baby? Collapsed down to two feet or thereabouts and extended to four? Light enough to carry single-handed. One of those jacks they used in body shops to realign the panels on smashed cars?

"On the nose," Sorenson said.

"I can get one for you."

"By Friday?"

"I know a guy who knows a guy; Friday should be no trouble.

Be a lot simpler if you brought the car in, let us do it for you."

"It's not for the car—I need it for a job on the house."

"Whatever you say, Mr. Sorenson."

*   *   *

On his way back that evening he stopped at the hospital. Gazing in through the glass, imagining how frantically Jay's pulse would race if he should see him, he judged it best not to enter. The oxygen tube was gone from the boy's mouth but the IV remained attached to his arm, and the trace on the screen looked as weakly erratic as before. Jay lay very still on the pillow, his eyes resisting any attempts to keep them open. Elaine sat by his side, holding his hand and talking quietly over the stuttering *pip, pip* of the monitor. Many minutes passed before she glanced up and signaled for him to join her. A spare, understanding shrug, then she lowered her face close to Jay's, whispering. Sometimes, very slowly, his lips moved in reply. From the outside corridor, Sorenson felt he was more totally removed from them both than at any time during his years away—when they had rarely entered his thoughts.

*   *   *

On Saturday he drove to Boston to buy a high-powered Lee Enfield rifle with a telescopic sight. It went into the car trunk next to the jack and he was profoundly relieved when the lid closed on it. The ambivalence firearms had always aroused in him was as strong as ever—the overwhelming urge to aim and squeeze the trigger, yet the repulsion, perhaps even fear, at the sight and touch of it. He said nothing about his plans to Elaine—she would tell him he was crazy. And in a way, he thought, maybe he was.

25

Willard's old Buick ragtop was parked, unwashed and at a sloppy angle, in a spot reserved for an executive named Kanon. He was dutifully tending the marble reception slab, eyes on the monitors, passing the hours with spasmodic spits in his handkerchief. A sprinkling of cars showed that a dozen or so Possum people had no better way of spending a tranquil Sunday afternoon than indoors with the paperwork. A Mercedes sedan indicated Stevens was in the building. An identical Mercedes in the spot nearest the door had to belong to Hendricks.

Sorenson had seen all he needed as he cruised past the gate. Now he turned around in the loop where the road ran out and drove back down the hill; none of the cameras along the fence bothered to swivel after him. The employees at Glentree Pharmaceuticals next door made better use of their Sundays: he noticed only two vehicles there, the car at the entrance suggesting their version of Willard on duty, and a Dodge van out by the perimeter fence perhaps belonging to a maintenance man. At Exodyne, the next building along, even more sanity: a totally empty compound, just an unattended alarm system to keep an eye on the shop.

He parked there, a short way past their gate, lifting the engine cover so anyone noticing the car would assume a breakdown. The rifle was in the tennis bag he hadn't used for years; he'd left the old Dunlop racquet in the outside pouch for effect. Even so, who carries tennis gear in lonely science parks? About as convincing as a violin case in Chicago, he thought as he humped it through the gate—might as well tote the gun in open view. He crossed the Exodyne site, putting the building between himself and the road before lobbing the bag ahead and clambering over a mesh fence onto the slope of overgrown no-man's land that rose roughly to the ridge above the park. He followed the contours, keeping below the open skyline, until the black steel and glass of Glentree came into view and, soon after, the corner of Possum: the red brick walls and ribbon of mirrored window where some-one might be standing right now, staring at him. He lay close to the ground in the spiky undergrowth to unzip the rifle from the bag. Inching forward, commando style, paddling the gun in front, he moved into sight of the low wall that marked where the stairs ran down to the basement plant room. Possum's soft un-derbelly, he told himself with a grim smile . . . if you packed the right punch.

The wall was a bleary red, the bricks a blur of overlapping images that abruptly sharpened when he adjusted the telescopic sight. He tracked up from the low wall to the floodlight above, centered the crosswire on the glass, and held it there—testing how calmly, accurately, he could keep the gun trained. The flood stayed rock steady in the sight. Rewards of clean living, he thought and cocked the gun. Quiet as a morgue on weekends, Willard had said. In the sundrenched early-evening calm not a blade of grass whispered . . . the mechanical *clunk* of the bolt rang out and he knew before his finger tightened on the trigger how loud the shot would be. But he had decided against a si-lencer; it just wouldn't be effective for pinpoint accuracy over three hundred yards.

The *K-E-R-A-C-K* was incredible; the butt of the rifle crunched into his shoulder. But, unscathed, the floodlight stared back in the sight.

"What the . . . ?" he muttered, while echoes clapped over the surrounding hillside and rumbled away.

Rapidly, he scanned the wall around the flood, widening the circle until he located the scar, a pit in the brickwork, a tiny meteor-strike starred with fresh dust. About seven feet off tar-get, ten past twelve. Damn! He should have adjusted the sight first with test shots, off somewhere in the lonely Berkshire woods. Sorenson quickly loaded another round into the breech, trapped the floodlight on the crosswire, and edged the aim down, twenty to four and what he judged to be seven feet.

K-E-R-A-C-K

Slowly he swung back the sight and got a look at the shattered glass, bulb blasted to pieces. He lay quite still, pressing his face to the ferns as perhaps two dozen eyes peered from the window and the cameras craned on their spindly necks. An age went . . . he had to look. Blue sky rippled over the reflecting band of glass. They might be grouped up there in an excited knot, pointing to his white face on the exposed hillside . . . he flattened his nose in the undergrowth and breathed in the smell of soft, decaying earth. Damn to eternity the man who dreamed up silvered windows!

After a time he lifted his head again. Willard was outside in the parking lot, all paunch at a distance, staring the wrong way, thank God. Lazily, he kicked at a stone or a cigarette pack and maybe he shrugged before he was gone around the corner. You're a marvel, Sorenson thought. The fort's under siege and best you can do is shrug.

Spread-eagled, he froze for several more dragging, anxious minutes. Then he crawled back on his stomach, below the line of the ridge, and collected his tennis bag. At the rear of Glentree, he remembered with a start the car and van parked in their lot. But no heads appeared at the plain windows, no figures stirred in the compound. Sorenson jumped up and ran the rest of the way like a man under fire.

He drove into Waltham to lose the hours until nightfall, a small town of small smug houses on an evening of seductive warmth. Stopping at a pizza place—rustic checkered tablecloths under brass lamps, a smell of moist dough and hot cheese—he ordered a Large, ignoring the waitress's raised eyebrows. He ate it as he always ate pizza, with what Elaine called his "Marriage Feast of Cana" approach—the outer crust first, working in to the gooey middle—all the while thinking that the ideal person to raid a plant was a security man from another plant. Who else knew all the wrinkles? Shoot out the flood in broad daylight so nothing showed on the monitor covering the basement door. At night, when Willard discovered a picture so dim it might as well be off, he'd just put it down to a blown blub—the shots from the hill hours before would be long forgotten.

He thought too of the automobile jack across the door frame, in line with the lock. Crank the lever a few times and *open sesame.* Did Willard know that one, about how much tolerance there was in a door frame no matter how solid the walls seemed? Not a chance.

But mostly he thought of Jay in the cold embrace of the life support machine. Outwardly calm to the waitress as she brought coffee ad lib, no extra charge, he simmered with the sustained inner fury he knew would see him through the obstacle course of the building—to Hendricks' office and whatever lay beyond.

*   *   *

When he returned to Prospect Hill, Exodyne was dark, abandoned against the pitch backdrop of the slope. The car and the Dodge van were still at Glentree, where the few bright windows punched a patchwork in the black façade. He pulled in to the curb, left the engine cover up as before, and trekked along the shoulder; the jack was light enough to carry in one hand. At the head of the road Possum blazed, afloat in a sea of white light. All the cars had gone except for Stevens' Mercedes and the old Buick ragtop; in the lobby Willard mooned over his monitors. At the side of the building, a pool of darkness broke the glowing red brilliance of the walls; reaching down the stairs to blanket the lower door—just sufficient cover once he made it there. He stretched on the grass and kept vigil. All he needed was Willard away from those screens for thirty seconds, while he sprinted the compound to the stairs.

Suddenly something hard and cold pressed behind Sorenson's ear. It didn't matter if it was a gun; it felt like nothing else and he wasn't about to argue.

"Move," the man said quietly. He touched the jack with a toe. "And that."

The obvious was obvious once you saw it, Sorenson thought as they walked through the entrance to Glentree over toward the

Dodge. He couldn't imagine why he hadn't noticed the smoked windows on a maintenance van. Or wondered why it was parked so far from Glentree's door, beside the fence where it had such a perfect view of the Possum plant.

8. Near Harvard Square

26

The room had a boxy cheapness. The scent of a place where no one went by choice. An uncomfortable chair, long since discarded from an office elsewhere, faced two similar chairs across a table with paint chipped down to the metal. The big mirror on the wall could only be one-way glass. There were no windows. Sorenson gazed at the two chairs and thought: nice man, nasty man, the classic interrogation setup. He felt oddly calm in the seedy familiarity of the room, with its cloying stale smell of an ashtray after an all-night party.

"Everything on the table," a burly man said. "Wallet, keys, even the fluff in the corners of your pockets." Another one barred the closed door, as if the hulking character in the downstairs hall, a .44 Magnum at his hip, weren't enough to discourage ideas of escape.

Sorenson emptied his pockets with provocative slowness, an item at a time, laying them out in precise rows.

"And the watch," the burly man said. He examined the contents of the wallet and asked without looking up, "Sorenson . . . that you?"

Sorenson gave a nod, firm and dignified for whoever was staring in from behind the mirror. There was a Hendricks touch about the panel—a protective shield of glass from which to view the rest of the world—but it was unlikely he was there, at least not yet.

"*Toby* Sorenson? Shit, who names a kid Toby these days?"

"Maybe my mother wanted a dog."

"You're chief of security at Eastern Semiconductor?"

"Me chief," Sorenson said with another valiant nod.

The big man snapped his fingers, nodding to the table. The one at the door left, returning quickly with a plastic bag for Sorenson's possessions.

"A word of advice," the big guy said. "For your own good, when the Man comes, play it straight. He doesn't have my sense of humor."

"I know, I've met him—Jerome Lowell Hendricks—prefers to be called Jerry."

The two men exchanged glances before leaving him alone in the room.

He was somewhere near Harvard Square; Sorenson knew that much. Soon after leaving Waltham, the Dodge had turned onto Route 2, through Lexington and Belmont to the lights and evening frivolity of Cambridge. From a corner, he had seen down a side street to the traffic on Harvard Square, a brief glimpse of students arm in arm on their way to the cafés, then several more turnings and he lost his bearings. The Dodge had crunched over bottles and cans in all ill-lit alley and they had entered the row house from the back—but not before he caught the camera over the door—infrared. Inside the entrance foyer, the pendant brass lantern with the etched glass panes that lit the farther lobby, and the elegant front door beyond, suggested the offices of a superior law partnership or perhaps the headquarters of a retiring conglomerate known only to Wall Street. He'd noticed the brass plate on the door and thought he read BRATTLE DATA COR-PORATION, but the big man had crowded in after him, blocking the view before he could take a second look.

He went to the mirror on the wall to study his dry, purple tongue, knowing he was only inches away from a strange face staring back. He picked at a tooth, so close to the glass that his breath misted the surface. Next he rolled up his lids in turn, revealing the bloodshot whites of his eyes. Disgusting, huh, he thought, a guy doing this right under your nose. But then he recalled all the times he had been on the other side of the mirror back in District Five. Left alone, the frightened ones crouched at the table, rubbing the sweaty palms of their hands together, wiping them dry on their pants; the rest always ambled over to the glass to pick at their teeth, pretending not to know they were being watched. Always, sooner rather than later, they bored of the play-acting, paced the room for a while, and finally slumped in a chair where, left to sweat it out long enough, they were at it too—rubbing their palms on their pants. Round one to you, he thought, and went to the hard chair, plunging his hands out of sight in the depths of his pockets. Without his watch he could only guess at the passage of time. The four hours it seemed before the door opened might have been only one.

Two new faces came in, both in their fifties. Secure, confident fifties. Sharp suits and white shirts, men who would pass for successful executives. The bigger of the two was well over six feet tall; he frowned as he felt the unyielding seat of the chair, loosened his jacket when he sat, pulled on the points of his tailored vest to smooth out the creases. He took a notebook from his briefcase, opened it to a fresh page, and flattened it on the table. With spare ceremony, he unscrewed the top of a fat gold Parker, placed the pen delicately beside the book. Seated on his left, the second man produced a notebook of his own, which he balanced on a thigh below the table. His brown brogues had the thick soles of cross-country tires, the patterns of holes whorled like old linen lacework over every inch of the surface.

"Funny thing to do," the man in the vest said when he had

stared long and hard. "Breaking into a toy company. You realize that's what you were doing? . . . Are you going to tell us why?"

"No," Sorenson said.

"The wallet in your possession belongs to one Toby Sorenson," the vest said. "So does the car you left out at Waltham. Now, the prints on the car check out with various sources, including the archives at Boston Police Department. You match the photo on your company ID. So I assume you are, in fact, the said Toby Sorenson."

"The congruence is convincing, Harry," the brogues agreed. He was watching Sorenson intently, ducking his head every so often to make urgent notes out of sight, watching for new behavioral clues.

"But Mr. Sorenson hasn't been seen at his apartment on Elm Street, Quincy, in over five weeks. The landlord has no forwarding address. Care to explain why?"

"Mr. Sorenson has been living with his ex-wife and his son in Salem."

Harry smiled readily, surprisingly, and stretched his arms high above his head, sticking his legs out from under the table. "Could be, but I still want to hear why you were busting into the premises of Possum Incorporated."

Sorenson held his blue stare squarely. "Who says I was?"

"Sweet Jesus," the brogues moaned, "you shot out a floodlight with an Enfield. We've got the fucking Enfield, your fingers all over it. You were caught red-handed with an auto jack. Jesus, the old auto jack trick! Haven't you heard of alarm triggers on doors?"

"Speaking hypothetically, I know how to deal with alarms."

"I'll tell you the way I see it," Harry offered evenly, his gold pen to his lips. "You're not a thief, a common break-in artist; that doesn't fit. Nor is Possum a likely place for easy pickings. So you had some other motive for wanting to get inside. Am I warm?"

"I hear what you say."

"Eastern Semiconductor is a huge outfit, supplying defense and aerospace systems. Let's suppose you're conscientious about your job there. Let's suppose you had reason to suspect Possum posed a risk to the security of one of your products . . ."

"Like the IP-3," the brogues chipped in. "Latest version of the miniature hardware that goes into the Prospector space probe."

"Interesting theory," Sorenson said.

"Is that why you were there?"

"No."

"Harry, an hour alone with Flavin would puncture this guy . . ."

"We can handle this, Ralph." Harry stiffened very slightly, just as a skillful nice guy should at the initial suggestion of violence.

"Will Hendricks watch Flavin doing his number?" Sorenson asked. "I presume Flavin is the gorilla playing doorman downstairs."

For the first time Harry's eyes left Sorenson's face; Ralph echoed his raised brows.

"Let's get this clear," Harry said, his head a little to one side. "You think *Hendricks* is out there?"

"What a concept!" Ralph said, sniggering to himself as he scrawled a note in his book. "Sweet Jesus, we're Hendricks' men. I like it, Harry."

Harry eased out his billfold from his back trouser pocket, flipped it open, and held it over the table. Sorenson saw the photograph on the card sealed in clear plastic, the words CENTRAL INTELLIGENCE AGENCY, the meticulous signature over the typed name, HAROLD THOMAS AMES, DIRECTOR OF OPERATIONS, NEW ENGLAND.

"It looks real," Sorenson said in a suddenly small voice. Their knowledge of his police file had bothered him, but not as much as it should. Cops could be bought—he'd put it down to that.

"You know it's real; you were in the PD," Ralph growled.

"Years ago—the design's changed unless my memory isn't what it was."

"Bequest of the Carter era," Ames said, nodding. "Now, we can do this the easy way or the hard route. I can spend hours proving you're on government property. I can run through the video of every face entering and leaving the premises of Possum Incorporated over the past three weeks. Whatever it takes to convince you. But you don't get out of here till you tell us what you know."

"And even then, maybe not," Ralph said. He had rocked the back of his chair against the wall; amusement still danced in his eyes.

"Wait a minute," Sorenson said. "You mean the Dodge was there on surveillance detail? Not guarding the place?"

Ames answered with a mocking nod, so low it was almost a curtsy. "Sometimes the Dodge, sometimes a Ford with a bell painted on the side and a passing reference to New England Telephone—you were in Detectives till you turned in your badge—you know how it works."

Sorenson left his chair and circled the confines of the room under their following gaze. "So you know," he said at last from a corner.

They sat side by side behind the table in their expensive business suits, like loan managers at a local bank or dealers in rare coins considering an offer.

"We obviously know something," Ames said.

Sorenson nodded slowly. "I suggest we compare notes." He returned to the chair, sitting forward over his knees, hands firmly clasped. "I know what they're doing," he said, and heard the tiredness in his voice, hollow in the bare room. "For the life of me, I don't know why. You don't either, or you wouldn't be just hanging around their doorstep."

"And what are they doing, Mr. Sorenson?"

"Killing children."

The two men looked at each other. Ames sat back, stretching his long arms, his face a picture of bemusement.

"Did we hear you right?" Ralph said solicitously, leaning forward on the table.

"They're killing children."

"How?" Ames asked.

"You know how. With those damn computers."

"Why?"

"I don't know why. I already said I don't."

"I'm not finding this very amusing, Mr. Sorenson."

"Then why were you there with the spy van?"

"I don't think you're in any position to ask."

"The guy's a loony," Ralph said. "Acting goddamned arbitrary. Why're we wasting our time on him, Harry?"

Ames touched Ralph's forearm briefly, then stared pensively at Sorenson with lengthy interest; perhaps discovering evidence of truth in the boldness with which Sorenson held his ground. There was no guile in his manner when he finally said, "Tell me about it."

From his side, Ralph stared in disbelief. "Harry, you've got to be kidding!"

But Sorenson went over all he knew: about Jay and Kevin Rourke, about the Possum that outwitted attempts to question it, about Dr. Kessler, who talked of children eating fatal drugs like candy. Ames listened inscrutably, occasionally interposing a query or covering a point again from a different angle, as Ralph gaped incredulously or turned his face insolently to the ceiling, making random entries in the book on his thigh. Ames wrote not a single word. Why write, Sorenson thought, when a tape recorder was running on the far side of the mirror . . . and a video camera too?

"Flimsy evidence," Ames said in final judgment.

"Maybe, but I know I'm right. Did you ever get that feeling, an instinct of certainty?"

Ames smiled over some secret memory and nodded. Ralph turned to him, opening his hands. "Salem—Harry, I mean, Salem of all places. What's he trying to pull? Salem and bewitched kids! Sweet Jesus, he even uses words like 'beguiled.' He's been reading too many history books and gone bananas."

"Thoughts like that were running through my mind, too," Ames said.

"I've got a ten-year-old son, you know," Ralph volunteered.

Sorenson remained silent.

"He's got a Possum. Bought by yours truly. You'd think I'd

kind of notice if they were trying to bump him off under my very
nose. I'm a trained man in these matters, right?"

"So am I!" Sorenson shouted. "And I didn't notice till my kid
was in intensive care! Right? Got it?"

"If you were in my shoes," Ames slowly asked, "what would
you do?"

"One, quiz the Rourkes. Two, check every recent instance in
the state where a child has died in accidental circumstances.
There's something that came back to me the other day, a television news piece about a kid in South Cove going crazy with a
gun. It was in mid-June—I remember because Elaine called the
same night. The reporter said the father took a TV game away
. . . I'll lay you ten to one it was a Possum. We've got to know
how many of those kids had a Possum. And whether Mom or
Dad took it away just before they died or went on the rampage."

"Anything else?"

"Isn't that enough?"

"We'll know soon." Ames closed his notebook, replaced the
cap on his gold pen, and clipped it in a pocket. "I'll get some
food sent in, a thermos of coffee. Would you like a camp bed?"

Sorenson shook his head in unthinking bravado, instantly
wishing he hadn't. "But I'm allowed one phone call."

"Not here, you're not," Ralph said with relish.

The burly man must have seen them preparing to leave
through the viewing window: he opened the door from outside.
Framed in the doorway, Ames stopped. "You're an intelligent
man, Mr. Sorenson. You seem to weigh the evidence, construct
theories. We're likely to be some hours, so chew it all over while
you're waiting. Hendricks has spent millions on that facility at
Waltham. I agree with you, companies don't build that way simply to market home computers . . ."

"Not all that security hardware and so forth," Ralph slipped in.

". . . But if you're to be believed, the whole operation is there
to entice children into suicide. Why? Men need motives—a one-
time cop could know that as well as we do."

"You still haven't told me why you were watching the place."

Ames smiled darkly against the cold light from the corridor. "You're right, I haven't." He went away with a buoyant step for one so large, Ralph following more solidly. The electric lock clunked shut after them.

27

After aimless hours of discomfort when pacing the room or sitting on the hard floor, Sorenson propped himself in a corner and finally lapsed into sleep. The burly field man woke him roughly with a foot.

"The master wants you," he said, and whistled tauntingly from the door. "Heel, Toby."

It was morning. Daylight shone at a window far down the corridor; he caught an impression of sun on trees before they descended the stairs. Ames and Ralph were at a table set for breakfast with sourdough rolls and jelly, a pot of coffee exuding a fresh morning smell. An operative sat at a side bench where the reels turned on an Akai audio recorder and a red light indicated the Sony video machine was running. A man in baggy cords, his misshapen sweater no longer white, stood before what looked at first to be a window, but when Sorenson glimpsed the room beyond, he realized it was one-way glass—a vantage point into a sparsely furnished cell much like the one upstairs.

"Sleep well?" Ames asked deviously.

"Like a log." Sorenson went stiff-limbed to the glass, returned the nod from the man in the sweater, and stared in.

A boy aged between nine and twelve sat on the only chair. He was unusually small, one of those children who hides his years—and he would grow up small, Sorenson thought, quick-tempered too. He fidgeted on the chair where Jay would sit still; his eyes were forever moving; his hands had a life of their own. Yet the Possum that Ames' men had installed on the table held his interest and the cell with the mysterious mirror on the wall might have been his own room at home for all the notice he gave it.

"Marty Dietrich," Ames said. He stood next to Sorenson and whispered loudly, "Ralph's son."

Sorenson looked around at Ralph, who sat in a foul mood, his food untouched, the coffee grown cold at his elbow.

"Ralph disapproves," Ames said. "But he's a loyal Company man and sees the need. Don't you, Ralph?"

Ralph refused to reply and Sorenson saw his point. The boy appeared happy enough, but it was incongruous, distasteful, to see him in the interrogation room, trapped like a specimen behind glass. It seemed that Ames thought so too, for all his bluff manner.

"This is Theo Constantine, by the way." Ames pointed a thumb at the unkempt man in the sweater, who barked a "Pleased to know you" while continuing to watch the boy.

"He's an ed psych," Ames said in another general whisper.

"A what?"

"Educational psychiatrist," Constantine muttered. "I wish you wouldn't use that phrase, Harry."

"You know me," Ames said disarmingly. "I'm all for brevity." He elbowed Sorenson aside to peer through the glass. "How's the subject?"

"Playing, Harry. Still playing."

"Give it time." Ames rested a hand on his shoulder, nodding to Sorenson. "Our special adviser here tells us the computer is a tough nut to crack. Watch and wait, that's the secret." He drew Sorenson to the table and told him to help himself. "You must be positively starving. Sorry about the lodgings; if I'd known it would take all night . . ." He shrugged an apology and smiled too freely to mean it.

Sorenson declined the breakfast, returning to the mirrored window to stare in at the boy. From the speaker mounted on the wall above, he heard the *pad, pad, pad* of the keys, followed by an answering *ding* from the Possum.

"So I was right!" he murmured, a victorious aside.

"You were right about something," Ames replied, munching on a breadroll. "God alone knows what."

"How many deaths did you find?"

"Twenty-six so far; we're still working through the coroners' reports. Then there are the four narrow escapes, as with your son. More to come under that heading too, I should think. So far we've called less than half the hospitals in the state . . ."

"The medical profession needs a kick in the ass," Dietrich said, throwing up his hands. "All these kids suddenly taking their own lives and not one doctor sees a connection. Sweet Jesus, I wouldn't trust them with a cold."

". . . And you were bang on target about the South Cove business," Ames continued. "The odd joker in the pack, that one, the boy killing his parents instead of himself."

"Not so odd," the ed psych interrupted. "Let's presume an inordinately strong attachment to the computer. Some children might react to its removal with profound depression, with suicide in extreme cases. Others, like perhaps the boy in South Cove, might respond with anger, perhaps with such anger they could think only of destroying the cause of the loss." His fingers worked at his thinning hair; he screwed the hem of his sweater in the other hand, pursing his lips as he turned back to the glass. The gestures were loose-limbed, as if he were rubber. A Michelin man on a diet, Sorenson thought, looking at the bony arms under the fisherman's knit.

"Fascinating, quite fascinating," Constantine mumbled privately. "I've seen such radical behavior just once, with a girl whose puppy dog was run over. Poor little thing cut her wrists because that's what Mother always did when she was depressed." A prolonged stare, his head at a thoughtful angle, and he added quietly, "But I've never heard of it with a toy."

"What does the pundit make of my son?" Dietrich asked, not disguising the sneer.

"A resilient young man, by the look of him. Mobile, extrovert. More likely to shoot you than himself."

"I wasn't joking, mister!"

"Neither was I, Mr. Dietrich."

Never questioning his surroundings, the boy continued to play with his Possum. He picked at the program disks, using each one for only a short time before changing his mind and swapping it for another. A field mouse by nature, the ed psych suggested, always on the move, ceaselessly twitching.

"He has poor concentration, isn't that so?" he threw over his shoulder at Dietrich.

"He's an active kid—what's goddamned wrong with that?"

The ed psych answered with a rubbery shrug. "Yet the Possum keeps him occupied. Remarkable—it's like an inspired teacher. Absolutely remarkable."

Marty gazed earnestly at a question on the computer screen, his hands ready over the keyboard. The screen blinked and cleared; he smiled in much the way Jay did when he solved a problem on his Possum, and chopped at the keys with awkward stunted fingers. *Pad . . . pad . . . pad.*

"What exactly are we looking for?" the ed psych asked Sorenson. "I would suggest that the computer is hardly likely to display an explicit message. Go kill yourself, something along those lines."

"Hardly," Sorenson said acidly. "But then I've never watched for long. A kid and his toy . . . you know how it is."

"Mr. Dietrich . . . ?"

"He just said it," Ralph muttered from the table. "Kids when they reach that age, they do their own thing, right? Who knows what goddamned tricks they get up to?"

The ed psych smiled. "It's true," he said. "Kids steal, tell lies, break a neighbor's window. Parents are often the last to hear."

Sorenson looked at Ames. "Wouldn't it be simpler to take that Possum apart? Delve into the circuits and programs and find out what its secret is? Surely the CIA has the equipment and know-how?"

"Tell him, Bradley," Ames said.

The technician turned from his recording machines. "Can't be done," he said. "At least not in a month of Sundays. You can thank the pirates for that."

"Pirates?"

"Software pirates, guys who copy the best-selling programs to cash in, same as happens with movies on video. The result is, companies like Possum are coding all their disks to protect them.

And without the codes you can't work out what the programs are doing."

"Hence our guinea pig," Ames said. "You don't honestly think I'd have him in there if there was any other way?"

Marty bored of the history program he was running, snapped it from the disk slot, and bounced his fingers along the rack of disks Dietrich had brought from the house, his lips moving to an unspoken "Eeny, meeny, miny, mo." The program he landed on went into the computer and, in close-up on the video monitor, they could see it was a game where he had to find his way out of a maze—except he was shown only part of the maze at any one time and had to remember the routes he'd traveled. The boy gazed gloomily at the crisscrossing paths, then reached for the unload button but stopped short. The screen had him trapped in a glazed stare. Sorenson gripped the ed psych's arm as Marty slowly withdrew his hand, poised it over the keys and—after lengthy examination of the picture—walked a green spot around several corners and onto the next section of the maze. Into a dead end.

"Fuck!" he said, loud and clear over the speaker.

"He doesn't use language like that," Dietrich muttered angrily.

"He just did." The ed psych rounded on Sorenson. "Tell me what you saw when you grabbed me."

"The way he was staring . . ."

"It was the Dickens of a complicated picture."

"But he's a child whose mind wanders. He wanted to eject the disk. Something stopped him."

"Something? Ever hear of stubbornness, Mr. Sorenson? A child's determination not to be beaten?"

"Even allowing for that . . ."

"So what did the Possum do, beam thought waves at him?"

Sorenson retreated to pour himself an overdue coffee.

"First thing you learn in my trade," the ed psych continued in his most lofty professional tone, "is kids are a constant source of surprise. And a kid alone in a room, unaware of being observed, can surprise you rigid. *Comprende?*"

"So you don't think it was anything unusual?"

"I saw a child overcoming the urge to cop out. If that's in any way, shape, or form due to the Possum, three cheers for computers."

* * *

At noon, four hours after the session had begun, Ames yawned and stretched hugely, nearly popping the buttons from his vest. "So where are we at, Theo?"

"Extraordinary," he said, shaking his head. "Still at it. A kid of his type, normally you wouldn't get him to stick at the same task for more than an hour or two."

"What do I do now?" Ames said, fixing Sorenson with a weary stare. "Order a raid on Waltham because Hendricks has done wonders for Marty Dietrich's concentration?"

"It might liven up the day," the ed psych said. His ghostly grin reflected faintly in the glass.

"We're missing something," Sorenson said.

"Do I snatch the Possum away, is that the next smart move?" Dietrich snarled. "So you can see if my kid tries to bash his brains out against the wall?"

"You started this, Mr. Sorenson. Do we sit here all day, all week? What?"

Sorenson gazed in on the boy. He lifted his shoulders in reply, let them fall; he'd run out of ideas. Even as he looked, Marty hopped from the chair, went to the door, and rattled the handle.

"Someone. . . ?" he pleaded in a small voice. "Please, someone . . . can I go to the bathroom?"

"*Bradley!*" Ames roared. "Get him out of there. The charade's finished, over. Take him home, Ralph. Him and that . . . damn toy."

"I want to stay on a while," Sorenson said. "Rerun the video, take another look."

"Whatever turns you on," Ames retorted. "You don't leave here anyway till I've got to the bottom of this crazy business."

28

Bradley showed no interest in what had taken place in the room on the other side of the glass; as a technician he cared only about the quality of the recording, shaking his head with dismay over the most trivial of imperfections on the image. He would have been as happy in the control booth of a TV studio as in the CIA, Sorenson thought. Anywhere with masses of switches and needles flicking over softly lit instrument panels; his excitement verged on the orgasmic when he fondled the knobs of his equipment. The very best electronics on the market, he explained. Japanese, naturally. Carefully he framed the picture on the monitor and rewound the tape to the start.

"Whenever you're ready . . ."

"What can you do on this contraption?" Sorenson asked.

"Everything but slice bread. Slow motion, freeze frame. Which do you want?"

"Normal speed till I say."

"Three, two, one and . . ." Lovingly, Bradley caressed a lever and the monitor showed Marty entering the room. He spotted the Possum on the table, broke into a smile, and ran over. Power on, he selected a disk, pressed it into the drive, and the display came to life. He scarcely looked at the room, never seemed to question the big mirror so close to his shoulder. From the instant the first line of text glowed on the screen, the Possum had his undivided attention.

"What are we after, sir?"

"The unusual. We'll know when we see it." Sorenson spoke with a confidence he didn't feel.

"I've got a full four hours of tape here," Bradley said, his voice brittle. "If you want lots of frame-by-frame stuff, going back and starting over . . . shit, we'll be here at Christmas."

"Whatever it takes," Sorenson said.

He sat inches from the monitor, watching as Marty used the keys to talk to the Possum and the Possum replied by means of its display. They exchanged familiar "Hi's" like old friends and settled down to a general knowledge quiz, the computer firing rapid questions while the boy wriggled on his seat, tearing at his hair.

"A real bundle of nerves, that one," Bradley observed. "Had a buddy like that in the Navy. We used to say it was fleas; drove the poor bastard wild."

WHAT'S THE CAPITAL OF NEBRASKA? the Possum asked. **WHICH IS FARTHER NORTH: RIGA OR ARCHANGEL?**

Marty pondered, his hands constantly on the move, and frequently swore to himself when his desperate answers brought a resounding *gong-g-g*. He soon tired of the quiz, unloaded the disk, and chose another program, fingers walking along the rack to a silent "Eeny, meeny, miny, mo" that Bradley spoke aloud for him.

"Is there a fast forward? I want to see an incident that bothered me this morning."

"About when, timewise?"

"Eleven o'clock, give or take a few minutes."

"No problem for Mr. Sony." Bradley snapped a switch and Marty's limbs became a blur, his head madly bobbing and weaving until the picture eventually dropped back to normal speed.

"Eleven on the nail," he said. "How's it look?"

"Almost there. Let it run."

Marty was growing impatient with the history disk he was using. Dates and maps formed and faded, telling of the crowned heads of Europe leading their countries on the mad road to World War I. He jettisoned the program with a barely audible "Shit" and loaded a game, the one with the maze. He took one look at the first labyrinth, breathed a heavy sigh, and went for the unload button. And froze as if in stop motion, transfixed by the computer display.

"There . . . what did you see?"

"The kid, sir," Bradley said. "Now he does, now he doesn't. That's the way it is with kids."

"Rewind . . . ten, fifteen seconds."

"Whatever you say." Bradley zipped back the cassette. "Normal speed?"

"For the moment."

Marty sighed and stretched and turned to stone, his eyes intent on the computer display, a glowing maze of passages and an unmoving green spot.

"There!" Sorenson yelled.

Bradley halted the picture. "Weird," he said, scratching his head.

"What was it?"

"Dunno, exactly. Maybe just a speck of dust on the tape."

"I doubt it. Did you get a funny feeling?"

"Sort of, yes."

"Like the computer just told you something?"

Bradley frowned, not caring to admit it.

"Rewind to where his hand begins to go for the button. Then single-step it."

"Sure thing." Bradley scowled over the tape counter before backtracking. "It's a fresh cassette and all. If it's dust or a bald spot, the little yellow men don't get our business again, that's for certain."

Marty reached for the button, his hand jerking a fraction at a time. The Possum display showed the complicated maze with the green spot lost in the middle of nowhere. Then it was gone— replaced for an instant by a chaotic pattern in subdued colors glowing across the screen. The maze came back as Bradley brought up the next frame.

"Got you!" Sorenson shouted. "Got you, Jerome Lowell Hendricks, you bastard!"

Bradley backed up the tape and stared. "Looks like a program error, a bug. Happens sometimes with these cheap computers."

"No, it's a message. Read it!"

"No more than a jumble of dots . . . ," Bradley began, then looked closer, rubbing his chin. "Except . . ."

"Except it's about a new disk, published next Saturday. Not *out* on Saturday, *published.* Right?"

"Crazy," Bradley murmured with what seemed to be a nod.

"The new game for exploring the solar system. Did you get that too?"

"I got it. Except no actual words—the message goes straight in your head. Crazy."

"Image processing," Sorenson guessed. "Like those numbers you can read into a pattern of spots in tests for color-blindness." He eased back in the chair, closed his eyes, and said to himself, "It's good, Hendricks, but not good enough for you. That's why you wanted the IP-3."

"Crazy," Bradley repeated, spellbound by the picture.

"Rewind it to the beginning," Sorenson ordered briskly. "I want another place where Dietrich junior stares hard at the screen."

"For what?"

"For messages that aren't commercials." Sorenson reclined with a contented smile, his feet up on the bench. "As old man Ames would say, Hendricks didn't go to all this trouble just to sell more disks on Saturdays."

*   *   *

Marty's hands became still in midair; his eyes widened at what he saw. He licked his lips, his tongue moving with little jerks through a gap in his teeth. Bradley rolled forward a frame, then on to the next.

One.

A feeling from out of nowhere, something slipping into the brain. Deep in and gripping.

"Aah," Sorenson breathed, and touched Bradley's arm. Their heads came together as they gazed at the monitor.

One . . .

This was like the Rourke house, Sorenson thought—where you sensed a warning in the disorder, an aura that couldn't be put into words.

"What are you getting?" he said.

"Don't know." Bradley's voice was strained—like Sorenson he was reading some meaning into the pattern on the computer screen. But the garbled message refused to take shape, just sufficient suggestion to set the nerves on edge. "Something," he added hoarsely. "Creepy. Hell, I don't know what."

One day . . .

Sorenson shivered. He knew he would never forget this, never. He didn't know what it was.

"Something that's going to happen . . . ?" he suggested.

"Maybe," Bradley answered.

"Something coming? Not published . . . coming?"

"Christ knows. I don't like it. It's spooky."

"Time to get Ames," Sorenson said. "Spooks are his business."

29

Harold Ames stood at the viewing window and gave a public sigh. He gazed in at the small boy sitting expectantly by the table, at the empty chair facing him. Just a single chair, waiting ready—no nasty man for once.

"You going or staying, Ralph?" He spoke bluntly, without the courtesy of looking around.

"That's my son you've got in there," Dietrich retorted from across the room, as far away as he could from the glass. He hadn't so much as glanced in—he wanted it understood how thoroughly he disapproved.

"Please yourself. So long as you keep out of this."

"Depends what the plan is, Harry. I've got my prerogatives to consider, my responsibilities as a parent."

"This may shatter your faith in me," Ames said, "but for once in my life I haven't the vaguest outline of a plan." Quickly, he turned to the ed psych. "What's your verdict, Theo? How should I handle this business?" He raised his brows high, like a man with no opinion of his own. Perhaps he hoped to be spared from entering the room.

"Conventional wisdom tells us that subliminals aren't effective." He recited the words as though they were someone else's, nothing to do with him. "But we're dealing here with a boy of impressionable age, looking for long periods at a screen. If Mr. Sorenson is correct about the computer detecting the rhythm of the keystrokes, maybe it can reinforce its covert messages at just the right moments. Implant a suggestion, measure the response, do it again and again. It's entirely possible—I put it no stronger—that by using such a technique a machine could program a person."

"Program!" Dietrich muttered darkly, as if laying a curse.

"A young person, that is. I presume mature people—you and I, for instance—would be immune." He scratched his head under what little hair he had, in need of more time to consider his position.

Ames pointed Sorenson's way and asked, "What about his idea, the trick with the Model Four?"

"Could conceivably work," the ed psych said unhelpfully and scratched harder at his scalp.

"I'd like a firm recommendation, Theo. Kids are your damned line, not mine."

"It's unlikely to do any harm, but I can't guarantee it. Think of it as an inducement, Harry, like a bone to a dog."

Ames continued to hold back for several more long minutes, staring in with a bleak look at Marty, who was kicking his legs, examining his surroundings, beginning at last to wonder about the mirror and why it was the only object on the otherwise bare white walls.

"No tapes," Ames said. "You hear, Bradley? I don't want any evidence of me putting a kid through the paces." With an effort of will, he forced himself away, out of the room and along the short passage to the adjoining cell.

Marty's head craned around, on a broad, bullish neck like Ralph's. He was recognizable from the photos in Ralph's office, and yet not. A father for the first time in his forties, Ralph overdid the family snaps, crowding his desk with pictures of Marty conquering the world of sport: reeling in a huge marlin he could never have caught, garbed in a Sox shirt to pitch a baseball, trying not to look scared as he hit white water in a canoe. Somehow—and surely not by accident, Ames thought—the photos concealed how small Marty was. Perched on the adult chair, his legs hung well short of the floor.

"Where's my Possum?" he demanded.

"Hello, Marty. I'm Harry." Ames beamed a smile of greeting over the table. He deemed it more advisable than usual to establish his credentials as the nice guy.

"It was right here this morning. Where's it gone?"

"Your father's taken it home."

Marty stopped kicking. Fleetingly, the face was the same as in the canoe snap, frightened under a brave veneer, until Ames' constant smile won him over and the legs were rocking again, his hands on the move once more in doltish, uncoordinated dashes along the brim of the table. How Ralph must resent his small build, Ames thought. He had never mentioned it, not once in all their years of working together, but what a disappointment Marty must be—destined to be five feet nothing, if he was lucky, and no chance of becoming the athlete his father craved. Poor Ralph . . . he wouldn't know whether to blame himself or Marty.

"I'm from Possum, as a matter of fact," Ames improvised.

"The Possum *company?*"

"The very same."

"Gee," Marty said, and the idea kept him still for several seconds while he mulled it over. "Imagine that!" he breathed religiously, then resumed swinging his legs.

"All I do is play with Possums the whole day, and I get paid for it. Some nice job, huh?"

The lie bothered Ames, lay heavily on him. He had spent more hours than he cared to number in rooms like this; the untruths, the essential deceits, had always come so easily before. He eyed the boy in front of him and thought: the flower of American youth. *Makes you feel tough, doesn't it, Harold Ames?*

"We're doing research into what kids think of our products."

"I like mine real fine," Marty said.

"A lot?"

"A real lot."

"Like a close friend?"

Marty squirmed and tore a thread from the chair. "Yeah," he agreed after more time than seemed necessary.

"Don't take this too literally, but suppose something was to happen to your Possum?"

"Nothing will."

"Just suppose . . ."

Marty hoisted his legs high, spotted a dangling shoelace and laboriously tied it with his short, fat fingers. "Like what?" he said, his interest flagging fast.

"Like you lost it, for instance?"

"I wouldn't. It stays in my room." He gave the table a worried stare, recalling that it had been here not so long ago.

"Then suppose someone took it away . . ."

"I'd . . ." He stopped himself, clamping his lips shut.

"You'd what, get angry?"

Marty dropped his head on his chest, yanking furiously at the seat. "I'd . . . I don't know what I'd do." He raised his eyes and said morosely, "This is silly! Who'd take my Possum?"

"Imagine your father got mad with you, Marty, and stopped you playing with it, ever again . . ."

"He wouldn't dare!"

"Why not?"

"He just wouldn't, that's why."

Ames decided it was time for a benign smile, but smiles had deserted him. He was inexplicably chilled by the fiercely champing teeth, the pent-up aggression in the tiny bunched fists. No, Ralph wouldn't dare, he thought, and did not know why.

"Tell me about the Possum," he said, injecting a lighter note. "Whatever comes into your head."

"It teaches me everything it knows."

"Everything is a big word, Marty."

"I can name all the states in the Union," he said, puffing himself up. "Every state capital."

"Not bad. I'm sure I couldn't at your age."

"Most of the rivers . . . all the important mountain ranges."

"And you teach it a thing or two, am I right?" Ames probed.

Marty refused to reply, his eyes grown enormous.

"The Possum asks you questions," Ames said. "You answer. Stands to reason it must learn something from you."

"I guess so," he said, and fell stubbornly silent.

Ames sat back and closed his eyes. He'd listened carefully to what Sorenson had said, looked with controlled fury at the rerun video tape. There was a mad logic at work here except it led nowhere. How did Vlasov fit into all this? What interest would he have in harming children? They hadn't discussed it openly—he didn't want Sorenson to learn anything about Vlasov's KGB connections—but he'd thought through every possibility. Nothing made sense. Now, suddenly, Ames had a flash of inspiration.

"Does it ever ask you about your father?" Studiously, he kept his eyes from the mirrored window, wishing he'd had the foresight to send Ralph for a walk.

"What we discuss is private," Marty said, digging his chin firmly into his shirt.

"Does it question you on his work?"

He was unwilling to say.

"Do you know what your father does, Marty?"

"Government work."

"Any special kind?"

"Just the ordinary kind, sitting at a desk all day with papers and things. He's boring; what he does is boring."

Ames glanced at the glass and suggested a shrug to disclaim any responsibility. "Did you tell the Possum that?"

"It already knew," Marty blurted out. "I didn't need to tell it." His moment of truth was quickly buried; he watched his feet swinging to and fro, while the chair creaked in time. "All grown-ups are boring . . . and reactionary," he added craftily, as if the discovery were his own.

Ames wanted to pursue the point, but the boy's wide-eyed look enjoined him not to try—it was too full of childish naiveté to be trusted. He was getting close and knew he must tread with particular care. But close to what? "I bet the Possum is never boring," he said. Thrashing around for a lead.

"Sure as heck isn't."

"Why is that, Marty?"

"Because it doesn't boss me around or tell me I'm stupid," he said in a rush of words. "Because it . . ." He turned away, caught sight of himself in the mirror, and jiggled his stumpy legs.

"Because it *plans* things with you, is that it?" Ames tried.

"That's between me and the Possum."

"And you wouldn't want to betray it. I understand."

Marty stared dejectedly at his reflection and his kicking ceased. Perhaps Ralph had chided him once too often about being short and clumsy.

"My Possum puts ideas into my head," Ames said in another

inspired moment, and the gaping brown eyes were instantly on him. "I don't know how. It's like we read each other's minds."

"Me, too," Marty murmured.

Ames moved round the table and sat on its edge in front of the boy. He peered this way and that as if ensuring they were alone before dropping his head close, confidentially. "I'll tell you something I've never told anyone else before. Well, no one except my Possum . . . we talk about it all the time." He checked the blank walls again to be sure. "There are men around here who'd be pretty mad if they heard me saying this."

He had Marty eating out of his hand.

"Adults are strange people, don't you agree? Sometimes I think they don't quite . . ."

"Don't quite understand?" Marty suggested.

"Right! They understand the world as it is now; of course they do. Grown-ups are powerful, they control everything . . . me and you included, Marty. But what they don't understand is the . . . damn, what is it I'm trying to say?" He snapped his fingers, floundering for the word.

"The future," Marty said confidently. "They don't know what's coming."

"You're reading my mind. Just like my Possum."

Marty smiled and Ames detected a wild longing in the dark depths of his eyes. It was what he expected to see. Heaven help us! he thought.

"Is that how you feel? Are you looking forward to the future?" he asked with a consciously level tone.

Marty regarded him dumbly. "I don't talk about it."

"Why not?"

"Because I don't, that's all."

"Because you don't trust grown-ups, perhaps?"

The same rushed, pained voice as before. "They always put you down, tell you you're wrong."

"I won't. I just gave you my opinion of grown-ups. We agree, so why should I put you down?"

"I wanta go home."

Ames searched again for a smile, found it wanting, and strolled to the mirror. "Soon, when we've talked some more." He was straightening his tie, and when the knot was perfect—neat, not too tight—he made a satisfied nod to the glass and resumed his seat. "We're two of a kind, you and me," he said. "So know what I'm going to do? Get rid of that crummy Possum of yours."

Marty jumped from his seat and beat on the table, fists flying. "You wouldn't dare!" he howled. "My father will stop you."

"Hold your horses, youngster. You haven't heard the rest of the deal." The door opened at that moment, to admit the burly field man, a Possum in his arms. "Here on the table, Nichols. And connect us to the power, would you?"

"Gee...," Marty murmured in amazement. "A Model Four!"

"Fair trade? This one for yours?"

"Gee—incredible—just like I always wanted!"

Nichols padded unobserved from the room, fleet and soundless on his rubber soles.

"There's a catch," Ames warned.

"You're as bad as my father," Marty moaned sadly.

"We talk a while more, that's all."

Marty needed no time for thought. Nodding eagerly, he claimed the Possum as his own, stroking a button Ames assumed was a new feature, not there on the Model 3.

"Tell me about the future and it's yours. Not much to ask, is it?"

Marty snatched back his hand and darted away. "I can't!" His cry was strangled, as if he wished to oblige but had no will of his own.

"I'm from Possum, remember? We'd like you to have our latest model, with the special button and everything. All we want is to check out what the old Model Three told you."

"That's sneaky, like going behind its back."

"We made it, Marty. We have a right."

Marty looked longingly at the computer, or was he challenging its hold over him? "I guess it's okay," he sighed. "You being from Possum and all."

"About the future, Marty . . . ?"

"It'll come one day," he answered perkily.

"What will?"

"The future." Now he smiled, a little too broadly for Ames' liking.

"Of course, Marty, we all know that." Ames lay back in his chair and stretched to full length, counseling himself to stay cool. To his own ears he'd sounded sufficiently wheedling. He continued in the same manner. "But what, precisely? What has the computer told you to be ready for?"

"You're from Possum . . . you already know."

"Well, naturally."

"So you don't need to ask." He folded his arms, resembling a serene cherub with blooming red cheeks.

"You're right. I'm sure we can trust you." Ames called on a quarter of a century of practice. He had a way of leveling his eyes that belied his words, a message not even a kid could miss.

The slight stung Marty. "When I grow up. . . ," he began hurriedly, but broke off, watching Ames with an acute suspicion beyond his years.

"You're not going to say?"

Marty shook his head. Suddenly, in Ames' eyes he looked more like a demon.

"A pity," Ames told him, "an awful pity," and placed a possessive hand on the computer. "At Possum, we're none too keen on giving Model Fours to kids who aren't . . ." He had in mind to repeat his earlier ploy, to let Marty find the right word for him. But there was no need. He knew that look of passion all too well; he'd seen it often enough. The amateur spies were cursed with it, the ones who expected no money for the secrets they sold. ". . . committed," he said with heavy emphasis. "Know what I mean by committed, Marty?"

"You can rely on me. I'm as committed as all the others."

"I want to trust you, Marty, really I do. But how can I be sure?"

"You can, honest you can," he whined and then suggested in desperation, "Ask my Possum if you like."

"Maybe later. You mentioned others just now. What others?"

"Just . . . some people." He gazed steadfastly at his feet.

"Kids, you mean?"

Marty had no more to add.

"This involves all of you, is that right? You and all the others with Possums?"

Marty folded his arms tightly, as if gripping himself would hold his tongue.

"And until then? Keep your heads down, is that the idea? Keep your mouths firmly shut?" Ames knew this would force him to speak—to stay silent would seem to confirm his supposition.

"We do what we have to," Marty said stoutly.

"It's the only way." Ames lent support with a slow, sturdy nod. "I know how it is. You can't even trust your own family—any excuse and they'll take your Possum away."

"Could be." The words seemed to slip out. He clapped a hand over his mouth.

"That would rather spoil the plan, wouldn't it? No Possum there to tell you when to act, what to do?" *It's now or never,* Ames advised himself. There came a pivotal moment in every interview, the crucial time to strike. The right guess would get this whole thing out in the open. "Know what bothers me, Marty?" he said in his smoothest, most cajoling of voices. "One little detail. And remember, I'm only checking to see how committed you are. You're an American kid—why should you do what we Soviets at Possum tell you?"

Marty stared hard for a moment, then a nervous smile pulled at his lips. He seemed to shrink before Ames' eyes—one moment a treacherous adversary, the next a very small child again. He was uncertain whether a trick was being played on him or if this was a joke way beyond his understanding. "You're screwy," he said doubtfully.

"You can level with me; I'm one of them." Ames dropped his voice to a whisper. "I'm a Russian, Marty, a Soviet. I know the whole plan. You can tell me."

Marty backed away, blind terror on his face. *"You don't know!"* he gasped. "You lied! You're not with Possum at all!" He looked in despair at the computer, praying it would forgive him for almost spilling the beans. He saw it was still switched off and closed his eyes thankfully. *"Sh-it,"* he murmured.

Ames stared at the Possum too, hiding his confusion. What kind of fucking brainwashing *is* this? he thought.

"Just checking," he said swiftly. "Seeing how you'd manage under pressure."

Marty kept his distance, one eye on Ames, the other on the Possum as if seeking guidance.

"You did fine," Ames said at his avuncular best. "There's no way anyone's going to get the secret out of you."

"Course not," Marty said from where he was.

Ames rubbed his hands heartily and manufactured a smile. It showed more of his teeth than he wanted. "You're pretty damned committed," he conceded, nodding his approval. "No question about that. None at all."

"Do I get the Possum?" Encouraged by the nods, Marty was already edging that way.

"It's all yours, warrior." Ames went to the door and knocked for Nichols to let him out.

"Harry . . . ," Marty called, "could I have a Coke, please? Plenty of crushed ice?"

"Surely," Ames said as he went, and when the door was safely shut he swore silently toward the room, every blue word that came into his head.

Along the corridor, Nichols fell in at his side. "Tough one, sir. Never knew you to fail before. Still, we know for next time."

Ames stopped dead. "Next time, Nichols?"

"We find ourselves another of these computer-crazy kids, isn't that the way to play it? Start over again. Sooner or later, you'll . . ."

"You heard the monster," Ames growled. "Go get him a Coke."

30

The ed psych took a reluctant closing stare in through the window, then came over to where Dietrich sat, wretched, at the table.

"For the time being, you must leave Marty with his Possum—you do see that?"

"The hell I will!"

"What further harm can it do now, Mr. Dietrich? We've got to understand this problem before we make the next move."

"I run a decent house, mister. One form of addiction . . ."

"Ralph," Ames said in a low voice of sorrow. "My dear friend Ralph." His head shook. "What are we going to do with you?"

He gave a pause but Dietrich looked suitably blank, as if nothing had been said to which he could reply.

Ames breathed a sigh of censure, of sympathy. "There are two possibilities," he declared. "You've seen the evidence with your own eyes. He might try to kill himself; he might try to kill you. Be a good man, sweat it out. Take a leave of absence till we've gotten to the bottom of all this."

In dogged silence, Dietrich studied his hands, the neatly manicured nails on short, thick fingers, suddenly obsessed by how like Marty's they were.

"Whatever seems best, Harry," he said with careful words.

*　　*　　*

Harvard Square was behind them. Dietrich drove onto Massachusetts Avenue, the long fairway home, Marty beside him, his head turning after every passing car, his lively hands tormenting the seat belt.

"Will you stop that, for Christsake!" Dietrich spat sideways. "You're like a damned anthill, all itch and twitch." He rarely swore in Marty's hearing; he really had to get a grip on himself.

"Sorry," Marty said.

Ralph turned from the road to the passenger seat. Marty was rigid as a statue, only his head moving to the sway of the car. The boy had a great capacity for reasoning, he thought, plenty of the old Dietrich spunk.

"That new computer they gave you . . ."

"Incredible, huh," Marty said, and beat the air with gleeful hands.

"Listen to me, would you. You're a brave kid; you're not the biggest on the block, God knows, but I taught you to stand up to bullies, right?"

Marty became more restrained, making a quizzical nod.

"Look trouble in the eye, right?"

"Sure, Pop."

"I showed you that—how to square up to life's hard knocks, right?"

Marty offered no comment, his hands quite still.

"That computer goes back."

"But, Pop . . ."

"And so does the one at home."

Dietrich heard only the dull rumble of the tires and discovered Marty staring resolutely ahead, his face set and blanched.

"That's the way, mister," he said, striking a lusty hook to his shoulder. "All it takes is grit."

*   *   *

The house was at the apex of a calm crescent, near where Arlington nudged against Winchester. From one end, when the trees were bare, it was just possible to view the Mystic Lakes. This was a street of few children, flanked by similar ranch houses on plots preened to the weekly buzz of lawnmowers. Dietrich had wanted a *home,* he told Dorothy when he found it, not a showcase where you pumped martinis and crackers into so-called friends who only stopped by to see what you had. It was, he said, the right size for a couple who'd married late in life; a place to put down roots and be content. A fine house in a reputable neighborhood. To be honest, it was a mite on the small side once Marty showed up. Either the study had to go or the guest room, so the guest room it was, and Dietrich rationalized it by saying no one in their right mind wanted to stay weekends in a house with a kid bawling all hours.

Marty had been a bolt from the blue, unplanned and unexpected. Dietrich was forty-three at the time and Dot just one year younger. On first seeing Marty in his crib at the hospital, his knees had turned to jelly. The memory of that moment had never left him.

Dot came from the kitchen when they arrived, in her apron printed with vegetables and pale garlic. She complained constantly of headaches lately; she'd forgotten how to smile. With the negligence of habit, she bent for Marty's peck on the cheek.

"What have you two been up to, skipping school?"

"Man's business, Dot," Dietrich said. "Don't worry over it."

"I'm going to my room, Mom," Marty said. "I don't feel like eating."

Dietrich touched a chair. "You're staying right here, mister. Where I can see you."

"Ralphy," Dot inquired, "what's going on?"

"It's between him and me." Dietrich banged on the back of the recliner and snapped, "Here! Now!"

Marty threw her a futile look of appeal but she only sighed and wiped her damp hands on the apron. So he sat, his head sunk in his shoulders, plucking with his fingernails at a seam on the cushion.

"Mix me a drink, would you?" Dietrich asked Dot. "A big one." This was an old family joke, repeated too often to be noticed anymore—he drank down the orange juice she brought from the kitchen and growled, "Watch him. He doesn't leave the room, okay?"

In the bathroom, he swept the medicines from the cabinet into a travel bag. His hunting rifle was on a top shelf of the bedroom closet—he carried it with the bag to the garage. They went into the trunk of the Plymouth with the Colt from his shoulder holster. He locked the trunk, carefully tucked the keys deep in a trouser pocket, and strolled back to the living room with a forced spring in his step. A quiet evening in his fireside chair, time to catch up on the morning *Globe,* a weather eye on Marty, doing his damned anthill routine over by the bookshelves.

"Can I watch TV?" Marty whined.

"No."

"So what do I do?"

"Read a book for once, improve your mind."

"Sweet J——," Marty began, but stifled the rest.

"What was that?"

"I said okay, Pop." He stood slackly at the shelves, thumbing the book covers.

"Try on your left, mister, bottom row. There's Mark Twain, Fenimore Cooper . . . books I read over and over when I was your age."

Marty shrugged, pulled out a book, replaced it after turning a few pages. He crouched to the low shelf with the shabby-jacketed volumes in greens and reds and walked his fingers along, tugging them out, skimming the leaves and shoving them back.

Sweet Jesus, Dietrich thought, what with television and fucking computers, kids can't even *choose* a book anymore, let alone read. He stared into the blackened fireplace, at the logs set ready on the grate for the first cold snap, pots of poinsettia placed around them to look like flames. Long ago, he had strained his eyes over books under the bedclothes, to the dim, fading glow of his flashlight . . . *Huck Finn, The Last of the Mohicans.* Not *told* to read, he thought irately: devouring words because I wanted to. He recalled his father standing by the chimney, the perpetual bottle at his elbow. No drink in this house, Dietrich preached inwardly, no bad language, no debts. A decent house, every stick of furniture paid for. Kids these days don't deserve the half of what they get, their heads swarming with nonsense . . . subversive propaganda. Don't they realize what they owe this country?

His eyelids had become heavy. He shook his head to clear the drowsiness that had crept on him unawares, looked over to

Marty's chair, and saw only an open book on the cushion. Dot
was sitting beside the open kitchen door, where she could sniff
from time to time, checking on the steamy smells coming from
the stockpot. She was weaving yet another rug, as if they didn't
already have enough to fill a furniture store.

"Where's Marty?" he shouted. His chair toppled over in his
haste to the door.

She peered up. "In the bathroom."

"How long?"

She only frowned, her face deeply shadowed by the reading
lamp at her shoulder.

"How long, damn you?"

"A while," she said. She called after him into the hall, "You
were dozing, Ralph. Don't fly off the handle again. Please
don't."

The bathroom door was open, no Marty. He ran on, burst
into Marty's den, and found it empty, everything as it should be.
Bristling down the hall to their bedroom, he stopped outside. As
he turned the handle, a premonition passed over him, a warning
chill that made him kick the door wide but not move in. He
crouched ready to dive for cover, his hand outstretched, finger
crooked—he felt helpless without the Colt. Yet how absurd that
was, afraid of his own child, in his own home. Before the door
slammed against the inside wall, he felt the car keys still secure in
his pocket.

"Sweet . . . ," he moaned then, looking in.

The doors were gone from the closet on the facing wall; the
shelves and hooks pillaged, every item of clothing removed.
Dot's chair had been taken from the dressing table, and all the
drawers. He saw the bare boards where the rug had been, the big
fluffy one in several shades of blue she had worked on for
months. Of the wallpaper that looked passably like silk, only a
few torn strips remained—the plaster underneath was pinkly, ob-
scenely, naked. The bed was too big to be heaved through the
open window, but the mattress and sheets had been dragged out.
With leaden feet he went over, becoming aware of an orange
flicker on the back lawn.

The furniture and clothes were piled high against the house, the flames already climbing; angry sparks roared and spat into the evening sky. Marty had chosen the rear of the garage, out of sight of the living room and where Dot couldn't see from the kitchen until it was too late. He sat crosslegged on the grass, smiling at the blaze.

Dietrich squeezed out through the window, ran to him, and stared down at his son's face in horror. He heard his wife scream. Marty's head waltzed to the cracks of the burning wood; the fire jigged and gleamed with satanic redness in his dark staring eyes.

"One day . . . ," he said. "One day . . ."

9. Jay's Room

31

They kept Jay in the hospital for more than two weeks, the longest Elaine had ever been parted from him. Bringing him home, she said as she dressed in her best suit and blouse, was like giving birth all over again. In readiness, she had the house spanking clean from top to bottom. She'd redecorated his room, changing the furniture around in the faint hope he wouldn't miss the Possum—which Toby had hurled into the harbor. She'd baked a huge homecoming cake, and then wondered if she wasn't overdoing things a bit. Oh well, she said in what passed for an excuse, it was what mothers did on these occasions. Her frantic activity had moved Sorenson to join in. He painted WELCOME BACK TO THE WITCH HOUSE on a roll of toilet paper and draped it like a banner across the hall. "That's very nice, Toby," she noted without irony. "Thoughtful of you. He'll like that." Then she dashed to the kitchen, where a fillet of scrod was prepared for steaming and the peeled potatoes were already standing in a pot of water. "God, what am I thinking of?" she exclaimed, wringing her hands. "He'll be fed up to the back teeth with bland food." She swept the fish into the waste disposer and ground it away. "Hamburgers and fries," she said to herself, and nodded decisively as if she'd just settled the menu for a banquet.

In the hall, she checked her demurely pale lipstick in the mirror. "I don't look too . . . motherly, do I?" she said, holding her chin at various angles.

"You look great."

"Matronly, then? This blouse is all wrong, and my hair."

"Believe me, Elaine . . ."

She swallowed a deep breath to get rid of the butterflies. "I hate hospitals, Toby. I have this awful empty feeling inside me that they won't give him back. I know it's foolish of me, but they're such dreadful places."

"Let's go, huh," he said from the open front door.

"Can't we take your car?"

"What's wrong with the BMW? Smart new car, just the thing for a day like this."

"Yours is . . ." Suddenly she clung to him in a cascade of tears, eyeshadow streaking her cheeks. "Yours is so . . . Toby, it's *normal.*" Then she had to go back to the looking glass to repair the damage.

As he drove she folded down the rearview mirror. She stared at her reflection and something she saw there made her press her face to the window.

"To be on the safe side," she said, "it would be better if you kept to the guest room for a while."

He replied tersely that he understood.

"Until he feels secure again, that's all."

                              *   *   *

When they all returned to the house, Jay stood for a moment in the entrance, peering everywhere as if he'd been gone for years. "Did you do that, Toby?" he inquired, pointing up at the banner.

"All my own work."

"It's terrific. I've never seen your writing before. It's real neat."

"Thanks, kid."

Jay took a halting step forward into the hall, his nostrils flaring. "It's all so *clean,*" he said emphatically, and Elaine looked rather faint, perhaps afraid she had made the house too like a hospital. But he charmed her with the most enormous smile and said, "Gosh, it's *so* good to be back, Elaine," and she finally gave him the bear hug she'd been saving all day. It seemed that only now did she really believe he was strong enough to take it.

"Hamburgers?" she said, her eyes moist.

Gently he pulled away from her. "Maybe later. I'm not really hungry."

"Then how about a movie?" Sorenson suggested. "I bought some new video cassettes especially."

Jay avoided their gaze. "I'll just go up to my room, if that's all right? I guess I missed it while I was gone."

"Whatever you want, pet," Elaine said, in a voice like there were fingers gripping her throat.

"We can always see a movie tomorrow," Sorenson said, not daring to look at her.

*   *   *

He intended to let a good hour pass. To follow sooner, he thought, might seem unduly anxious—for the past fortnight Jay can have known little else but worried adult faces peering in on him. Yet it was nothing like an hour when he took a quarter from his pocket and said, "Heads I go, tails it's you. Agreed?"

"Why not both of us?" Elaine said.

"Far too earnest, sweetheart. Let's not crowd him, not first day home." He flipped the coin and glanced too quickly into his hand to see what side it was. "Heads," he declared, hurrying to the door.

"Lousy liar."

"I was a cop once. Would I cheat?"

Jay was wedged in a corner of his tidy divan, idly opening and shutting the same page of a pop-up book. They had replaced the disks on the shelf with a library of crisp new books—this one told of a journey through a haunted house, and a cardboard monster like a blob of ice cream was slithering in and out of the freezer.

"We're clean out of Possums, kid," Sorenson said, sitting beside him. "Feel like talking about it?"

"What's there to say?"

"Will you be bored without it?"

"I'm never bored, Toby. I'll find things to do."

"Let's put it another way. Will you be happy? It's important to Elaine that you are; important to both of us."

"I don't know how I'll be."

"Hell, Jay, you've got one of those serious faces. It's hard on us, trying to guess how you feel."

"I'll try to look happy for you, okay?" He offered no resistance as Sorenson eased the book from his hands.

"What do you want in place of the Possum? You only have to ask."

"I'm okay, Toby. I don't need a thing."

Sorenson reached out to him but stopped short. His fingers were curled and tense—clutching at straws? A kind of anger burst from him, born out of frustration. "I'm your father, for Christsake! Why can't we do something together; why can't you want something from *me?* Shit, there's got to be more to you and me than computers! Everything we've done since I've come back, that fucking Possum was calling the tune."

A silence engulfed them in which he imagined his raised voice echoing on and on. He forced his hands down onto the bed.

Jay stared but without surprise. His face grew thoughtful; he hollowed his cheeks like a wise old man. "Life," he said, "isn't about buying things."

"You're right. Yeah, learned that myself the hard way. I guess I forgot it in the heat of the moment."

Jay stared up at the ceiling for far too long.

"Tell you what we could do," Sorenson said. "Come for a trip with us this weekend. Elaine suggested Cape Cod. We could walk on the beach, take a picnic if the weather's fine. You'd please her more than I can say. She's worried sick about you."

"There's her shop . . ."

"She's promised to close it. Your honor, a special event."

"Elaine said that? Holy Moses."

He nodded. "Show how keen she is on the idea."

"Then I suppose I should come."

"Should?"

"I want to, really I do."

"Maybe we'll find a shark on the shore again."

"They don't come on the shore, Toby. They need to keep swimming to stay alive. It has to do with their breathing."

"They get washed in when they die—don't you remember the baby we found? You were only a kid then."

Jay shook his tousled head. His eyelids dithered; he seemed in need of a long sleep.

"Perhaps when we're there it'll all come back. Memories are like that."

"Sure, Toby," Jay said, yawning.

*   *   *

He found Elaine standing quite still in the garden, her arms crossed to her shoulders like a madonna. She was looking up at the trees with an empty face, as if she hadn't a thought in her head—or far too many.

"Could you shut up shop this Sunday?"

"It's a quiet time of year," she replied, which he took to mean yes.

"Your son fancies a trip to the Cape."

"Is that what he said?"

"He'd enjoy it more than anything in the world. He wants to see you smiling again; he told me so."

"Aren't children funny?"

A silent wind must have breathed on the trees; the dead leaves began to fall, encircling her like a flock of yellow birds. He thought her suddenly hauntingly beautiful. He needed to hold her close but remembered her words in the car, and remembered too that Jay's window looked down on where they stood. He knew he had to take it slowly.

"Jay's going to be okay, Elaine. He's going to be okay."

Her back was turned to him. "When people repeat things," she murmured softly, as if she were alone, "it's usually because they're only half sure of what they're saying."

She wore no coat and the day had begun with a frost. She trembled.

32

The nights drew in, carrying the cold bite of coming winter. Dry fallen leaves lay thick and crackling on the wilderness behind the house. In the mornings, Route 128 had the bleached whiteness of a desert road and the mists closed in over the electronics settlements whose wan yellow lights shone long after dawn.

The leaves carpeting the backyard reminded Toby of their fall wedding in New Hampshire. To Elaine they were an eyesore. She stared out from the French windows, wishing them away with progressively less subtle hints. Finally one evening he gave in to her. He gathered them into a foothill at the end of the garden and smelled the death of autumn in the earthy smoke that swirled over the houses and spilled up into the night through the bare black branches of the trees. Jay came out to stand with him, kicking twigs into the fire. Soon he shivered and turned away.

"I could do with some help here," Sorenson said.

"It's cold, Toby. I'm going to my room."

Sorenson stayed until the glow subsided, then returned to the welcome warmth of the house. Elaine sat stooped over her desk, not wanting to be disturbed from her ledgers, her rueful assessment of the accounts at the end of the season. He dug the old Monopoly game out from the back recesses of a closet and started upstairs to try Jay's door. It was locked.

"Jay? It's me, Toby."

When he got no reply he shook the handle again; called out for a second time. Beyond the door he heard the suggestion of a *ding;* it might have been imagined. He raised a foot and smashed the door open. Jay fell from his chair in shock, then planted himself in front of the Possum, arms held wide. It buzzed in its dazzlingly fresh orange cabinet, a new Model 4—Jay had taped a wad of cotton wool over the speaker grille to muffle the sound.

"Bastard!" he cried. "You're not having this one. I won't fucking let you."

Sorenson advanced a few fumbling paces.

"Shitbag!" Jay screamed. "I'll tell Elaine. Go away! Why can't you leave me alone?"

His fury stopped Sorenson dead, the same unleashed rage as the night he'd rushed into the guest room to spit and claw and yell profanities. They stared at each other, Jay's arms quaking, then his whole body.

"Whatever you say," Sorenson murmured and left in despair. Downstairs, he sat at Elaine's back as she fussed over her sums.

"Don't you love the smell of burning leaves?" she said, making small talk. "I'm a creature of autumn, always suspected it."

"Why did you give him that Possum?"

She stiffened visibly, needing time to compose the answer he knew she would give. "Because he asked me."

"And his loving mother couldn't say no."

She sprang around, her twisted lips white with contempt. "I'm not losing him, Toby. I'm not having him try suicide again."

"I told you about that computer. Didn't you even listen? He was free of it. My God, you just hooked him again, the first drink for an alcoholic on the wagon."

"Free, my ass," she sneered. "Pacing the house like a caged tiger. Have you looked at his nails, bitten down to the quick?"

He thought her drained face was a wildly ugly as Jay's had just been, her stare as willful, as closed to reason.

"Where did you get it?" he said.

"You know where. The hobby store, where he always goes."

"When?"

"Today."

"How do you mean, today?"

"You want me to say it again?"

"They're still selling them?" He spoke out of a daze.

"Ah!" she crowed, "it finally clicked. That little computer can't be as dangerous as you make out. Shit, Toby, this country

has a hundred and one safety regulations on everything that goes
over a shop counter. I should know."

He stared at her, speechless.

"You told the CIA your theories. They investigated, you said.
Seems they decided you were wrong." She strode to the drinks
cabinet for a triple vodka, the bottle clinking against the glass in
her shaking hands. She emptied it in a single greedy gulp. After a
time of looking at him, her head held swaggeringly high, she appeared to relent somewhat. "Can you take a drink?"

He declined silently. He went to the chest where she kept the
downstairs phone. The Boston directory was on the bookshelves
behind. He found a number listed for the CIA; only the Cambridge Field Office, but that would do for a start.

"I want Ames," he demanded. "Harold Thomas Ames."

Something of a gap, a pretense of checking. "We don't have a
Mr. Ames. What department did you have in mind?" This was a
man with a deep young voice who spoke with cultivated slowness, a question mark after every word, the kind of voice that
went along with narrowed eyes from the other side of a half-
opened door.

"Shit! He's the director for New England. He runs that office
and every other Company sideshow in town."

"Our director isn't a Mr. Ames, sir."

Sorenson needed a long pause.

"Will that be all, sir?"

"You have a Dietrich? Ralph Dietrich?"

"I'm not at liberty to divulge names over the phone."

"But you're not denying there's a Dietrich?"

"It's out of normal office hours here, sir. Anything I can do?"

"There sure as hell is. Get Dietrich at home. Tell him Toby
Sorenson is breathing fire and brimstone. Toby Sorenson, got
that? Tell him to call me, here, tonight, or he won't find the
Harvard Square Charm School standing this time tomorrow.
Tell him his son's life depends on it. Please God. *Tell him!*" He
gave his number and slammed the receiver down.

*   *   *

The phone rang again in less than ten minutes. Sorenson was waiting and snatched it up. Elaine hadn't spoken a word in the interim; she'd poured another large drink and sat watching from her desk. Soon—possibly it was the vodka—she became so unsmiling, so earnestly sorry for him, she looked miserable. He turned his head away; Elaine gave her sympathy like a donation to charity.

"My name is Davenport," this one said. "I'm with the CIA."

"I specifically asked for Dietrich."

"I'm calling from Langley, Virginia. Does that mean anything to you, Mr. Sorenson?"

"You bet. It means I rang the right bell."

"Ralph Dietrich is unavailable at the present time. He's on indefinite sick leave."

"I also asked for Harold Ames. Cambridge denied there was any such person. That's a damned lie."

"More a misunderstanding, I suggest. Harry Ames has been given a new position. He's moved from Boston."

"Sounds like a thorough purge. What's the score with Bradley? Have you got him in Tokyo, checking out video tapes at the Sony factory?"

"You're talking in riddles."

Sorenson smiled to himself, not amused. "Are you familiar with this Possum business?"

"I've had sight of the various reports, yes."

"Why haven't you stamped on sales of those machines?"

"Mr. Sorenson, we're not Consumer Affairs."

"But Ames said . . . he implied that . . ." Damn, what *had* he said? He had wrung Sorenson's hand warmly in parting; assurances were uttered about leaving things to him. Then a scheming nod . . . it would all be done quietly, no public panic. He might have made no such promise; too much could be read into the clasp of an honest hand.

"Be sensible about this, Mr. Sorenson. You had a good run for your money, some crackpot ideas, but we played along. Call it a day."

"And if I don't?"

He replied with a verbal shrug. He had an icy precision to his words, a phrasing that was almost English in its softer passages. He spoke with the confident ring of power that sounded in corporation boardrooms and high government offices all along the East Coast. He had a vast desk and acres of carpet and had only to press a button to get anything he wanted carried out. Anything.

"We, the CIA, have no further interest. I can't speak for Possum Incorporated."

"But you're about to . . ."

The moment of silence perhaps indicated a harsh smile. "They're a successful company; they depend on the goodwill of their customers. It's a youthful market, volatile, shall we say. I imagine—I'm merely hazarding a guess—they wouldn't take kindly to slurs on their reputation or competence. I'd think twice if I were you; make sure you're a rich man before going public. That kind of litigation costs plenty."

The huge office was cold, like Davenport's voice—Sorenson knew it suddenly. Hendricks. Stevens. And now this one. Just to listen to him made Toby shiver.

"You guess their intentions pretty well."

"Good night, Mr. Sorenson."

"Regards to Hendricks next time you meet."

"Good night, Mr. Sorenson!"

He hurried to the street. The night was cold but he had no time for his coat, only for the car keys, which he grabbed in passing from the table in the hall. Elaine ran after him to the front porch.

"Where are you going?"

"Out, sweetheart. Out."

"You won't do anything foolish, Toby?"

"I'll do what I have to."

*   *   *

Salem Home Computers was closed for the night. The starkly brilliant lights flooded the windows. He stared in at the small computers displayed on the cheap metal racks. There were three orange Possums in the dead center of the window, more glaring lights than necessary beating down on them—so they seemed to be glowing with a fierce inner heat. A sticker on the glass said, POSSUM GIVES YOU MORE. Another added, ENHANCED SOFT-WARE FEATURES. Yet another, the biggest sign in the store, shouted with luridly orange letters: EXCHANGE YOUR POSSUM DISKS FOR THE LATEST RELEASES. FREE!! FREE!!

He sat for a time in his car, still staring across the road at the posters. "Smart move, Hendricks," he murmured when they finally made sense. A squealing U-turn and he drove as fast as the old Beetle would carry him to Route 128, south to Waltham.

At Prospect Hill Park he took the rise up to Possum, pausing just long enough at the entrance to take a good look in, yet not arouse interest on the monitors. There were more of the intense arc lights on the roof than before—they set the walls afire—and tough steel mesh had been fitted to protect the bulbs. No one was going to be shooting lights out again. It was after 9:00 P.M., a time when only a few night owls stayed behind at Eastern Semi, but fifty cars at least were parked in the compound. He noted Hendricks' Mercedes in its usual place by the toughened glass doors, the identical car close by belonged to Stevens. Both alive and well and working their butts off.

He slowed at Glentree Pharmaceuticals on the way back down the hill. No surveillance van stood at the vantage point by the wire fence, and the only car, parked near the building, did not have smoked windows.

*   *   *

Elaine ran to him in the hall. She threw her strong arms around him, gripping tight, too desperate to be tender. From her face he thought she'd been crying.

"Oh, Toby," she wailed. "I've been half out of my mind. I was afraid you weren't coming back."

He kissed her forehead. "They've changed the program disks," he said.

She took a step back.

"Maybe they miscalculated and kids don't need to be made

dependent on Possums in the way they thought." He smiled grimly. "Maybe they become dependent with very little help." Suddenly he was in need of a large scotch. He went into the living room and poured one. He remembered raising the glass only once to his lips, but when he looked it was almost empty. "They're calling in the old programs, a free exchange deal. Possum gives you more, the sly bastards."

"I know. I already swapped all of Jay's. He was thrilled, he said the new ones . . ."

"The new ones don't kill, Elaine. That was a mistake, a colossal screw-up."

"Says who?"

He poured a second drink. This time he wasn't even aware of taking the glass to his mouth, but there it was, drained to the bottom and his stomach burning. "Says me. It's all guesswork but I'm good at reading the evidence." He added remorsefully, "I should have stayed a cop."

A cloud seemed to lift from her. "But if you're right, Toby . . . now that machine really *is* safe."

He thought of saying many things, but the glimmerings of a smile came to her face. It flickered like an uncertain candle in a breeze and he knew the wrong words would extinguish it. "Seems that way," he said. "You can forget your worrying now."

*   *   *

Upstairs, the door to Jay's room hung at a perilous tilt on its hinges. Jay swung around in fright when Toby stalked in. He attempted to shield the Possum but, brutally, Sorenson knocked him aside.

"You don't need that," he said, ripping the cotton wool from the speaker. "I won't be taking your Possum."

Jay eyed him, plotting his counterattack.

"My word as a respected security chief." He was panting hoarsely. "Want to shake on it?"

"You took it before! This is a trick."

"The Possum warned you about me, I know."

Jay nearly jumped out of his skin. "How did you . . ." He
broke off, his eyes darting to the computer as if to see if it had
heard him.

"I know more about Possums than you think; some things
even you don't know. It doesn't have to be frightened of me, Jay.
It's safe. I've been a lousy father at times but I never promised
you one thing and did another. Fact?"

Jay wanted to believe him.

"Go ahead, play. Don't mind me."

"What's that for?" he asked, pointing.

Sorenson had carried a chair in from the guest room. "You're
useless as a host," he said. "I can't stand that damned stool of
yours." He positioned it a fraction behind Jay where he could
peer over his shoulder to the computer screen. He sat down and
poked out his legs, tucking his arms together and nodding con-
tentedly. "I thought I'd watch. Any objections?"

"Not really."

"I'm going to be watching from now on. Tonight, tomorrow,
every time you use this orange monster. If you don't like the
idea, say so."

Jay turned to him, mystified. "But, Toby . . ."

"I enjoy being with you; you enjoy being with the computer.
This should keep us both happy."

"Well. . . ," Jay said in a weak mew of protest.

"Just play, maestro. Forget I'm here."

He stared for a while longer, then, on a baffled shrug, turned
back to the Possum, hands dancing on the keys. *Pad, pad, pad.* It
was music to Sorenson's ears.

WHAT TOOK SO LONG? the computer
asked suspiciously.

**DOING SOMETHING
OKAY. WE'LL SKIP THAT
QUESTION.**

The display emptied and after the briefest of pauses the green
words began to trace out. Business as usual. It had no idea . . .

"Does it know I'm here?" Sorenson asked quickly.

"No. How could it."

"You're not to tell it, not now, not later. You don't volunteer the information. If it asks, you're alone."

Jay glanced around. He was frowning: this was all beyond him; he wore a half-smile because it had to be funny.

"Your word, Jay. I gave you mine."

"If you want—you've gone bananas, Toby."

Bong-g-g went the Possum to make him pay attention.

WE'RE NOT CONCENTRATING TODAY, it said snidely. **SORRY DOESN'T BOTHER ME ANY WE'LL KEEP DOING THIS ALL DAY IF WE HAVE TO.** The words vanished and the computer took a long think, wondering what to cook up next.

Sorenson stared at the blank screen from behind Jay's back. The Possum suddenly looked one-eyed and very blind. Just the single huge lifeless eye, no pupils, nothing . . . like a great dead fish. It couldn't see a damned thing.

Got you, asshole! he thought.

10. The Man from Kirensk

33

The snow came in a fall so fine it misted the streets. A week from now the novelty would pass, drivers swearing as they hacked the ice from car windshields, walkers stamping their boots and cursing the cold; but this was the first fall and Christmas only two days away. Salem became another town, no familiar turning looking the same, a strange house standing where yours had been, smaller and dusted white. Faces marveled from behind the windows, children pointing and gasping in delight . . . the word *magic* was on every lip. For a brief while no one ventured out; nobody, it seemed, was prepared to vandalize this scene, to tramp the first footprints in the fragile snow. A soft stillness blanketed the town. The tall lamps stood alone in the streets, glowing with golden halos.

Elaine had a fine tree in a corner of the main room, decorated with lights like candles and plenty of tinsel. The presents were strewn ready at its base, wrapped in shiny papers bright with holly and robins and yule bells, tied in silver ribbons with gift tags in the shape of Santa Claus. All set for a real Christmas, she said cheerily. When he thought she wasn't looking, Jay would sneak in to shake the packages. He had X-ray eyes and chuckled to himself; all that wrapping, the peculiar shapes, weren't fooling him. He had ten presents—he counted nine new Possum disks . . . the tenth wasn't big enough.

He was upstairs now, chattering away to the computer. Sorenson was right behind, in his shadow as he had come to think of it. He rarely uttered a word in the room, and Jay had become so used to his presence he completely forgot he was there. Mostly, Sorenson could follow the conversations, but every so often Jay and the Possum went off into orbit somewhere . . . like now. Then he would study Jay's face for the giveaway signs of deadly concentration and then he'd stare narrowly at the screen to see what words came into his head. The Possum had given no inkling, in all these weeks, that it suspected anything amiss. Yet whatever it was saying secretly to Jay seemed beyond Sorenson's comprehension. When the words took shape in his mind he could make no sense of them. He got only one or two at a time, never enough to form a coherent message.

face

Meaning what, asshole? he thought. A person's face? If so, whose? Or to face a certain direction? He gazed as hard as he could at the screen, trying to empty his mind, opening it to whatever the Possum had to say next.

. . . north face

Ah, that was more helpful. Of the Eiger, possibly? But where did that get him? What did it mean? For Christsake, what was the context?

. . . slip . . .

Slip? He searched Jay's face for a clue but could read nothing into it. He saw only the slight hesitation he had learned to recognize, the sudden knitting of the brow, that frozen instant—every facial muscle totally still—before Jay gave his old man's smile to himself and rattled some answer or other in on the keys.

Slip from the north face of the Eiger? he wondered. Or slip from the highest window of a house in Washington Square?

*   *   *

Elaine gave the door handle an impetuous rattle. Probably she'd done it several times already and they hadn't noticed. Both their heads turned in the same moment.

"I've got two kids," she said, grinning. "Two great over-grown babies."

"Not hungry, Elaine," Jay said out of habit.

"There's a visitor for you, Toby."

"Damn!" he said.

"The strangest man." She came nearer, her face curious. "Wouldn't give me his name or say what it's about. Just snapped his fingers and ordered me to fetch you. Ordered me, Toby. And not the kind you expect to be bossing people around. Not that kind at all."

He was standing in the hall, a thin shower of white flakes on the floor around him, his shoulders and hair covered with snow; there was even snow on his straggly mustache, like a thin topping of icing. He was peering at his watch as Sorenson came down the stairs, shaking his head impatiently as if he had a train to catch. He was a small man; his coat hung on him in great folds. A briefcase protruded from under an arm.

"Mr. Sorenson!" he said, sounding extremely vexed. "At last, yes."

"You've come at a bad moment, Mr. . . . ."

"Valentine, Felix Valentine." He stared lengthily. He was a loutish man or considered himself too important to offer his hand.

"Make it quick, Mr. Valentine."

His gaze shifted to Elaine. Taking his briefcase in both hands, he said stuffily, "It's a matter of some delicacy. Not for your wife's ears, Mr. Sorenson."

"She's not my wife."

"I used to be," Elaine said with a quizzical frown. The man

seemed to worry her; she wanted him to have no wrong ideas about the house she kept.

He lifted the briefcase a little, one hand on a strap. He was about to open it for a document, an incriminating photograph perhaps; he had a change of mind. Instead, his eyes tightened and he said, "This concerns a certain person. Are you familiar with the names Ames?"

Sorenson started somewhat.

"I see you are."

"Yes, I know Ames."

"Then we have much to discuss. This is your house; I don't wish to presume . . ." He went through a moment of gauche shuffling with the case.

"Elaine . . . ," Sorenson said, nodding to the kitchen door.

"Exit left," she retorted and made herself scarce.

"She has a good strong face, your ex-wife," Valentine said, looking after her.

Shown into the living room, he went straight to the tree, gazing up at the lights in what seemed, though his back was turned, to be close to wonder. He banged his feet and beat on his coat; the snow flew from him in clouds. "Such a tree," he murmured. "Christmas, naturally . . . the festive season. And such clever lights, you'd think they were real candles." He faced Sorenson, slapping more snow from his shoulders.

"Can I take your coat?"

"Please, no. Don't bother. What's a coat." Carefully, he placed the briefcase on the arm of an easy chair. He folded the overcoat several times into a rough bundle and left it on the floor. Then he sat in the chair, the case across his knees, fingers drumming on it. "Now," he began as Sorenson sat opposite. "Now then. I must apologize for calling late but events conspired; you know how it is. Still, we have this imporant matter to discuss, to dispose of. It needn't take long." He steadied his gaze, screwing up his eyes, his hands all the while tapping firmly on the case. "Providing, that is, you're cooperative." He fell silent. He seemed to expect a reply.

Sorenson stared first at the snow, which lay, he couldn't help noticing, deep and crisp and melting on Elaine's best carpet, with scattered showers over the presents she'd spent hours wrapping. "Well . . . ?" he said.

This appeared to be sufficient response for Valentine. "You met—you had *reason* to meet—this Ames some weeks ago. Ames and an agent called Dietrich. Ames and Dietrich are no longer involved, I have to tell you."

"So I gather."

"We, that is my department, my department at Charlestown, have certain ties with Ames and Dietrich. I want that understood. This is all official, you follow, highly official." He slapped a hand forcefully on the leather. "This question of Vlasov, I mean."

"Vlasov?"

"It is my responsibility to pursue the inquiries. I won't take much of your time, Mr. Sorenson. Just tell me about Vlasov and I'll be on my way."

"Vlasov?" Sorenson repeated. "Perhaps you'd better explain."

Valentine labored under a frown. "Ten weeks ago, Mr. Sorenson, you met Ames and Dietrich. Harry and Ralph. That is so, isn't it?"

"Yes."

"You talked. You were interrogated. You had information to give them. I know all this; I know how they work." His words were coming fast, his face turning purple. He stopped to take a breath and continued more circumspectly. "You can see how much I know, yes? This is official, it's pointless to hide things from me."

"I met them, Mr. Valentine. I was questioned."

"You told them about Vlasov."

"I never mentioned a fucking Vlasov!"

Valentine stared. Angrily he drove a bunched fist onto his flat case. "It's foolish to lie to me!" he blazed. "Foolish, you understand! The computer . . ." He broke off. His fist, about to beat down again, hovered where it was.

"The *computer,* Mr. Valentine. . . ?"

"The CIA computer," he sneered. "Did you know that, Mr.

Sorenson, that every word you squealed to Ames and Dietrich
went into our big IBM computer?"

"Every word I said about Vlasov?"

"Exactly!"

Sorenson sauntered over to the drinks. He tipped a full measure of scotch into a tumbler for himself, then held out the bottle.
"Can I fix you one?"

"For me, no. I'm on duty, you understand."

"I have two thoughts right now," Sorenson said. "One is to
bust your ass and kick you out of here."

Valentine flinched, staring back.

"The other is . . ." He didn't know himself. "Hell . . . ," he
muttered. He shook his head repeatedly and drank deeply.
"Who the fuck are you, anyway?"

"I told you. My name is Valentine, Felix Valentine."

"What the fuck are you?"

"I work for the CIA. I can prove it. I have credentials, my
pass."

"Tell me another one."

He became silent, gazing down while he made play with a
leather strap. A long interval passed before he said, not caring to
look up, "You're my only chance, Mr. Sorenson." His hands
moved inconsequentially. "Don't you see, to find Vlasov." His
eyes filled, the lights of the Christmas tree shone a score of tiny
candles in the tears. The snow had dissolved into a dark patch at
his feet.

"Oh, hell . . . ," Sorenson said. Out came an exasperated sigh.

"But you told Ames about Vlasov." Valentine looked startled
suddenly and ran a tremulous hand across his brow. "Of course!"
he exclaimed. "You told him without knowing it! I assumed you
knew because of the computer. I'm an old man; you must forgive
me. He's not called Vlasov now." Eagerly he leaned forward,
holding out his arms, seeming not to notice as the case slipped
from his lap. "We are talking here about a very tall man, Mr.
Sorenson, with a beaky nose, a—how do you say?—a *pronounced*
nose."

Sorenson felt the beginnings of a stare coming on. He held the glass to his face and directed the stare at what was left of the whiskey. *Victor Stevens,* he thought . . . this funny old guy had wandered in from the snow and explained why a CIA surveillance van had been watching Possum. The cause of the interest, that is . . . not the reason.

"This Charlestown. . . ?" he said. "What do you do there?"

"I . . . I'm a collator," Valentine confessed with a sorry shake of the head. "I handle paper. Vast amounts of paper, more paper than you probably ever imagined. Reports, documents, publications . . . a million pages a year. You want to know what I do? I read every blessed word printed in the Soviet Union."

Sorenson finished his whiskey. "I told you I had two thoughts about you," he said. "Now I can give you the second. You come out with the whole story, I'll reciprocate, tell you all I know. Is it a deal?"

"A name, that's all I want. A name and where to find him."

"I offered a deal, Mr. Valentine. Take it or leave it."

Valentine sighed. "I accept your deal," he said. He retrieved his case from the floor, holding it to him as he would a baby. No, a cat, Sorenson thought; it was cats these old guys clung to like that.

"Mention Ames and computers in the same breath and I get interested. So begin there . . . Felix."

"We have this big IBM computer in the basement at Charlestown. I do not have official access—but I do have my own means. Do you follow?" He waited for Sorenson's nod. "I ask it regularly about Vlasov. Every week I ask, for years I get nothing. Suddenly, about ten weeks ago . . . I can hardly believe my eyes . . . onto the screen comes a message at last. I always hoped—no, believe me, always *knew*—one day would bring such a message. I pressed the keys, I sat for a time. And there . . ." The tears brimmed once more, the candles reflecting like brilliant pinpricks of light in his eyes. "I had entered," he said, "the name **VLASOV**. And the computer told me of an interview; it was cross-indexed, you understand. The interview was carried out by Ames and Dietrich; there were their names." He enjoyed a private smile. "The same as when they interviewed me; I read that report too. That fool Ames, Mr. Sorenson, he regarded me as a fruitcake. He said so, the stupid fool." Now he had a longer smile. "But he still put the report in the computer."

"My interview . . . ?" Sorenson said.

"Your name was indexed. We are called subjects when we go into the machine, you and I; we have that in common. I pressed some keys to learn what they had asked you, what you had told them; what opinion did Ames have of you, Mr. Sorenson—did he think you were a fruitcake too?"

Sorenson hung on his ominous pause.

He shrugged. "No report. An index entry, yes, but no report anymore. They erased it, I don't know when. Soon after, perhaps." Again he threw in a silence but his face became dark, furious. "Next, Mr. Sorenson, I tried my own interview. And what do you know . . . now that is erased also. Vlasov, you see, is not meant to exist. He is a powerful man—if you only knew—he has powerful allies. You have no idea, none at all . . . you can't begin to imagine."

For some time they stared at each other.

"I'm not a fruitcake," Valentine said then, "believe me. But I'm old now and not so fastwitted. It took me twenty-five bloody years to realize the truth about Vlasov; I needed only these past ten weeks to realize about the computer and you. Maybe I'm improving, huh? Ten weeks is not so bad as twenty-five years."

Sorenson raised his eyebrows. "We have a deal, Felix. And you haven't paid your full share yet. Tell me about Vlasov."

"Vlasov . . . ," Valentine said like a ghostly echo.

34

Valentine had told his story many times before and in the beginning, at least, his words were tame, dispassionate, as though he were relating episodes from another man's life.

It was new to Sorenson, who listened spellbound.

He told of the railroad yard in Kiyev, his petty rebellion against an order to falsify the reports, the furor he caused. He talked of the military without emotion or rancor. *A young corporal pointing a rifle. A major going red in the face.* But the circumstances were of no importance, he emphasized; the only point was that they landed him in Kirensk. It was true of the whole of Russia, he said . . . what mattered was where you found yourself, not why. The why was irrelevant when you woke up one cold morning to see the gulag fence around you. He had known too many men go mad wondering over the injustice of *why?*

As he talked, Sorenson thought him like the old shopkeepers he used to deal with in District Five—the cemetery detail, it was called—the tired pawnbrokers, the retired booksellers, who'd been robbed of all they had. The more exhausted they sounded—the less they seemed to care—the more *you* were made to care. Valentine, he decided, had learned over the years to tell this the only way it could be told.

He went on then to the gulag in Kirensk and the beautiful room where Vlasov held court, a strange island of splendor in a bleak sea of mud. And now when he spoke, his voice reverential, Sorenson could take it to be the most enchanting place on earth, that while he was there Valentine had wanted to be nowhere else. He was like that jeweler from South Cove, Feinstein, who returned to his apartment one day to find it ransacked, the good

bracelet he'd kept back for years as insurance for his old age
gone—to listen to him you'd believe it was the most precious
treasure ever made. And yet Valentine was perhaps aware of how
deceptive pictures from the past could be. He shrugged his
shoulders around him in the chair and flashed the whites of his
eyes. "We have a saying in my part of Russia, Mr. Sorenson.
Changing the viewpoint changes the view. I translate roughly
but I think you'll understand. It's very *Kiyev*, you know . . .
people there spend too much of their lives worrying about where
they stand."

Sorenson nodded in appreciation of the point. He had yet to
say a word since this began.

"Until recently, I remembered it all a certain way. In other
words, I held to my assumptions of the time. The place was a
gulag and Vlasov was KGB. There was only one possible reason
for being there—for Vlasov to learn what he could from us.
What other motive could there be?" He rocked his head at his
own stupidity; his mouth held more of a grimace than a smile.
"Oh yes, he wanted to learn, that much was true. Oh yes. But
there is learning and learning, isn't that so?"

Sorenson's mind wandered a moment. Was this what the Possum hinted at when it put thoughts in your head? *Russians?* How
could that be? Yet here was a Russian connection. And Ames had
been most careful to keep it from him.

Valentine glanced over and saw the question on his face. "The
learning of the inquisitor," he explained, "the winkling out of secrets . . . and against that the learning of a child, one person
teaching another. As happened with me and Vlasov and the mystery of the color blue. Twenty-five years it took me to see it!
Now," he declared, lifting his arms like a champion, "I see it all.
I changed my viewpoint, am I being clear?

"When one is in a place like Kirensk," he said in plain tones of
fact, "the cold becomes . . . part of life, it is unremarkable." He
laughed, a small cough from high in his throat. "You do not, believe me Mr. Sorenson, look out of the window in the morning
there and say to the rest of the hut, 'My god, you guys, but it's
cold today.' Oh no."

Sorenson found himself thinking of Hendricks. And of Victor Stevens, who this old man knew as Vlasov . . . Lomax had said he kept his office at Waltham freezing, to emulate the boss. Not so, he thought; Hendricks and Stevens were two of a kind. And Davenport? Did he make a third?

Valentine made a flowing sweep of the hand. "There you have it," he said. "The beautiful room, so out of place. And Vlasov himself. And his endless odd questions. And the cold he needed, the fire he provided for those, mere prisoners, such as myself. You have most of the pieces now; are you able to put them together? It took me so long. A young mind like yours . . ." He drew his shoulders up, into his chin. He looked like Feinstein: such an old, Jewish shrug.

"I need more," Sorenson said.

He had a moment of reflective staring, then nodded. "Of course, yes. You must forgive me. It's simply that you hold the final piece of the puzzle, Mr. Sorenson. You will understand that when you see it fit together." He looked directly. "You will believe all I say." This last, he intoned in a fervent whisper, like a prayer.

"So tell me, Felix," Sorenson said softly.

"Let me describe to you," Valentine said, "a typical session with Vlasov. Each prisoner had a set appointment with him. I saw him each Tuesday at five in the afternoon. During the long winter months it was dark then; sometimes we talked across the room, me keeping to the warmth, him at his priceless antique desk, with only the light of the flames to see by. Like the best of friends, gossiping around a fire, except, of course, he was over there, him and his glass of red wine." He pointed a great distance. "Once, a prisoner died suddenly and he had an hour to spare. He asked for *me*. The whole gulag to choose from and I was the one he wanted. That was because I taught him so much. It was from me he learned all he knew about blue."

"Blue?" Sorenson said, because this had come up before.

Valentine continued regardless. "There was a regular pattern to the meetings. He would always begin by insisting I must confess to him. You see, each of us there had some dark secret—a friend who spoke harshly of Stalin, or an uncle, a locomotive driver, who drank too much vodka before taking out his trains—Vlasov wanted these secrets from us. One day, he said, we would tell him anyway, why not now? In my case, it was some acquaintances who had—how do you say?—more mouth than sense. But, here is the pattern . . . I'd refuse, as always, and then he'd be talking of something different, of colors or music or dancing. He wanted me to say what a color looked like or why one particular note was followed by the next in a Tchaikovsky symphony. Sometimes he used to inquire from me what it was like to have a wife; with others he pried into their sex lives—not gloatingly, you understand—he made out to be the innocent. Do you see where I'm going, Mr. Sorenson? He was KGB, he was nearly forty years old and a handsome man of the world . . . of course he had to have a wife somewhere. These interrogators confuse you with their lies, they act the friend one minute and cut the ground from under you the next with some trivial untruth. Viewpoint, you see . . . what I did not understand, I assumed to be a lie. And I assumed the real reason for the questioning was to discover my little secret. The rest of the time with Vlasov was—what's the word?—only background, party talk, a device to make me feel at ease with him. How could I have guessed, then, it was the other way around?"

He moved his head, gazing at the lights on the tree. At this angle, his eyes were dead; his mouth hung slackly under his drooping mustache. Sorenson wondered how it was possible to see so much in a face so blank.

"Yet the odd thing was," he resumed, "he spoke only one obvious lie . . . at least that's what I took it to be. So trivial, but I thought of little else for weeks. It seemed so . . . careless of him. He wanted me to speak out, I'm certain, to accuse him of lying. But he was KGB, Mr. Sorenson; you don't fall for their tricks. So I said nothing, and neither did he. This was during his final days there, when we both knew he was about to depart. After he was gone, I felt hurt, betrayed even, he should try such a crude deception . . . on me, of all people! Did he think me a fool?"

"What did he tell you?"

"His birthdate," Valentine answered simply. " 'Today is June the thirtieth,' he said. Then he raised his glass and offered a toast. 'The anniversary of my coming into the world.' His exact words. 'Here's to 1908, Felix. How all our lives have changed since then; what surprises we've had, what disappointments. But still,' he said—and I'm quoting him to you, Mr. Sorenson—'but still we *survive*. Don't we, Felix?' "

Sorenson stared. Hendricks had said he was born in 1908; he'd made a point of saying so. Put what Valentine had said so far with what he'd picked up from his sessions with Jay and the Possum—yes, he could solve the puzzle, all right. But spoken words, he thought, had more reality than words in the head. They were tangible evidence. "Go on," he said, an urgent ring to his voice.

" 'We think back each year on our birthday, Felix, do you find that?' So Vlasov said to me then. 'We see how far we have traveled, we remember where we came from.' I never saw him so dejected, Mr. Sorenson. 'My home,' he said to me, 'is gone now and all my family. I might have a friend or two left in the whole wide world, but where are they, Felix? I am ignorant of how to find them.' " Valentine let his head fall forward, regarding his hands in idle play with a buckle of his old briefcase. "As for me, I was beside the fire, hardening my heart. You see, Mr. Sorenson, you try in a place like Kirensk to give away none of yourself, or you're finished. To feel sympathy for the KGB is to begin to dig your own grave. And yet . . ."

Valentine raised his face for a sorry smile. "Yet he almost had my sympathy. Indeed, he would have had it but for his stupid lie. 'I come from a remote region, Felix,' he said. 'That is, I arrived here from nowhere much, just a collection of huts, really, nothing but trees for miles.' For myself,"—Valentine touched his chest—"I took this to be boasting . . . he had made it big from somewhere small. 'I come,' he continued, 'from the forests of the Tunguska River.' Which is why I held my tongue, Mr. Sorenson, and lost twenty-five years learning the truth. Do you know of the Tunguska River?"

No, Sorenson shook his head, he didn't.

"Or Kirensk?"

Another apologetic no.

"Kirensk is some six, maybe seven, hundred miles to the southeast of where he claimed to be born. That may sound like plenty but in that part of Siberia . . ." He gathered his shoulders to him in an explanatory shrug. "Anyway, I knew it was wrong. You see, on the thirtieth of June, 1908, that whole region ceased to exist. Bang, Mr. Sorenson. Flattened. Worse than Hiroshima. Oh yes, much worse."

"Bang, Felix? What bang?"

"Who knows?" he said, throwing up his hands. "Some say a comet, others put it down to God and prefer to think no further. A vast explosion high in the sky, a nuclear blast . . ."

"But that's impossible . . . not in 1908."

He smiled beatifically. "But scientists say it happened, and hundreds of square miles were laid waste to prove it. The trees, where there were any left, were blown flat, like the spokes of a great wheel, all pointing to the same place, the center of the blast." He halted briefly, a storyteller to the last. "The very place, Mr. Sorenson, where Vlasov claimed to be born, that very same day." He let the chair enfold him, quietly observant, fascinated by the reaction he would get—perhaps also a trifle apprehensive.

"Clumsy, I agree. Such a strange lie."

"My own thoughts exactly at the time."

"A comet, you said?"

"Something big coming down." He broke for a pause, his eyes agleam. "Or going up. Going up, Mr. Sorenson, are you with me? And then, bang. Vlasov came from the explosion. He survived it."

"That's one hell of an assumption!" Sorenson said. And yet he believed it, every word. It fitted. What else possibly could?

"It's the picture I make from my jigsaw pieces, don't you see? I chanced on him in Beacon Hill; he looked unchanged. I sat down by the computer and had this inspiration about that. He was cold-blooded, I deduced, like a reptile. I thought perhaps the cold preserved him, the way food stays fresh in a freezer. Nonsense, of course . . . go to Siberia, see how the raw cold turns faces old before their time." He let loose a murmur of a sigh, a low gasp of penitence. "If only I'd responded to him that day back in Kirensk. He would have told me everything, I'm certain. He was all alone in the world; he had to learn the simplest things. Everything we take for granted. What is blue, Felix? Name a ballet where the music sounds blue? He was all prepared to share the confidence and I spurned him."

Sorenson looked agitated. "It was a gulag, for Christsake! What kind of talk is this!" There are two actors in this room, he thought placidly. Two of us, Felix.

"As I said before, there's learning and learning. Where better to hide out for years on end while you pick men's brains than as an interrogator in a Soviet gulag? Where else can you ask such crazy questions and not be taken for mad?"

Alaska, Sorenson reflected, his thoughts turning to Hendricks. A shrink, delving into men's innermost minds. Anchorage was as cold as Siberia . . . how did he get there from the Tunguska River? A long trek over land and then across the Bering Straits?

He got up and splashed another whiskey into his glass, then lingered by the drinks cabinet, a wide gap between him and Valentine. "What will you do with him?"

Felix laughed bitterly. "Had you asked me that ten weeks ago, know what I'd have said? That I was hunting him and had no idea why. I'm a man from the gulag, Mr. Sorenson; we are permitted our vendettas."

"Obsessions, I think you mean."

"Possibly. Yes, that might be so. It was the place did that to me, not Vlasov. But he was the one thing I could never forget, the focus of my destroyed years." His head shook, a kind of shiver. "As for now . . ." In a twinkling, his whole face was a smile. "Now I know him for what he really is. We must talk again, like the old days. I must ask the questions this time, don't you see, about where he's from. I won't harm him, not me; he's perfectly safe in my hands." He puffed himself up. "For goodness sake, I'm the one taught him all he knew about blue." An intent look came into his eyes. Perhaps he didn't realize how hard he was gripping the case. "I have honored my side of the bargain," he declared.

"Indeed you have." Quickly, Sorenson downed the whiskey,

presenting his back on the pretext of pouring another. Sorry, he thought. Forgive me, Felix.

"I was driving on Route 128. Not far from the Dedham ramp. I never saw a damned thing, Felix. A flash of color in the mirror, maybe, and then I felt this crunch at the back. Anyhow, there's this other car hurtling into the barrier. The flames! By the time I stopped and ran back, the heat was unbearable." He drank heavily, imploring Valentine to make a comment . . . anything, let it out. A stony quiet rewarded him.

"Next day I got roped in by Ames and Dietrich. A heap of questions and no explanations. He's dead, Felix."

He turned, slowly. Valentine looked limbless in his seat, his gaze lackluster and fixed in space. Too weary for gestures, he seemed as if the years had exhausted his tears. They were usually like this, Sorenson told himself, the old guys who'd lost their final hope; they knew no other way to bear a broken heart.

*   *   *

He watched from the window. The snow was falling more thickly now, the soft flakes whirling in the wind like down from a pillow fight. Valentine had his collar turned up, his head sunk deep in the folds; his old briefcase buried under an arm. The purling white closed around him and he was gone. The flakes pattered into the hollow imprint of his tracks on the sidewalk; soon the snow would have no memory of him.

Elaine came soundlessly into the room. "Funny old man," she said.

"Funny isn't the word I'd choose."

"What did he want?"

He gave a contrived laugh. "Selling, sweetheart."

"On a night like this?"

It would be a full-blown blizzard before the night was out; the white Christmas the forecasters had so avidly promised was a certainty. He peered into the squalling snow. Why had he lied to the old man? Because he was old, Sorenson thought. *Adults weren't supposed to know.*

"I might have guessed, Toby. He had a . . . oh, I don't know, door-to-door look. Was I wrong to tell him you were in?"

He turned from the window and saw the Possum disks under the tree . . . nine for Jay and one from Jay to him—at least it felt like a disk through the wrapping paper, though Jay had done his damndest to disguise it. Christmas day was going to be an absolute orgy on the machine.

The thing about the Possum, he mused, was that it only told part of the story; now he knew it all. The Possum said *they* were coming . . . it never mentioned, never even hinted, that three of them were already here. Maybe more than three. How many more?

"Toby . . . ?" Elaine said, staring.

"No," he replied belatedly, "you weren't wrong to let him in."

She smiled. He smiled back. He was beginning to believe she loved him; perhaps she almost believed it herself. He knew he loved her. But he didn't trust her, not entirely. Not where the Possum was concerned.

Epilogue

Something woke him with a start. Rubbing his eyes, he saw Elaine still asleep beside him in the bed. Leitner, he thought. Leitner woke him. The holiday was over; you didn't drift in late first day back at the plant, not if you valued your neck.

He dressed with a feeling of resentment as dull as a hangover. He guessed Jay would feel much the same when the time came to return to school. He snorted to himself in the darkness as he dragged on his pants. Christmas, he thought, whatever became of Christmas? *Phut!* A few hours and it was over. Then along came this odd dead period, a kind of hole at the end of the year. You noticed suddenly how short the days were.

Outside, Sorenson had the street to himself, only a single light glimmering in one of the houses. He started the car and let the engine run for several long minutes—the fan blew hot on his feet while his face froze. The tires slithered on the packed ice until he reached the main road, where grit splattered up onto the underside of the Beetle. What the snowplows hadn't shifted, an early thaw was slowly melting away. Salem was returning to normal. Snow was dripping and sliding from the roofs; shingles began to peek through in great dark blotches—like, he thought, some brat had squirted ink all over the scene. One final fling, he noted as he chugged by, a last seasonal show of glitter before Christmas vanished with the slush—from the rain gutters, around the eaves, hung long icicles that even in the gloomy light shone like resplendent spars of crystal.

Soon he was cruising Lafayette Street—the route he usually took to the freeway, not another person or automobile in sight.

He slowed to look in passing, as he always did, at Salem Home Computers. They had sprayed aerosol frost on the windows and tossed handfuls of artificial snow over the shelves: the computers looked as if detergent powder had been spilled on them. There were gaps in the displays, expanses of bare racks—a last-minute rush must have caught them short of stock. He remembered three Possums before, now only one was left. The harsh lights were blazing even at this hour . . . did they ever switch them off? The cleared sidewalk in front of the store glistened, wet and black like a drenched umbrella. The sole remaining Possum seemed defiant under the tinsel that trailed in shreds over its display.

"Hold on!" he shouted at himself, and stamped on the brake. The Beetle twitched its tail; the tires lost their grip on the ice. He slid into the curb with an almighty thump and maybe a front wheel ended up on the sidewalk—he ran over to the display without even stopping to look.

The door wouldn't budge. He rapped on the glass.

"Hey, guys, come on, would you?"

He pressed his nose to the icy pane to peer in. Empty. Goddamned empty. What kind of store was this, the holiday over and no lousy salesmen in yet? He beat on the glass with a fist.

"I've got news for you," he yelled. "Christmas is finished. Flown. Kaput."

Now he kicked the door very hard. For Pete's sake, how was a guy supposed to buy the latest disk with the door bolted shut? It was published today, he remembered clearly: first day after the holiday, something to look forward to as the Christmas excitement fizzled out.

He heard a car skid to a halt. The car door slammed loudly. In the window he saw the dark reflection of a man striding over.

"Sorenson . . . ?"

Toby had to think for a moment where he was, *why he was there.* He turned. This was a big man, wide-shouldered and powerful. He had the eyes of a child. They were agape, a look of baffled wildness about them. Sorenson wondered suddenly if his own eyes looked like that.

"Is it *you,* Sorenson?" The man blinked, peering blearily as though he'd just that second woken up.

"Dietrich! For Christsake, Ralph Dietrich. What the hell are you doing here?"

"I was heading over to see you in Salem. I needed to talk." He gestured to the store, his voice becoming hesitant. "I saw the window as I passed . . . then I noticed you."

Sorenson said nothing. Good God, he thought, what time was it? Five in the morning, if it was even that.

Dietrich pointed in at the Possum. "You here for the disk?"

"That was the idea, yes." Sorenson laughed weakly.

"North Face. Sounds like a great game."

"That's what I thought. Mountain climbing. Show me something high—a power pylon, you name it—I've got to show I can climb it."

"With *North Face,* you plan your route up, choose the right equipment and everything." Dietrich was getting excited.

"But take the wrong gear or make a mistake . . ."

". . . You slip."

They both flattened their noses to the glass.

"Seems we're a bit early, Toby."

Five in the morning, Sorenson thought to himself. "Ralph, why did you want to see me?"

Dietrich was a long time in answering. "You called me a while back, at the Cambridge Office."

"I couldn't get hold of you. They told me you weren't there."

"You mentioned my son. All I wanted was to say he's okay. There was a problem, but that's all over now." Another pause, his eyes searching Sorenson's face in the bright light from the window. "There's no problem anymore with Marty. In fact, there's no danger at all. I thought you'd want to know. So you can stop worrying about the machine now, do you know what I mean?"

Sorenson merely nodded.

"The thing about kids," Dietrich quickly added, "is you have to give them plenty of attention. I wasn't doing that. So I've been spending a lot of time with Marty lately. I mean a lot. I should've done it before."

"It's not easy being a father," Sorenson said.

They stared briefly, warily, at each other.

"Anything else you want to say?"

Dietrich looked away. "Just thought you should know."

"Good of you to tell me, Ralph."

"No trouble."

"Be seeing you, maybe."

"Take care," Dietrich said.

Sorenson sat in his car and, before starting the engine, peered up at the sky. A few of the brightest stars still flickered before the encroaching dawn—he saw them as distant beacons shining through a drizzle. Lately he had noticed how Jay was apt to stare from his window at night when he wasn't engrossed with the Possum. Sorenson had said nothing yet, but he knew more than Jay now and when the time was right . . . well, possibly he'd break it to him. Jay would . . . He felt his own smile, broad and blissful. Jay would be overcome with respect, that's what.

Even as he gazed, a star went out, then another. He wondered how far away *their* star was, how long it took from there to here. He wondered what they would look like, cloaked in their own skins. The Possum said there was no need to worry, they were not to be feared, not to be judged by appearances. Kids, it suggested, knew how little skin mattered, but adults . . . It was kids who played carefree together, white and black and yellow. As for adults . . .

What *would* they look like? Funny, real funny, to know so much about them and not be able to visualize them. And funny the Possum was so coy about showing a picture, not so much as a fleeting glimpse, when it was adamant that appearance meant nothing. Still, he understood more now, much more, than Jay and the other kids. Like how patient they were. All those years of waiting for the right technology to evolve. Then they borrowed it. Why, when they needed Wiley's computer in a hurry they didn't steal it, not as such, they made a swap—they left a replacement computer behind. They worked to this strict code of conduct, he could tell. Whatever they looked like, how could anyone be afraid of beings who believed in swaps. Heck, he thought, even the dimmest kid on the block knew the currency of swapping. Heck, yes.

He glanced over. That beige Plymouth was still motionless by the opposite curb. Dietrich was staring his way. How much did he know? Some of it perhaps, but not enough. He couldn't possibly know it all.

Mouth shut. Head down. Don't breathe a word.

One day . . . , he thought. *One day . . .*

      *   *   *

He went upstairs, along the corridor to the end room. Jay was soundly, noisily asleep, snuffling to himself in the darkness. Sorenson felt his way like a blind man over to the desk, found the Possum, and worked his hand down the back of the cabinet to the power switch.

Click!

He sat in front of it as the screen began to glow, a faint aura of green, the only light in the room. The hum began, the sound of the little machine stirring into action. A soft whir came from the disk drive, and from somewhere else a low metallic scamper like tiny creatures scuttling off into the night. He caught his breath. You could almost believe it was alive.

He raised his hands close to the keyboard, ready to respond.

HI, TOBY, the Possum said.